To Tom

Whiskey Riley

Jerry McGee

Jerry McGee

EsJay Press   Keizer, Oregon

ESJAY PRESS
4310 Shoreline Dr. N.
Keizer, Oregon 97303

© 2000 Jerry McGee

ISBN: 0-9672772-0-5

Library of Congress Catalog Card Number: 99-65949

Cover design by Bruce DeRoos

Book design and layout by DIMI PRESS

Printed in 12 pt. Palatino

DEDICATED TO

THE MEN WHO WORK UNDERGROUND

Credits and Acknowledgments:

Evelyn Hoxsey, cover painting
Robert Keilbach of Keizer, Oregon
Fort Vancouver Regional Library staff

Contents

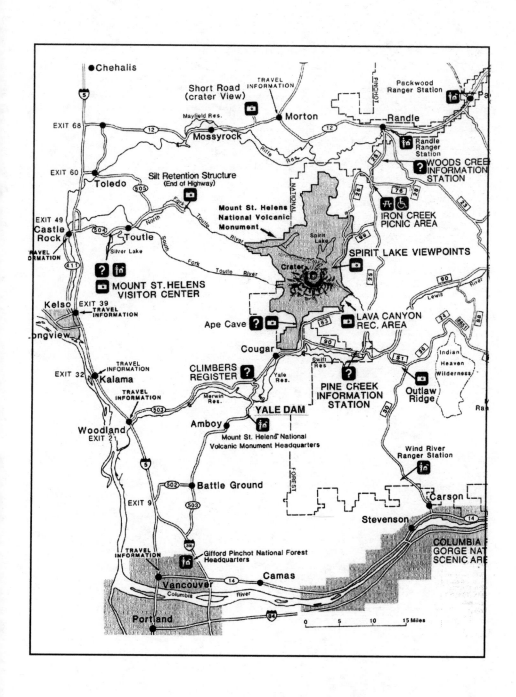

Chapter 1

Leaving The Valley

The short article in the *Vancouver Columbian* said that only a few would be hired at first, but eventually over two thousand men would be at work. It said the dam would be "in the shadow of Mt. St. Helens."

Could this be our way out of the Valley? Could this be the answer to the question that was the center of many discussions? How could we possibly make enough money to go to college? We wouldn't make it staying in the Valley that much was clear to me. If we could get on at this dam project maybe we could do it.

"Only Union men would be hired," the article said. O.K., so how do we get into the Union? That would need to be worked out.

Mt. St. Helens was prominently seen from our Valley although it was forty-five miles distant. Mt. St. Helens was not the weather vane Mt. Hood was, nor was it observed to determine crop planting like Silver Star Mountain. Mt. St.Helens was just a thing of beauty. That was its only function. It was a giant ice cream cone with a perfectly symmetrical crown. I had never been to St. Helens and I had never met anyone who had. Although we could see it, clouds permitting, it was remote and inaccessible.

The article said, "Men in the heavy construction trades will be coming from around the world to work on the project." If strangers could come from all over and find work in the shadow of "our mountain", men who had not even seen the mountain, then maybe some strong farm boys could get on too. The mountain was more ours than theirs. How did these people even hear about a dam being built on the Lewis River?

There were five of us at the start, but the plotting and planning quickly scared our work force down to two: Jerry Curtin and me. The others wanted to go to college probably as much as we did but not if it meant leaving the security of the Valley to look for work.

Jerry and I made a promise to each other to give it a try. We would leave the day after graduation. There was no reason to wait.

Mt. St. Helens was always a place of mystery as well as beauty , but now it had become a source of hope.

Leaving for Jerry Curtin was not a big thing. His family thought it would be like taking a graduation camping trip.

They thought we would be home, as soon as we got cold or hungry. In my case however, leaving was different.

"You're leaving aren't you," Mom said. I didn't reply.

"I thought as much. Were you going to say goodbye?"

"Probably," I said.

"Your brother didn't say goodbye but I understood. Will you join the Army too?"

"Korea doesn't interest me much and besides you have already given one son. That should be enough. No, I want to make some money. There's a big construction job starting up on the Lewis River. We're going up there to try to get on it."

"I didn't know you knew much about construction, Son. Your Dad did some carpentry work for awhile."

"I don't think it's that kind of construction work, Mom." I could tell she was worried but she would never stand in my way if she thought my mind was made up.

Mom was a little lady. She had worked hard all her life to raise her family of five on whatever ten acres could produce and on the returns of small jobs. I was the youngest by quite a bit. My oldest brother was killed in the woods and I can barely remember him. It seemed that Dad was always sick. He just gave up when we got the word that my next brother was "lost" in Korea at a place called The Iron Triangle. Dad died a month to the day after they told us about my brother.

I was the last so now she would be alone.

"Mr. Kilmer said he would pay you a full man's wage this summer, and even up that to a $1.25 when you're bailing. That's a fair wage Son. Family men don't get any more than that. You were always able to get along with Kilmer, which is more than most could say."

I have to admit I was proud when Mr. Kilmer asked Mom if he could talk to me about working for him as soon as school was out. I had no idea that he would offer me a full man's wage. I was big for seventeen but it was not my size as much as it was the fact, as he told Mom, that I had been taught to work and he knew he could count on an honest day from me.

"You gave your word to Kilmer. He's counting on you Son."

She was not trying to convince me not to go or to make me feel guilty. She just hoped I would do what was right.

"I stopped by Mr. Kilmer's yesterday afternoon on the way home from school," I said.

"What did he say when you told him you were leaving the Valley and wouldn't be able to work for him?"

"He couldn't believe it. He said he couldn't hold the job too long. I told him to go ahead and fill it. Mr. Kilmer shook my hand and said he guessed he would be seeing me in a couple of weeks or sooner, but then, if I do come back he may not be able to pay me quite as much. But Mom, then Mrs. Kilmer belted me on the back and gave me a bear hug that could have ended my whole construction career right there on the spot."

"Mrs. Kilmer hugged you?"

"Yeah, did she ever. Mrs Kilmer said, 'no, you won't see this one in a couple of weeks. He ain't coming back to the Valley.'

'She said we will hear about this one but he ain't coming back ' She said I'm going to make something of myself."

"She always was a good judge of horse flesh," Mom smiled.

Mom had more to say and so did I but neither of us spoke. Her silver hair glistened in the half-light of the room as she fussed with packing my work clothes into my denim duffel bag. My socks didn't really need to be rolled and I'm sure I didn't need an extra, handkerchief but I sat quietly on the edge of the old bed and let her fuss.

"You said, we. Is Deirdre going with you?" she said without looking up.

"DeDe? My gosh no. Jerry Curtin. I'm going with Jerry Curtin. He will pick me up early in the morning in his car. DeDe has no idea I'm leaving, as far as I know."

"You ought to say goodbye to her."

"She is a special friend as you have guessed. But we're leaving first thing in the morning, Mom. There are many friends I would like to say goodbye to but there just won't be time. "

"Still, you should say goodbye to her or her feelings will be hurt."

I wanted to change the subject . "You haven't asked me what I intend to do with all the money I'm going to make," I said.

"I know what you have in mind and you know I approve," she said. "How many times have I told you that you'll have to leave the Valley? There will be nothing here for you. The way out of the Valley is to get an education. It is my prayer that you get a college education."

"I will get an education Mom. I am going to go to college. I know I can do it but I can't make it working for Mr. Kilmer.

It's too bad that I have to leave the Glen but it's the things I've learned in the Glen and the strength that I've gotten from you that give me the gumption to try. I love every rock and oak in this valley, and I'll miss my friends and the neighbors that have been so good to us through the hard times. And I'll miss you most of all. But I just have to go."

"I know."

"As a child I could never understand, as I listened to you and Dad talk about the old folks how they left Antrim, Ireland, how they could leave a land they loved so much. But tonight I know how they must have felt," I said.

"The brave ones leave. It has always been so, "she said. "I will have pancakes ready for you and Jerry in the morning. Good night now."

"Mom, you don't have to fix anything for us."

"Breakfast will be ready at 5:30. I won't call you twice."

"When did you ever call us kids twice?" I laughed. "Good night Mom. I'll see you in the morning."

I wanted to say, "I love you very much Mom, " but I didn't.

Chapter 2

The Union Hall

The Union Hall opened at 7 AM and we were there on time, along with sixty or so other men. Tables formed at once for card playing. We sat on a bench at the side of the room. At the far end of the poorly lit basement room was a caged office with a middle-aged woman fussing around inside. The room soon became so filled with smoke you could cut it with a knife. Everyone seemed cheerful enough. There was a lot of good natured banter with an occasional burst of loud laughter. The games seemed to be friendly. They weren't playing poker. I know how to play poker. Whatever the game was, everyone knew how to play it. The art of shuffling and dealing was obviously a thing of status.

At eight-fifteen the door opened with a clatter and three men poured in. Two of the men had business suits on, but no tie which seemed, odd. The third man hung back behind the other two. This man was wearing a brown-felt hat which he took off and waved at everybody. He was wearing a white shirt open at the neck like the first two.

An old fellow sitting next to me said, "That's Big Al, the business agent for this two-bit outfit. "

I wondered why they called him "Big". He was a short guy in his forties with a beer belly hanging over his belt. Al walked from table to table greeting what appeared to be his long lost friends. The card games came to an immediate halt as Big Al approached each table. One man offered Big Al a gigantic cigar which was eagerly lit by one of the men in the suits.

The men at most of the tables stood, each man shaking Big Al's hand or slapping him on the back. The man sitting next to me, who had identified Big Al in the first place, spoke softly to no one in particular, "Now ain't that a chunk of shit."

Al was still making his rounds of the playing tables. I noticed that he never looked at the men on the benches but paid attention only to the men at the tables.

The phone rang loudly in the office cage. The entire room suddenly quieted down as if someone had pulled a zipper across their mouths.

It's for you Mr. Madrid," the lady in the cage cooed.

"No kidding. Now that is a real surprise," mumbled the man on the bench next to me.

Big Al took his time to stroll the length of the hall to take the call. He turned a quarter of a turn away from the crowd and talked softly into the phone for several minutes. The telephone conversation had everyone's attention. The conversation was broken occasionally by a chuckle from Al.

"Rosie, my pad," he said.

The call lasted about fifteen minutes with Big Al scribbling down notes and saying, "Uh huh, uh huh."

He handed the phone back to the lady and disappeared into the cage.The card games slowly resumed at a lower noise level. Before long Big Al walked back into the center of the Hall. Everybody gathered around him except for a few men sitting on the benches, who never stirred, including the old grump that had been sitting next to me. Jerry and I crowded up into the pack. It was clear that there was going to be some, important announcement.

Big Al began reading off names from a pad of yellow paper. He would read a man's name and with a flourish tear off a slip of paper about the size of a playing card. He seemed to know right where each person he named was standing.

As a name was read off a hand would come forward to take it with a "Thank you Al, thank you."

After a man got his slip of paper he would walk quickly to the cage where Rosie was busy writing out what looked like receipts and collecting money. After thirty names, or so, in this manner, Big Al slammed the pad closed and turned abruptly to retreat toward the cage. One man in the crowd who was not called, put out his hand to stop Al.

"Al could I talk to you?" he asked.

"Later. Can't you see I'm busy?" Al said.

Big Al quickly disappeared with the two men in the suits, inside the cage.

A few men strolled up to look at a clip board hanging at the counter at the cage. Most of the men, however, began to straggle toward the door and to the steps leading out of the dungeon.

I nodded to Jerry and we meandered up toward the cage and the clip board. Rosie appeared all smiles and teeth.

"Pardon me, is this the list we are supposed to sign?" I asked.

"Oh my, haven't you boys signed the list yet?" she said.

"If you want to be called you should be on the list. Of course you have to be a member, but if you're not, I would be happy to take your initiation fee and get you all signed up. Shall I sign you up boys?"

"How much did you say it was?" I asked.

"Fifty dollars in cash. We don't have the capability to take checks. Fifty dollars and of course your first months dues.

We like to collect two months dues at a time."

"Fifty dollars?" Jerry stammered.

I was hoping Jerry would ask about the monthly dues, but he didn't.

"Now boys, I can't stop you from signing your names on the list but you will need to pay the initiation fees and dues before you even could expect to be called out for a job. You understand. In cash," she said.

"We will just sign the list for now and join in a little bit. If that's O.K.," I said.

"Whatever you boys say." Rosie moved her attention to others.

I signed my name with the dull pencil that was hanging from a string. I put my thumb under the page number and tipped the clip board so Jerry could see the number. We were signing on page forty-four. Each page had twenty names or so on it.

Many names were crossed out but it was obvious that if we had to wait to work our way through this list it was going to be a long wait.

"My God. I don't have any fifty dollars, do you? I only have forty three dollars and some change," Jerry said.

I reached inside my coat pocket and removed an envelope Mom had shoved there as we were leaving. I knew it was her egg money. I had protested when she gave it to me. But she had insisted. I opened it up and carefully counted out thirty eight-dollars, a five dollar bill was the largest denomination.

"We have enough for one of us to join," I said.

"That's no good. We are in this together ," he said.

"For the price of a cup of coffee I will give you some advice." It was the old grump. He had maneuvered to where he could see our entire situation unfold, even to how much money we had. He could see our hesitancy.

"Come on boys, I won't roll you," he said. "I'm a harmless old coot."

He started toward the stairs and we followed. Out at street level the air was fresh and a sprinkle of rain had begun. The old man broke the silence.

"What do they call you?"

" My name is Jerry Curtin," Jerry said, extending his hand. The old man never took his hands out of his pockets to receive the hand shake.

"My name is Jerry too," I said. "Jerry McGowan." I didn't offer my hand.

"I didn't ask for your name. I said, what do they call you?" the old man said.

"It is a little confusing since both of our names are Jerry, well actually Gerald, but..."

The old man interrupted, "I'll call you Slim, and you're Mac".

"Actually I'm a bit on the heavy side, but if you want to call me Slim I guess that's O.K.," Jerry said. "I'm sorry but we didn't catch your name."

"I didn't throw it," the grump said. "But what would you call me if I didn't have a name?"

Jerry, or Slim, said without hesitation, "I would call you the Old Man."

"I would call you the Old Grump," I said.

For the first time the frown left the old man's face and he broke into a genuine grin, showing more holes than teeth.

"Call me the Old Man," he said.

It was only half past nine when we sat down at the table in the coffee shop. Neither Slim nor I drank coffee but the Old Man ordered three cups. When the girl asked if we wanted anything else the Old Man ordered a butterhorn. We both declined.

"So you're going to make your fortune on the dam," he began.

"We hope to get on the dam," I said.

"You won't make it out of this Hall on the price of your initiation fee. It will take some side money," the Old Man said.

"I have been watching for a week now and I am convinced that a little something under the table will be needed. I can pretty much predict who is going to get their name called each time. It has nothing to do with that list you signed or how long you have been waiting in the Hall. I have seen new faces come in a half hour before the call and with a wink and a nod go right out to work. I'm an old Union man. These clowns don't know it but I have been an agent in much bigger ponds than this one. This isn't the way it has to be. If I were you I would forget this Hall."

We didn't say a word.

He continued,"If you really wanted some good advice, I would tell you to turn around and go on back home. But you don't want that kind of advice I bet."

He offered us a cigarette but we declined. He allowed a long silence to let our situation sink in.

"Not all Union Halls are crooked. If I were you I would try the Hall in Longview," he said." It is run by the widow of an old Union man. I hear she is honest. In fact, the initiation fee may even be less. How much money do you have between you?"

"About eighty dollars," I said, fudging just a little.

"That is a damn little grub stake to be striking out on,"the Old Man said. "Here is what you ought to do. As soon as I finish my roll, why don't you give me a ride down to the Del Monte cannery. They're unloading boxcars of cans today.

Damn hot work if you take it. They'll put you right on," he said. "If you work right through lunch hour and don't complain you could quit about four or so, and still make it to Longview for the evening call, which is at 6:30. This call would be for the graveyard shift at the dam.

This Hall, in this two-bit town, doesn't open up for a grave yard call. The lady in Longview comes down to open up for an extra call, as I hear it," he said.

"Will the job at Del Monte's be done by four?" I said.

"Hell, Mac, we're not talking about getting the hay in. They don't give a damn if you quit or not. They write out your check whenever you say. For most of the crew quitting time will be shortly after a bottle of Muscatel has been earned," the Old Man said. "This will give you a little walking money and it sounds like you will need it. Where is your car parked? You do have a car? You didn't come in by oxen or something did you?"

"We parked over by the convent," Slim said.

"Hell, that's in the opposite direction. Why did you park over there?" the Old Man said.

"There aren't any parking meters over by the convent," I said.

The Old Man laughed for only the second time.

"I will just have another cup of coffee with Mac here and you go get the car, Slim," he said.

Slim reached for the bill the girl had placed on the table but the Old Man picked it up first.

"This one is on me boys," he said.

Slim came over to the box car I was unloading. "I think we had better check out if we're going to get to Longview yet this evening. "It's almost four," Slim said. "We have an hour and a half drive ahead of us."

Our checks came to $6.45 a piece.

"Will we see you in the morning boys?" the boss asked.

"We're not sure yet," I said.

The Old Man was standing in the open door of the third box car. As we passed by him Slim yelled, "Good by Old Man, and thanks for coffee and the advice."

The Old Man gave us a little wave and started to go back inside the box car.

"Say, how do we find the Union Hall in Longview?" Slim yelled.

"Hell, I don't know. I've never been there. Ask somebody," he said. He turned once again to go back to work and then, with what must have been an afterthought, he slid down from the boxcar and extended his hand. I took his handshake.

"Good luck to you boys. Don't be telling your life story the first night on the job. Keep your eyes open and stay together if you can. You'll do all right."

"Good luck to you Old Man and thanks again for your help," I said.

The Old Man would not be the last of the honest people we would meet in the months ahead, nor would he be the last to say, "Good luck", and sincerely mean every word. If there would have been more time we could have learned much from the Old Man. In time we learned who the"Old Men" were and who the "Phonies" were and in the construction game there are plenty of both.

Chapter 3

Longview

By the time we reached Longview, Mom's pancakes had worn off. It had already been a long day but it was going to be a longer one. We decided not to get anything to eat until after we found out what the Union costs would be. We didn't know whether we would be driving home yet this evening, and if so, we would wait and eat at home and save what money we had.

It wasn't too hard to find the Union Hall. We napped in the car until a pleasant looking-lady arrived at six and opened up the doors. A dozen men were hanging around, and we all went inside.

"Help yourselves to the coffee, fellows, if you don't mind the afternoon's leavings," she said. "I am hoping to get a call from M&K about 6:30. If we do we will probably get a request for only five or six men. These three fellows are first in line. They were here this morning and again this afternoon. If the call is for more than that we will talk about who we should send out. Is that O.K.?"

This lady was going to be fair. The Old Man was right about her. At 6:30 the phone rang. The lady talked a few minutes, took some notes, thanked the caller, and hung up.

"That was it, M&K's personnel office at the dam. They have sent in a call for four chucktenders. Any of you three want to go out as a chucktender?"

All three men shook their heads, no, with out any hesitation. It didn't appear as if they had to give it much thought.

"O.K., that opens it up," she said. "Any one want to go out as a chucktender?"

Nothing but head shakes greeted her question. The men started moving toward the door. Slim and I looked at each other and without a word between us, we started toward the front of the room.

"A chucktender you say? Is that on the dam?" Slim asked.

"Now where else would they be hiring chucktenders for a graveyard shift?" she smiled.

"I guess you're right there," I said.

"Can you make it to the office at the dam by 11:30 tonight?" the lady said.

"You bet we can," I said.

"Then that's fine boys. Let's get a dispatch slip all made out for you. I have to collect an initiation fee, unless you are already members of the Union, and one month's dues, before I can dispatch you to the job. If the fees and dues are too much at this time, you can sign to have them taken out of your first three weeks paychecks. They pay weekly but you will have to work a full week before you get your first payday. The initiation fee is thirty five dollars and the dues are two and a half a month. Once you're on the job they will just take the dues out of the first check each month. That way you won't have to worry about being behind. Does this sound O.K. to you?"

"Sounds fine," I said. "We will pay it all now."

All seemed to be going well. A heck of a lot better than we had dared to hope. The lady peered over her glasses as she was filling out the dispatch slip. "You know you have to be eighteen to join the Union."

I am sure she caught the look on my face but before I could say anything Slim laughed, "Of course we know you have to be eighteen. Let's get this thing going."

"Here you are. Just ask for Mr. Nelson and give him your dispatch slip, and the best of luck to you," she said.

We practically shouldered each other getting through the door.

"Jerry you know I'm not eighteen," I said.

"Yeah, I know it. That's why I answered before you had a chance to be too honest. But remember, she didn't say, 'are you eighteen?' she said, 'Did you know you had to be eighteen?' and yes, I knew that."

My Mom's last words to me were, "Be a good boy." I think she would understand this little deviation from the perfect truth, even though she would never have approved of it.

"Wait a minute," Slim said. He ran back to where the lady was locking the door.

"Excuse me please, but how do you get to the Yale Dam site?" he asked.

She laughed. "I don't know for sure., I know you have to go to Woodland and then up the Lewis River from there but that's as good as I can tell you. Except, I know it's a long way up the river. There's a Shell station in Woodland. I direct men there. Ask them at the station.

You will need a full tank of gas anyway. You shouldn't start up the river without a full tank of gas. Stay together if you can when you get to the dam and you will do just fine."

We thanked her and were off to Woodland, Washington. That was the second time today that a stranger had advised us to "stay together".

"By the way," I said, after we were under way, "What's a chucktender?"

"I have no idea," Slim said. "What ever it is, it can't be too hard for us. Right?"

"Yeah, right."

It was raining hard and the swipers didn't work right. Every few minutes Jerry, or should I say Slim, had to reach out the window to manually work them. But that was no big problem. The car hummed right along and before we knew it we saw the exit sign to Woodland.

"I think I know what a chucktender might be," Slim said, breaking a long silence. "They have this big camp up there where all the men stay. In the camp they have this big mess hall where the workers eat. I heard a fellow say how great the food is. I think a chucktender has something to do with making the food or serving the food."

"That's not really construction work but at least we will be in the area and maybe we can transfer to a real construction job after we prove ourselves in the mess hall," I said.

"Turn the dome light on Slim, I want to see if chucktender is one word or two on the dispatch slip."

The dim light from the ceiling of the 1936 Chev came on barely increasing the visibility in the car.

"It seems to be one word," I said,squinting in the half-light.

"What's your point, Mac?"

"A chuck wagon that serves food is two words, so a chucktender should be two words. But on the dispatch slip it's one word. The lady in the Union Hall probably didn't know the difference I bet."

"Yeah, probably not," Slim said.

But something else jumped out at me as I read the dispatch slip, really for the first time. "It says here 'rate of pay $1.90'. Holy cow! Do they mean an hour? That's over fifteen dollars a day."

"Let me see that." Slim very nearly ended everything on the spot as the car lurched up on the highway divider.

"It says seven days a week. We could make over a thousand dollars this summer. Could that cover a year in college?" Slim asked. "I can't imagine why those other guys didn't take the job. They just didn't want to wash dishes and peel potatoes and stuff I guess. For a $1.90 an hour, dishwashing doesn't sound too bad to me," Slim said. I agreed.

Slim pulled into the Shell station in Woodland.

"I'll get two dollars worth of gas. That'll be about ten gallons or so and I better get a quart of oil. Why don't you dash into the store and buy something for us to eat? Your Mom's pancakes were great but that was fourteen hours ago, and they weren't meant to last like Lend Lease," Slim said.

I bought a large loaf of Langendorf bread, two quarts of milk, and two Baby Ruth candy bars. I came out to hear Slim in a big beef with the owner of the gas station.

"He doesn't think my money is any good," Slim explained.. "He won't take our Del Monte checks."

"I would go ahead and take a chance on the check mister," I said. "The last four places we didn't pay at all." I put on my most menacing face and stood up close in front of him. And anyway the gas is in the car. What are you going to do, drain it out or something?"

"You construction stiffs are all alike. There's not an honest one in the lot," the owner said. "You come in here, from God knows where, and try to run all over the decent people. I'll cash your worthless check just to get you out of here, but not because you scare me sonny. I will cash it on one condition, that you never come back."

I think the guy meant it, too.

That should have ended it but Slim had to get in a parting shot.

"The only reason I would ever come back to Wood-berg would be to buy a station across the street and give gas away until you had learned some manners."

"The name is Woodland. Woodland and I will be here long after you're gone, sonny. You can count on that," the owner said.

Slim dug out, spraying gravel on the pumps and the attendant.

"Did he say how far up the river the dam is?" I asked.

"No. Do you want to go back and ask?"

"I guess not. He doesn't seem to be in a good mood to-night."

"It's a long way, that I know, but we will be there by 11:30 or my name's not Barney Oldsfield," Slim chuckled.

Fortunately, I think, the speedometer was broken ,so I didn't know for sure how fast we were cornering the curves.

"Hey, that old duffer called us construction stiffs. I wonder how he could tell by just looking at us that we are real construction workers?" Slim said.

We discovered in the months ahead that the term "stiffs" would have a less than endearing ring to it.

Chapter 4

A Little Surprise

We screeched into the camp, mud-splattered and all, at 11:00. We quickly dug into our spare clothing to find a clean shirt so as to make a better impression on the head cook or whomever. It was not hard to find the headquarters where the personnel office was located. The whole area was lit up like mid-day. Trucks were being loaded with men, pickups were taking off in various directions and there was generally a lot of friendly noise and action.

"This is sure a highball outfit," Slim said.

The buildings were all made of rough-cut timber, very practical but not fancy. I had heard that they had built their own sawmill to cut their own lumber.

"We're looking for a Mr. Nelson," I said, to the man on the other side of the counter.

"That's Nelson over there. He's busy right now but take a seat on the bench and he'll be with you as soon as he can.

In the meantime you can fill out these papers. Next of kin stuff you know."

Eleven thirty came and went. We had turned the paper work in and just waited. I could see in the back that Mr. Nelson really was busy. Still, I had hoped we could start right at 11:30 so we could get in a full shift. I wished my white shirt was not quite so wrinkled, but I would say that

I looked more presentable than the other guys who were waiting with us. Maybe the other guys may be going to work in different places so it may have been O.K. for them to be a little grubby.

"Pardon me," I said, to a fellow sitting at the end of the bench where I was sitting. I would guess he was in his early twenties. "Are you a chucktender too?"

"What?" the fellow said in a loud voice.

"Are you going to be a chucktender?" I repeated.

"I don't hear too good. Did you say chucktender?" he said. His voice was even louder than before. I nodded, "Yes."

"No. I'm a miner," he said. He turned to continue talking to the other guys who also talked too loud for the size of the room. They must all be hard of hearing.

"My God, do they have their own mine up here? Now that is something."

At 1:30 in the morning Slim went up to the counter again.

"Say, we can see everybody is pretty busy around here and all but my friend and I kind of wanted to get to work yet tonight. If that is all right with every one."

The man smiled, not in a snotty way, just a smile that indicated he had heard Slim's point of view before.

"Relax a bit. If you can find an empty bench stretch out and take a snooze. I'll call you when the warehouse is ready to have you come get your gear. They have a big order they've got to get out first. Nelson said to have the new hands just wait here out of the rain where it is warm, until they're ready for you. If you're worried about getting your time in, don't. You've been on the payroll since you left Longview."

"You mean we've been getting $1.90 an hour just sitting here on the bench?" I asked.

He smiled again. "That's right. And it pays the same whether you're sitting up or stretched out," he said.

I heard what he said but I couldn't believe it. Slim heard it too and was asleep in less than a minute. I sat there wondering how they could get a dam built paying men while they slept.

I guess I had dozed off when the man they called Nelson came over and shook us awake. "Sorry to keep you waiting, but this has been a busy night," Nelson said. Nelson was a graying man in his fifties. Probably too old to take a regular job.

"Just leave your rig parked where it is until you get off work in the morning. Then I would ask that you move your car down to the big gravel parking lot. M&K is a good outfit to work for and I think you will like it here. The pickup will run you over to the warehouse where they'll get you all fixed up. I'll leave you now. Good luck to you."

We could have walked to the warehouse easy enough. The warehouse was as big a building as I had ever seen. It was light as day inside but a little chilly.

A man took our papers. "What is your boot size?" he said. "Leave plenty of room for heavy socks."

He soon came back with a load of stuff that he kept putting on the counter. "O.K. here is your hardtop, unless you have your own. The headband adjusts. Do you know how to put in the liner?"

Before I could answer he had snapped in a webbing that went inside the helmet and placed it on my head, took it off again, adjusted it, and gave it back to me.

"Try on your boots and diggers. Do you want a rain jacket? Some don't like the coat but I would take it along anyway. Use it if you want to. Here are your rubberized gloves. Pick up a new pair each week. Otherwise they will get pretty rank."

We looked over the so-called "diggers", trying to figure which was the front or back. They looked like fishing waders that city folks use. The boots were just like a farmer's boots, only they were black instead of red. The toes were big and very hard.

"Steel toes," the man said. "No corners cut on safety here."

"I guess we will be in a lot of water judging from this gear," Slim said.

"No, not too bad. The pumps have kept ahead of it so far."

"Oh, that's good," Slim said.

"Let me have your hardtops and I will have your handle stenciled on it while we do the rest of the paperwork. What do they call you?"

"I'm Slim and this is Mac."

"Good. I like the short ones," he said.

Slim was still trying to get a feeling for our new assignments without asking anyone right out.

"I guess the hardtops are because we will be working around some equipment," Slim said.

"I guess you could say that all right," He rolled his head back and laughed. "You guys all have such a sense of humor. Frankly, I admire you guys. I don't have the guts to work underground.

This job doesn't pay as much as yours because you work seven days and we only work five. And then you get ten cents more an hour for going underground. I wouldn't trade with you. Money isn't everything is it ? It's what you like to do that counts. Yet, I don't see how you can do it."

"Oh, you get used to it," Slim said. He glanced at me with a strange look on his face.

"There's the flatbed now. Take these hands to the new portal. Good luck."

It was now 5:30 in the morning and the river valley was getting ready for another day. The lights around the head-quarters cast a strange hue.We bounced along a dirt and gravel road winding ever downward toward the river channel, which was in a tremendous gorge at this point.

Slim leaned over and shouted in my ear.

"Do you have the feeling that we won't be working in the mess hall?"

"Not unless they serve the food underground," I said.

We drove along the river at water level for a quarter of a mile, and then the road made an abrupt turn away from the river and we were up against a solid mountain.

There it was. The new, or west, portal of a major diversion tunnel. The tunnel would in time carry the water of this raging river around the construction site of one of the largest dams of its type in the world.

The sun was coming up over the Lewis River Gorge. It would normally be a sight to behold but on this morning in June of 1951 I was too preoccupied with other thoughts to appreciate the wonders of nature. And dead tired too by this time!

Chapter 5

We Will Make It Some Way.

The first few days whirled by - - the two of us completely overwhelmed with things we didn't understand. No one seemed very well organized. There was a lot of just plain standing around. It took us two shifts to "drill" one "round." I got the feeling we didn't do very well. I didn't know where I was supposed to be or what I was supposed to do or whom I was supposed to help.

Slim attached himself to a miner called Red. Red seemed to like him and told him what to do.

There was a lot of hand-shovelling with short handled shovels called "mucking out." At least I knew what to do at those times. I was scared most of the time. Slim didn't seem to be as afraid as I was.

At the end of our second shift we tried to see if we could get into the sleeping quarters at the camp. The fellow we talked to just laughed at us.

"There ain't enough bunks for the miners and the supervisors let alone room for some dumb chucktenders," he said.

He said that he thought that they would eventually build more bunk houses, but that would come much later. So, for now, sleeping in the car was the best we could do. It wasn't too bad.

On our third shift one of the miners noticed that neither Slim nor I had lunches.

"Where's your nosebag?" the miner asked.

"Oh, we forgot to bring our lunch pails," I said.

"No one forgets their nose bag," the miner said. "Look, I stay in camp and we make our own lunches from the stuff they put out for us. I've got more than I can possibly eat here. Take one of these sandwiches, and these cookies are too damn hard anyway. Take these."

"If you're sure you don't want it," I said, "it's appreciated."

I have never eaten a better sandwich in my life. I tucked the hard cookies into the pocket of my shirt for later use. I tried to put the cookies away without the miner seeing me but I am sure he saw it.

The next night the miner brought what amounted to a double lunch. He gave half of it to me. Another miner had done the same for Slim. I tried to thank him but he cut me off. "If you stay around this game long you'll find out that we take care of each other. Some day, some where, it will be your turn. When I see you come with your own nosebag I'll know that you have worked things out. Until then, I'll just make a little extra."

He had no idea how much that meant to us. The loaf of bread we had gotten at Woodland was long gone. Slim had found out that we could get a pay "advance."

"They say we can get up to 50% of what we have coming while we wait for our first check. Payday is Friday, so if we ask ahead of time we could get about forty dollars in advance. What do you think?"

"Where would we spend it and on what?" I asked.

"I thought I might run into Amboy between shifts on Saturday. I might buy another pair of wool socks. I don't know what else," Slim said.

We had been to Amboy before but we had always come from the south. From the dam you would come from the north to reach Amboy. Every summer our Legion baseball team came up to Amboy to play a double-header with the

Tum Tum Legion of Amboy. I will never forget the fir tree
that stands in center field. This damn tree required all kinds
of special groundrules, which I suspected, were tailored to
fit what ever team they were playing. If you look at a map,
Amboy is only about ten miles away from the Yale Dam
site. The nearest city such as it is.

Slim had not specifically invited me to go to Amboy with
him which I thought was unusual. Even for good friends I
suppose it's a good idea to get away from each other at
times. Since he didn't ask me to go I volunteered that I
would just explore around camp and see what I could learn.
The weather was fine so I didn't mind not having the car
for a roof over my head. Slim said he would be back in
plenty of time to catch the truck down to the tunnel.

I didn't worry much when it got dark and Slim wasn't
back. I spent quite a bit of time in the warehouse. Their
business was fairly slack and they didn't seem to mind if I
hung around. I even started to like their coffee. Coffee
drinking seems to be a must in the world of warehouse-
men. I went outside and looked around the big parking lot
every hour or so to see if Slim had returned but perhaps
parked somewhere else. The problem was my diggers and
boots were in the trunk of the car. Most of the other tunnel
workers hung their clothes in "the dry shack" on ropes
which they raised to the ceiling by means of hooks and
pulleys. But there hadn't seemed to be any room for us and
our clothes so we had been taking them "home" with us.

When the truck left to go to the worksite Slim was still
not back. I would have to work tonight without boots or
diggers, which wasn't going to be good, but I had no choice.
For the first time I realized how dependent I had become
on Slim.

Fortunately, Slim finally arrived in a pickup about fifteen minutes after the shuttle truck had delivered the rest
of us to the tunnel. He had my gear with him so all my

worries were for nothing. He also slipped me a candy bar as a bit of a peace offering.

I didn't get to talk to Slim until after the shift was over. He had lots of important "hot" news.

"They're waiting for some guy named Whiskey Riley to arrive from some place to take over our shift," Slim said. "I met Red in Amboy and he told me lots of stuff.

Red said we'll know when Whiskey Riley gets here because they'll fire the Shift Boss we have now. He says this Whiskey Riley really knows his stuff and there will be a lot of changes around here."

"Like what?"

"Red says the men on the east portal are already getting 'bonus' money for drilling more than the minimum ,but there are only a few miners on our side of the mountain who know what they are doing. Red says Whiskey Riley will keep a few and can the rest."

"Is that supposed to be good news?" I asked. "If this Whiskey Riley guy fires everyone who doesn't know what they're doing, he'll sure as hell fire us."

"Not according to Red. Red said he would pick me as his chucktender," Slim said.

"That's great but what about me?"

"Jeez, I didn't go into everything with him. By that time he wasn't feeling so hot anyway. That's why I was a little late. I had to help him into the bunkhouse. Only he couldn't remember which bunk was his."

"What was wrong with him?"

"He was a little sick or something. Maybe we had too many beers at Nick's Tavern in Amboy," Slim said. "He didn't make it to work at all. I guess it's all right to miss a shift once in awhile."

"Did you get your socks?"

"No, I guess I spent a little too much at Nick's. Red hadn't cashed his check yet so we spent part of mine."

He caught the look of disbelief and disgust on my face.

But he hurried on. "You don't have to go all the way to Amboy to cash your check. Red showed me another place right at the turn off coming into the jobsite. Say, this is some place."

"Cashing my check hasn't been a big worry of mine but thanks for the information. I will remember that," I said.

"Oh yeah, I called home from Amboy," Slim said. "They wanted to know if you wanted them to take any message to your mom. I said not particularly. Just that everything is going great. Was that O.K.?"

"That's exactly right," I replied. "Mom would just worry if she knew how we were eating and where we were sleeping."

"Dad said he would drive over to your Mom's place, but I didn't think you would want that. Oh yes. I almost forgot. Deirdre Driscoll left home."

"She did what? DeDe left home? Where did she go?"

"They don't know for sure. Apparently she left a day after we did. They think she caught a bus into Vancouver. That's about all anyone wants to speculate," Slim said.

"She probably went to try to get a job in a restaurant or something. I know she wanted to go to college next fall if she could swing it some way. That is really something.... So DeDe left too," I said.

There was a steady rain tattooing the roof of the car as we settled down to get some sleep. I was dead tired and the cooling rain was welcomed. Sleeping in the day time was not easy at first but we were getting use to it. The sound of the rain on the roof of the car would soon lull me to sleep and I needed it.

I had not been to sleep very long when I heard someone pounding on the driver's side of the car. It was Mr. Nelson the personnel officer.

"Uh-oh," Slim whispered. "I knew we should have moved the car to a different area each day."

Nelson didn't seem to be too upset but he was insistent.

"Are you the two Jerrys? McGowan and someone else?" he said.

"I'm Jerry McGowan," I said. "This is Jerry... ."

He didn't let me finish. "Come with me," he said. Nelson started to walk off. We had our shoes on in-a flash.

"It was good while it lasted," Slim murmured.

Mr. Nelson walked at a quick pace toward the bunk house. On the porch of the bunk house we met a man who was obviously waiting for Mr. Nelson.

"Bill, here are your new roomers. Get them set up and everything," Mr. Nelson said.

"Sure thing Mr. Nelson. You bet," the man said. "Come on with me boys. Let me show you the Yale Hilton."

Mr. Nelson stepped aside to let us pass.

"Thank you Mr. Nelson. This will sure beat sleeping in our car," I said.

"No need to thank me. Business is business."

"What was that all about, do you suppose?" I asked in a low voice to Slim.

"Beats the hell out of me but let's not ask too many questions."

The man in charge stopped in the hall of the bunk house.

"You boys go get lost for about an hour, then come back. Your room will be number twenty-three and your bunks will be numbers four and five. I will sign you up and all that sort of thing."

It was obvious that he wanted us to disappear and fast. So we did. On the way back to the car I said to Slim, " Whoever was in bunks four and five didn't know of these new arrangements."

"Do you think they threw someone out? " Slim asked.

"I think they did but I can't figure out why we get the shot at it."

I have never had a better night's sleep, or should I say, day's sleep. The best part of it all was that living in the bunkhouse meant we were eligible to eat in the mess hall.

A bed and three meals a day, what more could a person want?

For the first time since we landed here I had the feeling we really would make it.

Chapter 6

So That's A Chucktender

"We have got to find some way to know what is going on," I said. "Do you think you know Red well enough to ask him some questions?"

"I'm not afraid to ask him," Slim said. "I will see if he can get together with us after supper this evening."

Slim had good news. "Can I hit you up for a couple bucks?"

"Sure, except I only have a dollar seventy-five left from my Del Monte check. I didn't take a pay draw like you did," I said.

"Give me what you have, that will do," Slim said. "Mogen David only costs a dollar and a quarter."

I kept fifty cents and gave him the rest. "What is Mogen David?" I asked.

"A bottle of wine," Slim said. "Red said he would tell us all we need to know for a bottle of berry Mogan David. Do you want to run into Amboy with me after work?"

That evening we gathered in the day room of the bunk house. Slim got three glasses from the mess hall. He poured about an inch of berry wine into my glass, three inches into his glass, and filled Red's glass to the brim.

"I learned about mining from my Dad who took me into the shafts when I was fourteen years old," Red said.

"Everyone in my Hollow in West Virgina worked in the mines. Mining is all I know...... That is damn good wine. Fill my glass with a little more and I will tell you what you need to know to get by as a chucktender."

"You know by this time that a chucktender is a miner's helper," Red began. "The miner is the brains and the chucktender is the brawn. Do you know why they call you chucktenders? Have you noticed the two hinged clamps at the end of each drill? Those clamps swing up and guide the steel and hold the steel when the hole is being started or collared. Those clamps are called the 'chucks.' When the miner has drilled deep enough to have the hole well collared he will wipe the air with his hand. That means you take the big wrench, which is called the chuckwrench, and swipe the clamps down off the steel. You swing toward the face with all your might. The miners like a chucktender that is strong enough to knock the chucks down with one swipe. Got it so far?"

"What is the face?" I said.

"The face? Jees, it's.... just the face. The rock we are drilling into is called the face. The daylight end of the tunnel is called the portal. So the end we drill is called the face. You walk out of the portal and into the face. Got it now?"

"I think so," I said.

"So that's why they call you chucktenders. You tend the chucks," Red said.

"More wine?" Slim suggested.

"Don't mind if I do," Red said.

I passed my glass over to Slim but he poured Red's glass to the top,an inch in his own glass,and skipped mine. I hoped this would be a good investment.

"Now tending the chucks is not the most important thing for you to do," Red continued. "Changing the steel fast and smooth is more important. Every miner will have their own methods but the idea is to reduce the time that the miner is not operating. A good team of miner and chucktender can make footage on others if they work as a team and learn to make a quick steel exchange. The steel is in four foot lengths. You start with four-foot steel called the "starter." Then you go to an eight foot-steel, and in very rare case you might use a twelve-footer."

"Why don't they call us steel changers?" I said.

"What? Cause they call you chucktenders. If you ask dumb questions like that I'm just going to drink wine," Red said.

Slim frowned at me. "He didn't mean anything by that, Red. Here, have a little more wine."

"Now this is a big, I mean big, tunnel," Red said. ,"It is forty-two feet from floor to crown, and that is damn big. Now I don't know that much about die-version tunnels. It's not like a coal mine. But they tell me that they intend to run the whole damn river through the mountain by this tunnel we're drilling."

"They call it a diversion tunnel because they intend to divert the river through it while they build the dam high and dry," I offered.

"Where did you learn that?" Slim looked surprised.

"The guys in the warehouse explained it to me," I said. "After the dam is built they will close off the diversion tunnel and run the water through the newly built dam to make electricity."

"You don't say," Red said. He appeared perplexed. "What will they do with the hole in the mountain that we're making?"

"Nothing. It will be of little use once the dam is built. They will plug it. They could reopen it to make repairs on the dam or stuff like that. But the primary purpose for the tunnel is over when the dam is built."

"Well tell me this," Red said. "Why are they building the dam way up here in this Godforsaken wilderness where there is nothing but trees around? Can you tell me that?"

"I don't know. That's a good question and I will ask someone," I said. "I do know that this is a special kind of dam. It is called an 'earth filled dam."

"Now I know better than that," Red said. "They make dams out of concrete. Dirt would never hold up."

I shrugged.

"Explain the 'jumbo' to us." Slim said.

"The scaffold that we drill off of is called the jumbo. You have to have some way to drill forty-two feet in the air. So they build this steel frame on tracks or some way to move it back and forth. In this tunnel they have stripped down a Uke, you know, a Euclid truck, and mounted the jumbo on that. In most tunnels the jumbo would fill the whole tunnel, but in this case the tunnel is so big that we drill one half and then we move it over to drill the other half. Say, I'm a bit dry. Do you have any more of that sweet stuff?"

"No, the bottle is all gone," I said.

"Jees, did you only get one bottle for the three of us?" Red looked like he was going to cry.

"Keep talking Red. Mac can round up some more. Can't you Mac?" Slim said.

"I don't know how without running into Amboy again and besides I have already dropped a dollar and a quarter into this guy and look at him he can barely sit upright. "

Red started to cry. I mean real tears.

"You guys don't like me. You were just giving me wine cause you had to. You don't like me."

Now the sobs were uncontrollable. The jerk was bawling his head off.

"We will get you more wine tomorrow, Red. We like you a lot. Do you like that Mogen David berry?" Slim was almost pleading.

Red jabbed his finger at me. "He don't like me. He thinks his shit doesn't stink like mine."

I went off "What I think, is that I can't afford your information. You drank that bottle like it was soda pop. That was fortified wine. And as for me liking you or not, well, if I had some information that I thought could help a person out I wouldn't hold him up for a swig o'rot-gut before I told him what he could use."

"Go easy on him , Mac. You're just going to get him mad," Slim said.

But Red didn't hear most of what I said. He had slumped over and had gone to sleep.

Slim helped Red into his bunk. Red woke up enough to offer to the Washington wilderness his version of *"Irene, Good Night. "* Every other verse Red changed the words to "Irene I'm tight."

I decided Red had given us enough good information so that we could at least ask half-way intelligent questions, and maybe look like we sort of knew what we were doing.

Chapter 7

So What Is A Chucktender Again?

So, a chucktender is the miner's or driller's helper. The chucktender is the brawn and the miner is the brains but they have to learn to work together as a team. Voice communication is impossible because of the noise. Everything has to be by hand signals between the two. A pair that has worked together for awhile can almost read each other's mind.

The drilling machine itself is mounted on a gigantic frame made of cast iron six inches in diameter. This large frame is called the "jumbo." Usually it will fit the entire face of the tunnel. In the case of the Yale tunnel however, the jumbo only covered half of the width of the tunnel. The tunnel was just too big at forty-two feet in diameter. Forty two feet is a large tunnel.You can put a two-lane highway through the center of the Yale tunnel with room to spare.

On a river the size of the Columbia a tunnel would not be practical. Can you imagine the size a tunnel would have to be to divert the Columbia River? With dams on the Columbia, the strategy is to "split" the river with coffer dams that sheer the river to one side while they build half the dam on the other side and then reverse the process to build the second half. The drilling machines are mounted on "decks" or platforms, one above the other on the jumbo. On theYale jumbo there are four such decks where the miner's work. Each deck has its own name. For example, the floor or ground level is called "the lifters". The second deck up is called "cut deck" or "swing deck". This deck is hinged and split in the middle. Each half can be raised and lowered. The swing deck is raised anytime the jumbo is moved. If the deck weren't raised the jumbo driver, or "truckee", couldn't see where he was backing the jumbo. The third deck is called the "hoosier deck." No one was ever able to explain the name to me, but you can be sure there is a story behind it. The top or fourth deck is called the" arch deck." There are five drills mounted on each level, except for the arch deck, where there are only three drills.

Noise is a major factor. Consider the noise level when all eighteen drills are hammering. Imagine eighteen jackhammers all running simultaneously in a confined, non-sound absorbing-space. Talking is out, I can tell you that. The drill isn't exactly a jackhammer, however. First of all, the steel bit rotates. The machine, or hammer, is much larger than the biggest of jackhammers and there is a stream of water that runs under very high pressure down the middle of the steel. You call these drilling machines "liners,"never jackhammers.

The miner controls the machine by levers. There are levers that move the machine right and left and another set for moving the machine up and down. The control that regulates the pressure of the drill bit against the rock face is called "the screw."The whole system is powered by compressed air. The squealing and whistling, and the thump, thump of the compressed air just adds to the noise level.

The decks, which are made of four inch by six inch rough-cut timber, serve as a shield over the heads of the miners,except for the men who work on the arch deck. The arch crew must work totally unprotected. The chucktender works in front of his miner and usually right at the face of the tunnel. The chucktender will try to keep his head and shoulders under the cover of the deck above him but his arms and hands must be exposed whenever they change steel or tend the chucks. Any rocks that are loosened by the drilling process will slide and slip right down the face of the tunnel. If a rock slab is loosened by drills on the levels above you it will slide and slice until it comes to rest on the lifters at ground level. A slab of rock breaking off like this will give no warning. The splitting rock could be making a thunderous sound but neither the miner nor the chucktender will ever hear it over the noise of the drilling machines. Anything and everything that becomes dislodged during the drillout is most likely going to come to rest on the bottom level. This is one of several reasons why the lifters are considered to be in the worst place to work from the standpoint of survival.

When miners talk about rocks, and rocks falling, they don't mean something the size of a baseball. Something that size would be called "gravel." A "rock" is something the size of a 21-inch TV, up to the size of a small car. Boulders are larger still. Miners have a saying in the tunnel, "Don't worry about the rocks but watch that damn gravel." If you are caught between a rock and your steel you will lose something like an arm or a leg, if not your head. In most cases the person caught is going to be the chucktender, and he is most likely going to be killed outright by a rock. But if you get hit by gravel you might just wish you had been killed outright. Gravel will cripple you for life, whereas rocks will just kill you.

The most dangerous time is right at the beginning of a drillout when the miner is trying to get the bit started into the rock. This part of the operation is called "collaring" the hole. When the miner is collaring the hole the face rock will often fracture and split off. This is also the very time that the chucktender must tend the chucks. This same situation is repeated every time a new hole is started. Each miner will drill from six to eight holes in a typical drillout. So the process of collaring occurs at least that many times. It is not uncommon for a miner to try several locations before he can get a hole collared. A drillout can take four to six hours.

After the holes are drilled out, the miners and chucktenders walk out of the tunnel to a powder truck which has been radioed to arrive just minutes before the powder is needed. The powder is stored in a "powder magazine" some distance from the mining operation.

The chucktenders start carrying in the boxes of sticks of powder. Each box weighs fifty pounds and each chucktender will need to bring in two boxes of powder. It is a status thing for the miners to have a chucktender strong enough to carry a box of powder on each shoulder. It may be a status thing to the miners but to the chucktenders it is hernia time. And what does the miner carry while the chucktenders are packing fifty-pound boxes of powder? The miners carry about eight ounces of "primers". A primer is the electrical "fuse." It is a metal cartridge about the diameter of a pencil, and three inches long. The miner will need at least one primer for each hole he has drilled. Oh yes, the chucktenders are expected to be back at the face of the tunnel where the holes will be loaded, before the miner gets there. I had to take two trips. I just couldn't carry two boxes at one time.

The loading process is simple enough, but the miner must pay close attention and get the right primer in the right hole. Each primer is numbered to correspond to the split-second timing of the primer. Each miner must coordinate the timing of his primers with the primers in the holes above him as well as on both sides of him, or there will be hell to pay when they try to set off the blast. So during the loading process the tunnel is uncharacteristically quiet. This is spooky because only a half-hour before loading you can't hear yourself think because of the racket. Adding to the eerie silence is the fact that the light is very faint during loading. All electricity is cut off to the area so that only light such as it is, comes from floodlights set up at the portal of the tunnel or from rubber-encased flashlights.

The chucktender places a stick of powder into a hole and pushes it to the end of the hole with a long wooden tamping stick. The miner shoves a primer into the soft powder of the second stick and plays out the attached wires while the chucktender is running that stick of powder to the end of the hole. This time, however, the chucktender doesn't tamp the stick as hard. In fact the primer stick is pushed to the end rather gingerly. The holes are filled and tamped to within six or eight inches of the collar.

The air gets heavy during the loading because they cut off the air blowers pumping in fresh air. All in all, it's not the most pleasant of assignments, and I was always glad when we had completed the loading.

The final step is to wire all the primer wires together. Wooden stakes are driven into holes on both sides of the tunnel and bright copper wire called "buzz wire" is stretched across the face of the tunnel. The stakes keep the wire from touching anything that might short out the buzz wire. The two wires from each primer are twisted onto the buzz wire and the entire system is wired together and attached to a lead wire that is reeled out of the tunnel to the detonator.

The Shift Boss will yell at the top of his voice, "fire in the hole." He will wait about thirty seconds and again yell, "fire in the hole," and on the third time he will quickly raise the handle of the detonator and plunge it down-setting off the blast. In old westerns you will often see the plunger in the air, but in real practice the plunger is never raised and allowed to sit there. Too many things can happen with the plunger in the air, all of them bad.

After the blast, the air pumps come back on to push fresh air into the tunnel and at the same time force out the blue-gray powder fumes which spew from the portal.

The rubble from the blast is then removed. This is called "Mucking out." At Yale we had electric mucking machines which loaded the rubble into giant Euclid trucks. The

"Ukes" had to be pulled in and out of the tunnel by cable wound on a huge drum powered by a "donkey engine." The trucks could not go into the tunnel on their own power because of the carbon monoxide.

Besides the miners and chucktenders there are other workers in the tunnel. For example, each shift has a "nipper". The nipper is a handy man, a fixer, and a scrounger. He is quite often an experienced miner who does not drill anymore for one reason or another, but he pulls a full miner's wage.

Then there is the "truckee." This man drives the jumbo in and out of the tunnel. There is a "rigger" who operates the donkey engine, and finally there is the supervisory staff. The supervisors are, the project engineer, (the guy we never see,) the walking boss, (who is over both portals), and finally the shift boss, or,"shifter." The shifter is in total charge of the men on his shift. To the miners, the shift boss is the most important person on the job if not in their lives. The shift boss gives the day-by-day orders and hires and fires.

The last thing necessary to complete the tunnel job is to describe"the dry shack." The dry shack is a long hall like building made of rough-cut lumber. The primary purpose for the dry shack is to have a place where the workers can hang their diggers to dry out between shifts. The dry shack has a gang shower, wooden lockers for street clothes, a pot belly stove, benches, and a table. The dry shack doesn't smell like a bed of roses, not quite.

Most miners will buy a new set of working clothes only at the beginning of a job. They will wear this one-set of clothes until the job is done and never wash them out or anything "dumb" like that. It is a tradition among tunnel men to burn their work clothes in the pot belly stove at the end of their last shift on the job.

Now you know all that I had learned by the end of the first week.

Chapter 8

Whiskey Riley Arrives

"They say that this Whiskey Riley will be here some time this shift," Slim said.

"They've been saying that for several days,"I said. "I don't know if that's good or bad for us."

"No, they say he's out now. No one says where he has been, but he's out now. Red is certain ," Slim said.

We were all sitting around eating our lunch except for some of the crew who were in a fairly lively crap game. A black Buick rolled to a stop in front of the dry shack. The crap game came to a sudden halt and the plywood table disappeared from sight. We couldn't see who was in the back seat of the car but some of the miners recognized the Project Engineer who was driving and the Walking Boss in the front seat. Something was about to happen and everybody knew it. I had never seen the Walking Boss, let alone the Project Engineer.

"Hey, Shift Boss, that looks like your replacement," a miner said.

"I 'spect you could be right," the Shift Boss replied.

"Ain't you gonna go see?" the miner said.

"I'm eating my sandwich," the Shift Boss said.

No one had gotten out of the car yet. The Shift Boss finished his sandwich, took one more drink from his coffee mug, and threw the rest on the ground. Now he got up in no particular hurry and turned to walk to the car.

"You might just as well take your nosebag with you," another miner scoffed.

The Shift Boss tucked his lunch pail under his arm and started nonchalantly toward the car. He was through and he knew it. There was no protest, no whining, or anything like that. The Nipper stepped forward and said, "Goodbye, Little John."

"Goodbye, Nipper."

To tell the truth I felt sorry for the guy.

As the Shift Boss approached the car the back door opened. Out lumbered the biggest man I had ever seen. Later I learned that he was six feet ten and weighed over three hundred pounds. He wore a different type of hard-top. It was rust red with a short bill in front. There was a clip in the front for a light to hang. I had seen this type of hard top on three or four other miners. The hardtop made the man look even taller. Our ex-Shift Boss got into the back seat of the car without saying a word, and the car roared away up the grade.

Whiskey Riley had arrived. He walked slowly over to where the men had assembled for the crap game. Whiskey Riley didn't say a word but looked slowly into each face in the circle.

His gaze stopped at one man.

"Hello Turk," he said. "What's the situation here?".

"There ain't no situation. That's the problem," the man called Turk said. "I'm glad you're here, Whiskey."

Whiskey turned to the group of silent men. "It looks like chow time is about over. Why don't you hands just go on doing what ever you were about before the dinner bell rang. It looks like you're about half drilled out. Why don't you all just finish the drillout? I'll just watch a bit."

People moved. It was funny. I had not seen the area clear so fast before. The problem was, as I knew, there were more men than there were drills, and everybody wanted to be drilling when the new Shifter came around. Everybody tried to get up the steel ladders to the cut deck or the Hoosier deck. No one wanted on the arch deck or the lifters.

Red grabbed Slim and they headed directly for the middle lifter. So they got a machine. There was no place for me to go so I picked up a short-handled shovel and started digging a little channel for water to drain away from the lifters. All I could do was try and show the guy that I was willing to find something to do even if I didn't know what to do.

I felt awkward because anyone could see I really wasn't needed. Most of the other guys who didn't get a machine just stood around and tried to look real interested.

Whiskey Riley went from deck to deck standing behind each driller in turn. I felt he looked right at me on several passes but I never looked up. I just drained more water. I hoped it would at least look better than doing nothing.

Other men just milled around trying to stay on the opposite side of the jumbo This went on for the next three, long, long, hours. Whiskey made a final round and motioned to each miner that he was going to cut the air off in ten minutes which meant they should pull their steel back from the hole they were drilling. The air went off and the area became quiet. Whiskey Riley motioned toward the dry shack.

"Let's have a chat," he shouted.

The dry shack was warm, stuffy, and dead silent. The screen to the dry shack door closed with a loud bang as Whiskey Riley came in .

"I shut it down boys, before someone got hurt," Whiskey said.

Whiskey Riley produced a small flat metal flask from someplace and downed the contents. Slim whispered to me, "I don't suppose that's soda pop."

Whiskey Riley spoke to no one in particular. "That must be the hardest rock in ten counties. I have never seen so many hung steel on one face in all my born years. It looks like a porcupine swished its tail against the face of that tunnel."

One poor guy thought he should laugh at what he supposed were Whiskey's efforts at humor. He was the only one who laughed, and he soon wished to hell he hadn't. Whiskey Riley turned and glared right at him for what seemed like a godawful long time.

Nipper, do you know how to use this phone?" Whiskey Riley asked.

It was a regular, conventional phone, but Whiskey Riley did not appear to know how to use it.

"Sure Mr. Whiskey, or, uh, I mean Mr. Riley."

"See if you can get someone for me to talk to at the other portal if that thing will reach the other side of the mountain," Whiskey Riley said.

The room was still very quiet so we all heard Whiskey's end of the conversation.

"Who am I jawing with? Who? O.K. Jackson. I need to chat with you a bit. You what? What? You don't say. So do I take it that's your last word? I get your meaning Jefferson. What? Oh yeah, I mean Jackson. Maybe I'll be seeing you around Jefferson." Whiskey hung up the telephone.

"Boys we got a few too many hands here! As you heard I called the other portal hoping they had room for some of you. They don't. Jackass, or what ever his name is, said he had been expecting my call and he wanted to know what took me so long," Whiskey Riley said. "It seems that they put all the ex-cons, greenhorns, and other misfits on one shift so they wouldn't foul up the whole project. Can anyone here guess which shift they put them on?"

A high squeaky voice came from somewhere in the back of the room. "I can't imagine why they would put a top hand like you in this tub of shit. You think about it. Why wouldn't they put you in charge? You're the biggest misfit that ever walked God's green earth. You ain't worth nothing and you never will be. They set you up this time you big clumsy, ignorant, hillbilly".

"Clumsy? Clumsy?" Whiskey Riley took offense.

While the squeaky voice continued his diatribe, he was winding his way through the crowd of men which parted quickly to let him by.

Whiskey Riley stood square in front of the oncoming man.

"Tennessee is that you?" Whiskey Riley bellowed. "I would've thought that some shit-eating dog would've got you by this time."

Whiskey's big arms shot out like lightning, pinned the guy's arms to his sides, and lifted him clear off the floor in a ferocious bear hug.

"Put me down Whiskey, put me down," the man called Tennessee begged.

The two men stood there eyeing each other. "I never thought I would see you again," Whiskey said. They hugged each other again and I thought I saw actual tears well up in each man's eyes. I felt embarrassed for the big man, but he wasn't too embarrassed to take out a big red handkerchief and blow his nose twice.

"What do you make of that?" Slim whispered.

"Turk, you're my arch man. Pick five miners. You decide who will run the machines and who will be the chucktenders. But have them all be miners," Whiskey said.

Their reunion, was over and Whiskey had begun the task at hand.

"Set me up will they. We'll see by Gawd", murmured Whiskey.

"Take your time ,Turk. I want the best men on top. Keep me an arch in the shape of an egg and we will probably live to work another job."

"Picking the five best from this bunch won't be too hard," Turk said. He quickly pointed to five men who gathered around him. All five had the same type of hardtop for hanging a light on, which meant to me that they must have worked together before.

"I want the rest of you who claim to be miners to stand over there." Whiskey Riley had begun his organization.

Whiskey Riley went up and down the line tapping shoulders indicating for some to stay and for others to move over toward the door.

When he came to the man called Tennessee he hesitated.

"Tennessee, I want you to break yourself down to a chucktender and work on the outside lifter. Do you have any problem with that?"

"If that's where you want me, that's where I'll be," Tennessee said.

When he had finished picking miners there were at least ten miners left.

"Nothing personal, boys," Whiskey said. "I don't have a spot for you hands. You can get your time at the end of the shift."

One of the unselected miners said, " I'll break back to chucktending. I don't mind too much."

Whiskey paused. "As I said there's nothing personal, but maybe you didn't notice that I have a whole army of chucktenders."

No one else said a word of protest or complaint. Whiskey turned to his new crew of miners. "Now boys, you pick your own Chucktender. Better get one you can bring up right because training them will be your first job."

Several of the miners motioned to their chucktenders at once. Red picked Slim.

I remembered how it was in grade school when the team captains chose sides for a game of ball. You hoped you would be chosen early and prayed you wouldn't be the last one. That's the way I felt now, only on the playground everyone eventually did get chosen. But not everyone would be chosen for this ballgame. Man after man around me got picked. It was down to the last four miners when one called Johnnie pointed at me.

Johnnie was the miner who had brought an extra lunch for me before we got into the Yale Hilton. I was beyond relieved . I really needed the job. I averted eye contact with the fellows not selected. I knew they needed work just as much as I did.

"That's it, boys. School starts tomorrow." Whiskey Riley said. "Good luck to you other hands. Maybe I'll see you on another job."

In less than half an hour Whiskey Riley had brought some degree of organization to the chaos. However, ten miners, about twenty chucktenders and some others were out of work. I felt elated, but at the same time I felt sad for those now out of work. I managed to sit next to Johnnie on the ride back to camp.

"I want to thank you for picking me," I said. "I need this job."

"Everyone did. I picked you because you're the tallest, and you have 'Mac' as your moniker on your hardtop. I 've never met a Scot I couldn't trust."

I didn't think this would be the best time to tell him that I actually was a "Mick" not a "Mac" even though Mac was on my helmet. I glanced at Slim. He just smiled but did not give away my ancestry.

Red and Slim went off some place but I showered and went right to bed to get some sleep before the room got too hot. Tomorrow was going to be a big day and besides all of that we would get our first full paycheck. Slim's check would be "light" because he took a pay draw, but, I didn't.

Chapter 9

The Miner's School

I don't know what time Slim got to bed but I could see he didn't feel too good. That was too bad because I figured today was going to be a big day.

Whiskey Riley gathered us all around to explain his "school." Like most men who have worked in the tunnels for any length of time, Whiskey Riley had an obvious hearing loss. He more than compensated for this loss with his booming voice.

"Take your nosebags with you, gents, cause you'll be eating in the tunnel or at the portal from now on," Whiskey Riley said. "We'll meet in the dry shack at the beginning of each shift. If there are any instructions or orders you'll get them then. Other than that there ain't any drilling going on in the dry shack so there ain't no reason to be there."

Whiskey turned to go out the door.

"Oh yeah," he said. "I'm the first man into the tunnel each shift and I'm the last one out at the end of a shift. That goes for when we shoot too. Is that understood? When there's nothing to do you can sit down, or sleep, or play crap for all I care but do it where I can see you. Don't be crawling off someplace to sleep."

He turned again to go out the door.

"Oh yeah, another thing. Crap on your own time unless you got the runs or something. That shaft already smells

like a horse barn. No one pisses in my tunnel. You go outside to take a leak and that's on your own time too."

"I want to talk to the arch men up on top of the jumbo.
The rest of you go to your machines and start training your
chucktenders the way you want them to work for you. I
want everyone to use the standard hand signals. Don't anyone get original on us. I want you to start by slapping the
'babes' butts."

"I don't want to hear any drilling till after dinner time,"
he said. "I want those babe's butts spanked first. After chow
time we'll collar holes and drill a four-foot round but we'll
let the day shift load."

Whiskey had been sitting on a corner of the table during
most of this oration. What happened next became a ritual
that would occur each day at starting time for the next several months until the job was over . Whiskey pulled out his
pocket watch, took a long look at it, and stood up. When
he stood up we stood up and then came his famous
line,which I have been told was his trade- mark: "Well boys,
let's get closer to it. All I want to see is assholes and elbows, and both of them turned up." With that pronounce-
ment he led his army into battle.

Johnnie and I were assigned the middle lifter, so we were
on the floor of the tunnel and right in the middle. On the
machine next to us was Tennessee, and his miner whom,
they called Easy Money.

"When Whiskey said,' spank the babes' butts', he meant
start at the very beginning, with the basics," Johnnie explained. "So this is a chuckwrench. You stand with it in
your hands this way and facing me. When we change steel,
 and we'll get into that, always lay the chuckwrench in the
same place. The day that you have to look for your wrench
is the day we got big problems between us. There are four
large nuts to tighten and loosen throughout the drillout.
This nut is called number one."

He raised one finger. "These two nuts are called two's, and here is number three. The nuts are numbered in the order they are used most. So which one would not be used much?"

I tapped the number three nut.

"That's good," he said.

"When I raise one finger and clench my fist what do you think I'm talking about?" he asked.

"I would tighten down on the number one nut right here," I said.

"And what do you suppose you do if after you have tightened the number one nut I keep my fist closed and shake my fist at you?"

"I think I would try to tighten the nut still more," I said.

"You got it. And I mean a lot tighter," Johnnie said. "Now you see why I wanted a long armed chucktender. I want some leverage on that wrench. Now, you see those two steel guides that swing up to hold the bit? Those are the chucks. That's what you're suppose to tend. Now you know why they call you a chucktender."

I nodded my understanding so far.

"Now let's review what I've told you so far. You parrot back everything I've told you. Give it to me just like I was a greenhorn and you were the miner. Go ahead, do it."

"This is a chuckwrench. You hold it like this. No, don't stand there. Stand facing me." I repeated every word just as he had given it to me and even including his expressions. He liked it. When I had finished repeating my first lessons to him I said, "You learn fast for a greenhorn."

"I didn't say that. You just put that in," he cackled with laughter. I was relieved that my attempt at humor was well received.

And so the morning went. Johnnie went into great detail and I appreciated it. He didn't just say the nut had to be tight but explained the function of the nut and the consequences that would result if the nut wasn't cranked down enough. He seemed pleased with me and the way I was catching on.

"I have had stronger chucktenders but I ain't never had a smarter one," he said.

We ate our lunch together under the stars at the portal to the tunnel. It was a frosty spring morning without a cloud in the sky. For the first time in two weeks I felt comfortable, because I knew I would soon be earning my pay. I didn't have to feel guilty anymore. The best part was, I knew I had made the team.

We drilled a short round after dinner. Whiskey Riley watched over the shoulder of each miner in turn. Every so often he would signal the miner to shut the machine off and he would shout instructions in the miner's ear, with a lot of gesturing. I noticed he would not leave a miner until things were going smoothly. When the miner did something that pleased Whiskey he immediately praised the miner, usually with a thump on the back and a thumbs up motion. He even gave me a thumbs up when I responded to Johnnie's clenching fist.

On one pass Whiskey motioned Easy Money to one side. I could sense that he was telling him something about Tennessee. Tennessee knew it too, and tried to look the other way. There were so many interesting things going on that I was actually sorry when the shift came to an end.

After we had eaten supper Slim and I compared notes. Red had told Slim some things that Johnnie had not told me and vice versa. For example, Slim and I had taken some cotton from an alka-seltzer bottle to stuff in our ears. Red said get rid of the cotton. He told Slim that the cotton absorbs the noise and damages the hearing even more.

The hand signals we'd learned were identical. We drew a picture resembling a drilling machine on a piece of brown paper. We drew in the nuts about where they should be. We practiced the hand signals and quizzed each other on them until we could respond without thinking .

The Truckee came in and he was all excited too.

"Whiskey Riley said he wanted me to back the jumbo in on its own power. He said he didn't want to take the time to hook up a pulley to have the donkey engine pull the jumbo in each time," Truckee said. "That means there will be fumes in the tunnel so he says I have to back the jumbo in and into position on one pass. Whiskey Riley says he'll help me practice tomorrow after you guys have drilled out."

"Do you think you can do it?" I asked.

"Whiskey says he will put a man on each side with flash-lights to help guide me," the Truckee said.

"That will help but do you think you can do it fast enough so the tunnel won't fill up with gas fumes?" Slim said.

"Whiskey said he watched me steer it in by the tow line and pulley. He says I can do it, Truckee said.

"If Whiskey Riley says you can do it, then by God, you can," Slim declared.

"That's what he said. But boys he don't know I ain't driven anything bigger than a Franz bread truck. But he says I can do it. That's what he said." Truckee repeated him-self as though saying it often enough would make it come true. Maybe it would.

Truckee was much older than Slim and me and it was good to see a man his age get as excited as we were. I hoped I could show a burst of such enthusiasm when I am in the mid thirties.

Truckee went on, "He said he wanted me to learn to run the mucking machine too, as soon as I can, and then he wants me to learn to operate the donkey engine. The prob-lem is I'm a teamster and those jobs are Operating Engi-neer jobs. I tried to explain that to Whiskey but he went off to something else."

"Maybe they don't have unions where Whiskey comes from," I said.

"Whiskey says every team has a back-up pitcher. No team can be dependent upon one man," Truckee said.

"What if he says the same thing to Blackie the donkey jockey? I can tell you there'll be hell to pay. Those damn Operating Engineers will shut a job down just for the fun of it."

The next shift was more training and practice. Whiskey told us we were getting better but that we still had to think too much about what we were doing.

"Boys, I want your reactions to be like rabbits making little rabbits. Fast and spontaneous," Whiskey said.

Now that was an example we farm boys could understand.

"Mac, can I borrow your tamper for a hole?" Whiskey Riley, asked. " Let me show you. You go tap, tap, tap. But how did I go?"

"More like, thunk, thunk," I said.

" Right, try it once. You ain't gonna hurt that powder. It takes a one hundred pound whack to set it off."

"Tomorrow we will have a real school in the dry shack," Whiskey announced at the end of the shift.

"How in the hell would you know a real school class?" Tennessee asked. "You ain't never seen the inside of one."

"Then I guess I better have some help from a highly eddycated stiff like yourself," Whiskey joked.

The Truckee came by again after shift.

"Hey boys. You can't guess what Blackie told me. He said Whiskey Riley told him today that he wanted him to learn to back the jumbo into the face of the tunnel. Whiskey said that he had been watching him and said he was a good hand. He said, he thought Blackie would catch on to it real fast. But Blackie is all nervous about doing it right."

We roared with laughter. So much for Whiskey's union problems.

" Whiskey Riley should be selling snake oil," Slim said.

We all stayed in the dry shack at the beginning of the next shift. There was a high level of expectation in the air.

Whiskey came in, the screen door banging behind him. He had a four-by-eight-foot piece of plywood,which he handled like a sheet of typing paper.

"Find a place to sit boys. This here school is now in session," Whiskey said.

He went over to the stove and got the iron-poker to use as a pointer. When he turned the plywood around so we could see the other side there was a very good likeness of the face of the tunnel painted in brown. "This here is the face of the tunnel, boys." No one could doubt it because Whiskey, or whoever had painted it, was a fairly good artist. The painting had a three-dimensional effect.

"We're going to learn about loading and shooting," Whiskey Riley said. "When the blast goes off, there has to be a wedge blown right out of the center, here." Whiskey tapped the graphic with his poker. "That's called "pulling the wedge."That's followed instantly by the lifters going off, here. The wedge and the lifters have to go off first in split second order to give the rest of the shot some place to go. That's why they call them the lifters. They lift the bottom up and out."

Johnnie turned to Easy Money and whispered loud enough so I could hear. "Did you know that?" Easy Money shook his head, "No." So this school was not just for the green- horns. Even experienced miners were learning new things.

"The ribs go next, and last is the crown," Whiskey continued. "That's why we use time-delayed fuses. You can't have it all going off at one time like we used to do in the coal mines. This way we reduce the rock fracturing beyond the tunnel alignment. This is controlled blasting," Whiskey said.

"If you could watch the blast go off, which I don't exactly recommend, you would see the center pop out first. Then the lifters will lift, then the rest will go off in a circle from the center to the ribs and finally to the crown. Any questions so far? You have noticed, I'm sure, that each primer has a number on it. The number relates to the split-second timing between the fuses. I said split-second, not seconds. If someone screws up and we get these numbers out of order, you can see there will be hell to pay. Right? The numbers are what make the series work. Now if the blast goes off out of order some fuses may be snuffed out by the blast and not explode. This will not make me happy. I will definitely not be happy. What happens is it will leave huge chunks of the face sticking out. We want the face to break clean. If the face is not smooth, it means that the Truckee can't get the jumbo up snug to the face. And what that means is that our chucktenders will be much more exposed. They won't have any cover over them from the jumbo. This means that the likelihood of having to break in new chucktenders goes way up. No one wants to train new chucktenders, now do they? But as bad as that is that ain't the worst of it."

Some poor chucktender made the mistake of asking, "What is the worst?"

Whiskey turned slowly toward the poor guy.

"The worst thing is for a chucktender to interrupt the Shifter just when he is getting warmed up." There was a life-threatening frown on his face.

"Now dang it all. I have to start all over from the beginning. When the blast goes off there's got to be a wedge come right out of the center..."

Everyone roared including Whiskey Riley. The poor chucktender joined carefully in the laughter.

"Turk, will you explain to these hands what we get if the holes don't explode in the right sequence?"

Turk was a quiet man but I think he was pleased to be singled out as a man with experience in such things.

"Well Whiskey, you're talking about a 'bootleg' or a 'jack-rabbit hole,' Turk said.

"And tell these hands what you mean by that."

"Whiskey showed you on his drawing that you can't get the jumbo up against the face because a block of rock is sticking out. That's because, as he said, the powder in the holes in the rock outcropping didn't go off." Turk was getting into it now and he took the poker from Whiskey's outstretched hand "Now what do we have to do? We go back in and re-drill that rock outcropping. You hope to hell you are drilling in between the old holes. Only you can't tell for sure exactly where the old holes are located because the face is all shattered. Even if you knew for sure where the old holes were collared you'll have no way of knowing the angle of the old holes and you stand a good chance of drilling across an old hole. It takes about a hundred pound whack to set off this stuff and boys your hammers are hitting a lot more than that. If we leave very many rabbit holes someone will die. It's as simple as that. I don't mean that we'll lose one or two men. We will lose that many this summer anyway. I mean we would lose half the crew."

"That's the place where you're wrong, Turk," Whiskey Riley said. "On my crew we won't get that many killed, 'cause as soon as I can determine who fouled up, that'll be the guy who goes back in to drill out all by himself."

During the entire summer whenever we would shoot a round all the experienced miners would listen very intently at the moment of the blast. They could tell by the sound whether it was a good one or not. All the blasts sounded alike to me, in spite of Johnnie's coaching as to what to listen for.

"When it goes BARROOM, ROOM, ROOM, ROOM, its a good shot. When it goes BARROOM, ROOM, BARROOM, ROOM, ROOM we got big problems," he said.

We had only two minor jack rabbit hole situations come up over the entire summer. Johnnie and Easy Money credited Whiskey's rule of letting the culprit drill it out by himself as the reason we had so few. Whiskey applied his rule on both of those occasions.

"What would happen if the miner said no thank-you and quit on the spot refusing to drill out the jack rabbit holes?" I asked.

Johnnie's answer came easy, and it was a shocker.

"Whiskey Riley would kill the man and then drill it out himself." Johnnie gave no indication he was anything but serious.

Whiskey made one other change in the loading process which all of us chucktenders appreciated.

"I noticed that the chucktenders have to carry all the powder," Whiskey said. "From now on the chucktenders will carry a box and so will the miners."

I don't think any of the miners minded.

By the third week under Whiskey Riley, we were drilling one round and part of the next in each shift.

"At this rate we will soon be on 'B' money,"Johnnie said. Bonus or 'B' money would mean seventy-five cents a foot for chucktenders and a dollar a foot for miners for everything over eight feet in a shift. That could mount up fast.

"Now you can see why we hillbillies all came crawling out of the backwoods," Tennessee said. "Consider this. After a series of nasty strikes John L. Lewis finally got us $14.05 a shift in the coal mines. Out here our regular time is $16.40 a shift for miners, and with another four dollars or so a shift with 'B' money it would be possible for us to make over twenty big ones in one shift. This country is not as nice as West Virginny, that's for damn sure. But they pay you a hell of a lot more."

Chapter 10

Tennessee

I got to know Tennessee pretty well, or at least I thought I did. We worked on adjacent machines. My miner, Johnnie, and Tennessee's miner, Easy Money were good friends too, we all helped each other out. At lunch time Tennessee would always eat apart from the rest of the crew. He always had such a sad look on his face, like he had lost his best hunting dog. He was experienced underground and had held miner's positions on other jobs. I figured he could teach me a lot. So I took to waiting until I saw where Tennessee was going to sit to eat and then I would join him. He did not seem to mind my questions and always gave me complete answers without making me feel stupid for asking.

If anyone else got up and came into Tennessee's area he would watch them from the time they got up until they left. If more than one person walked toward him he would try to keep his eyes on both of them, turning his head like an owl. I have seen those same eyes on animals we used to trap as boys in the Glen.

Tennessee was friendly to me and I could get him to laugh. He thought I talked funny. When it was time to return to work he was twenty feet out in front of the pack , except when Whiskey walked with the pack. Then he would hang back and be twenty feet behind the crew as we headed back into the tunnel.

One day I sat down first and called to Tennessee to join me. I had a question about why we were hanging, or sticking so much steel all of a sudden. A stuck steel really slowed things down. I also wondered about the big pipe they were hanging on the side of the tunnel wall.

"I got a couple questions for you Tennessee," I said.

Tennessee looked around. The nearest worker was fifteen feet away.

"You bet Mac. Let me roll this rock around to sit on and you have at it."

Unfortunately Tennessee bent over at the waist to roll the rock. His back-sides stuck up in the air as he was facing me. A miner walked past and couldn't resist Tennessee's hind end waving at him in the air. He poked Tennessee in the butt with his thumb.

The next thing I knew Tennessee had slugged me in the chest and thrown an upper cut that caught me flush on the point of my chin. All the time he was shouting something. I was flat on my rear in the mud. His blows kept raining down on me and he was shouting, "Goddamn it! Goddamn it!"

Whiskey Riley saved me from getting really hurt. Appearing from out of nowhere, he wrapped his big arms around Tennessee and just smothered him down with brute strength.

After a few minutes Tennessee said, "Let me go Whiskey, I'm O.K."

"Who set you off Tennessee?" Whiskey asked.

"I don't know. "

I was still sitting in the mud all this time rubbing my chin, and Whiskey was attending to Tennessee when it seemed to me that I was the one who got thumped.

Whiskey lowered his voice and put his arm slowly around Tennessee's shoulder.

"You know this won't be the last time this happens."

"I know Whiskey. I know." Tennessee collapsed in despair with tears streaking the dust on his face.

Some of the crew saw some action, thought a fight had broken out and started circling around. Fortunately, Tennessee's miner, Easy Money, interceded. " Fun's all over boys. Let's go about our business now," Easy Money said.

Whiskey Riley went on talking softly to Tennessee,"I can't tie a can to every stiff that gooses you. We have gone through this before Tennessee. I wish to God I could help you."

"You have helped me more than you should already. I'm not asking you to do it anymore," Tennessee said.

"Tennessee, do you want me to give you the 'cure'? Whiskey asked.

Tennessee's eyes widened. "Oh God, don't do that Whiskey. I don't think I could bear another cure," Tennessee said.

Whiskey nodded his head in understanding. Whiskey finally looked at me. I was still sitting on my pants in the water and mud. He held out his big hand and pulled me up.

"He didn't mean to hurt you, Mac, " Whiskey said.

"Christ no. I didn't mean to hurt you," Tennessee confirmed. "I can't help it."

"I don't get it. What the hell was that all about?" I asked.

"I'm goosey," Tennessee said. "I don't want you talking to me anymore or sitting by me. I will hurt you real bad some time. I don't want to hurt you, Mac. Christ, you're about the only friend I got."

Tennessee walked off to sit by himself.

The next evening as we were getting dressed to go to work Easy Money came into our room.

"You ain't never seen a man that's goosey, I guess, " Easy Money said.

"I've never heard such a thing before," I said.

"Well it's a nervous condition. I don't know what makes a man that way. But Tennessee is sure goosey," Easy Money said. "If someone jabs him in the ribs or gooses him in the butt he will fly off on whoever is in front of him. So the guy who may be minding his own business is the one who will get lumped. It's too damn bad but that's why Whiskey put Tennessee on the outside lifter, so there wouldn't be people working behind him or on his blind side. He put Tennessee with me because he knew that I already knew he was goosey. It's too damn bad too, 'cause he knows his rock as good as anyone and he should have a drill of his own."

"Thank you for taking the time to explain it to me. I thought at first I had done something to set him off," I said.

"No, not so," Easy Money assured me. "If Tennessee really hurts somebody, Whiskey will send him down the road. Or if it becomes too much of a sport for the rest of the crew, now that they all know he's goosey, Whiskey will let him go. Whiskey doesn't want to bunch Tennessee because he is a good hand. And because he is Tennessee's brother-in-law. Tennessee is married to the sweetest little girl that ever came out of the West Virginny hill country. That little girl is Whiskey Riley's kid sister. Remember if you can, Tennessee may be goosey, but he is a good man."

That evening at lunch time I waited until Tennessee had chosen his spot to sit. I waited until he looked up and made eye contact before I started walking slowly toward him and sat down facing him.

"I will never goose you Tennessee. I like to talk with you about things that are going on and ask you about what I don't understand," I said.

"Can I go on eating with you?" I asked.

"You'll probably get hurt some time if you do," Tennessee said.

"I will take my chances, unless you really don't want me sitting here." I said.

"You mean you don't think it's funny to goose me?" he said.

"No, I don't think it's funny but I'm not saying I won't laugh at it sometimes. Although I won't be laughing at you. All I want is to be able to ask you questions about the tunnel," I said.

"Go ahead," Tennessee said.

"Go ahead and what?"

"Ask me your questions."

"I can't think of any," I said.

We sat there in silence for the rest of the lunch break.

The next evening Whiskey Riley stopped me as we were going into the tunnel.

"You've made a friend for life in Tennessee. You can count on Tennessee 'going out' for you any time."

He could see that I didn't understand his terms.

"Going out? That means if you get in a fight or something like that you'll never have to worry about your backside if Tennessee is around. He would cover your bet in a crap game in a minute. You know things like that. That's what 'going out' means. That's what the Scots in the mountains say. They go out. and Tennessee will go out for you."

I thought to myself, will I ever receive a higher commendation than that?

When the word spread around the crew that Tennessee was goosey some of them could not resist the "fun." Easy Money had predicted it would happen. At times it really seemed humorous but most of the time it was just plain cruel.

Slim thought this was the funniest thing he could imagine. The more inappropriate the timing, the "funnier" it was. One shift, the jumbo had pulled back away from the face a few feet to allow the chucktenders a chance to clean some rubble off the arch deck. Tennessee was standing at the edge of the arch deck just looking down to the floor of the tunnel. Somebody, and I will always think it was Slim, reached out with a shovel handle or something and goosed old Tennessee. Tennessee let out a scream and jumped into space.

With arms and legs pin-wheeling and screaming, "Goddamn it! Goddamn it!" he landed thirty five feet below into eighteen inches of water. By some miracle he wasn't physically hurt, but I am sure he was hurt, by all the laughter. Slim was still laughing and talking about it over supper.

There was one time that even I had to laugh. A bunch of us decided to drive in to see a war movie that was playing at the Bee Gee theatre in Battle Ground, Washington. They had this Sunday matinee showing, and Tennessee went along with us. The seats in the Bee Gee would be fine for midgets, but if you had any legs at all the seating was tight. Tennessee went out to the lobby to buy us all a bag of popcorn. He came squeezing back to his seat right at the most dramatic and quiet segment of the movie, trying his best to balance five bags of popcorn. I don't know if Tennessee was goosed on purpose or by accident but he got goosed. Popcorn flew ten feet in all directions and Tennessee screamed out his old standard,"Goddamn it! Goddamn it!" And all the time he was beating the daylights out of a logger and his date who had the misfortune of sitting in front of us. By the time the lights came on, Tennessee had managed to crawl on all fours up the aisle to the side door where he slipped outside.

We were left trying to explain to the logger that we weren't the ones who had slugged his girl. Each time we got the logger and theater manager half convinced that the culprit was gone, one of us would start to snicker, and we were in serious trouble all over again.

Unfortunately for Tennessee,the frequency of these episodes was increasing. One morning at the end of a shift where he had been goosed several times since lunch ,Whiskey Riley decided something had to be done. We were all in the dry shack showering or hanging up wet diggers when

Whiskey Riley said, "Someone get the door. Stand back boys, give Tennessee room to fall."

Whiskey Riley turned to Tennessee with a look of paternal anquish on his face. Tennessee figured out what was coming.

"Tennessee, I'm gonna 'CURE' you,"Whiskey said. There was absolute assurance in his voice.

Tennessee's eyes narrowed to slits. Whiskey was no longer a friend; he was the enemy. Tennessee glanced at the door to escape but he could see it was blocked. He would have to fight and fight he did. He was no match for Whiskey Riley. Whiskey got Tennessee down on the wooden table, pinning his arms to his sides, and he started tickling, jabbing, prodding, and all other manner of goosing. Whiskey bounced Tennessee on the table, which then fell-over and they rolled on the rough floor. At one point they rolled, up against the potbelly stove, which had a pretty good fire in it.

Tennessee was screaming and cursing at the top of his lungs and at the same time he was trying to land good punches on Whiskey. In fact, one of Tennessee's blows landed on the point of Whiskey's nose and the blood spurted everywhere. Whiskey, on the other hand, was not trying to duke it out with Tennessee. Whiskey was just wrestling him and goosing him as part of the "cure". Whiskey gave no attention to the heavy blows targeted on his nose which I'm sure was now broken.

This "cure" treatment lasted twenty minutes. Tennessee finally stopped screaming, and dropped on a bench totally exhausted He could no longer resist Whiskey's prods and pokes. Whiskey sagged down on the bench, facing Tennessee. Both men were huffing and puffing. The room that had been a bedlam turned quiet as a church.

The two men sat there just looking at each other and breathing hard. Finally Whiskey reached over and picked up a broom that had been knocked to the floor. He jabbed

Tennessee in the ribs with the broom handle. He jabbed him a little harder. Nothing happened.

Whiskey stood up to his full 6'10" height and with great pride of accomplishment he announced, in a great booming voice,"Tennessee, you're CURED."

Just at that critical moment a miner standing behind Tennessee whistled, and jabbed Tennessee in the butt.

"Goddamn it! Goddamn it!" Tennessee screamed and lit full bore into none other than Whiskey Riley ,who was still standing directly in front of Tennessee. The look of surprise on Whiskey's face was a sight to see. His"cure" had lasted less than three minutes.

Chapter 11

Poker

We would usually get back to camp around 8:30 each morning. Slim and I, along with most of the crew would eat our supper, which was really more like breakfast and then turn in for as much sleep as we could get before the rooms got too hot. I could usually find a Portland *Oregonian* newspaper in the day room which, I would read until I dozed off to sleep. Reading a morning newspaper the same day it came out was a treat for me. At home our paper came by mail and it would always be at least two days old.

When we woke up we would stroll over to the mess hall once again. There was no set time to eat. There was always a meal waiting for us. The thing that amazed me was the fact that they had some kind of meat for every meal. We made our lunches from the stuff they put out on a long counter. There would be several kinds of lunch meat, cheese, lettuce, and always fruit of some sort. We could fill our thermos with either milk or coffee. I took milk.

It amused me to hear some of the guys complain about the food. It is probably the best food most of them had ever eaten in their lives.

Working seven days a week, or seven nights in our case, gave me a weekly take-home paycheck of $105 and some change. That was after they had taken out board and room and a few cents for some insurance which I didn't understand. The miners got twenty five cents an hour more than the chucktenders. The Shift Boss got twenty five cents an hour more than the miners, and the Walking Boss another twenty five cents. What could a person possibly do with all that money?

We got paid Friday mornings when we got off shift. The men working day shift got their checks at 5:30 as they went off shift, but the poor guys on swing shift didn't get off shift until 11:30 at night when the time shack was closed and wouldn't open again until eight o'clock Monday morning. I didn't see that as such a big problem. They would get their money sooner or later. But the swing shifters wanted it sooner. To make their point, they tipped the time shack over and said they would tip it over every week until someone could get out of bed and open the shack to pay them. They only had to tip it over once to make their point.

One evening after supper Slim popped into the room with some news.

"Some of the guys are going to play a little poker. Do you want to join in?"

"Sure," I said. My brother had taught me to play poker. It's a good game. On the way down to the day room where the game was forming Slim gave me the "ground rules."

"It's penny-ante with a quarter limit on raises," Slim said. "Do you have any money? Get a couple of bucks for us."

I had some change and I had cashed a check at Nick's in Amboy. The other uncashed checks I had stuffed in the bottom of my duffel bag. I got a couple of bucks for myself and gave Slim a couple. I think he expected more.

The game was fun. Tennessee was there along with Red, Truckee, and a fellow called Little Joe. we played mostly five card draw and seven card stud.

"Real poker," Red said.

A big pot would be 75 to 80 cents. Every once in a while someone would call for a crazy game like baseball, or spit-in-the-ocean, or high-low takes the pot, games like that.

This began a nightly routine with about the same men in the game each night. At least in the beginning. Sometimes a second or third table would have to be set up. I would lose 50 to 75 cents each night but it was fun to see how long I could last before I lost my predetermined limit. It was an enjoyable way to spend a few hours each night before we went to work. I began to notice, kind of in the back of my mind, that the number of players and the size of the pots were increasing slowly but surely. This was O.K. Everyone was having a good time.

One week I had not played for several evenings because I had found other things to do. As I came into the day room Tennessee sidled up beside me. "I would skip this game tonight if I were you," he said.

"How come? Why do you say that?" I asked.

"These aren't 'boys' playing tonight. These are "men".

"I don't get it."

"Look around you. Do you see anyone you know?"

I scoured the room and there were a few I recognized but at least half of the players were strangers.

"Who the hell are these guys?"

"I don't know for sure," Tennessee said. "They aren't from the job I can tell you that. "It's my guess that they are pros out of Portland here to make a killing. This is no penny ante game. At that, table over there they have been opening for a buck."

"A buck to open? My God I wouldn't last a single hand at that price," I said.

"Let's just watch from a distance," Tennessee said. "This will be all mainline poker tonight, none of those wild games here."

About this time Slim wandered in. I frantically waved him over to the side where we were standing.

"Stay out of the game tonight Slim," I warned. "Tennessee says the room is full of professional card players."

Slim looked slowly from table to table. "By God, is that right?"

"Do you know any of these hands?" Tennessee said.

"It looks like every table has a couple of construction stiffs that I do recognize but the others just aren't dressed right," Slim observed.

"You got that right," Tennessee said.

The strangers weren't dressed too different, yet something was different about them.

"Take a look at their shoes," Tennessee said. "Do you know any stiff who wears shiny shoes?"

"That means they got money," Slim said.

"Yeah, they got money and they damn well intend to have more before this evening is over," Tennessee said.

"They don't scare me any," Slim said. "They can only draw one card at a time, same as me."

I could tell what was going through Slim's mind.

"You don't get it do you?" Tennessee said. "These Yonikers make a living on this game. They're not here to have fun."

Slim wasn't listening. He turned on his heels and darted out of the room.

"I've got a bad feeling on this one," Tennessee said.

Slim returned in a few minutes with a roll of one dollar bills. He stopped where we were standing and whispered his big secret to us.

"I only got thirty dollars in this roll, but I got them all doubled over so it looks like I really have a wad, doesn't it?"

"Oh yeah, it will sure fool those pros," Tennessee whispered back sarcastically. But Slim didn't hear Tennessee. Slim waltzed over to the nearest table and said in a steady voice, "Is there room for another hand in this game?"

One of the Shiny Shoes vacated his chair at once and went to a another table.

"Thanks, buddy, I didn't mean to chase you out," Slim said.

"I could have waited for an empty chair."

"That's no problem," one of the Shiny Shoes said. "Glad to have you, friend."

With Slim at the table it made the score two Shiny Shoes to three construction stiffs. The Shiny Shoes sat across from each other.

"Slim is about to learn a thirty-dollar lesson called sucker poker," Tennessee said.

"I don't know," I said. "Slim is pretty good. Maybe he'll do better than you think."

"Yeah, maybe." Tennessee said.

On the second hand Slim won a little pot. He glanced over to where we were still standing and winked. Several hands later he won another little pot. Then he folded a couple of times with about two dollars of his money in each pot. Neither of the Shiny Shoes had even won a small pot as yet. In fact it looked like they had stayed in on a couple hands when it seemed like they should have folded.

Five card draw was the game when the first major pot developed. The game was jacks or better to open. The first player to the left of the dealer was a Shiny Shoes. He passed. The next player, a stiff, he passed. The next player was the second Shiny Shoes and he opened. Every one stayed in for the first round of bets. The first Shiny Shoes called for two cards. The stiff called for four. The next Shiny Shoes called for three, and Slim called for three. The other stiff and the dealer called for cards too, but I couldn't see exactly how many.

"What do you think each of them got?" Tennessee whispered to me.

"The guy who drew four cards probably has an ace and a prayer," I said. "The first Shiny Shoes that opened has got to have a pair of jacks or better or he couldn't have opened. I would guess he has a high pair with maybe an ace kicker. The first Shiny Shoes who passed and then drew two cards is a question mark. He probably has a little pair, too small to open but he is hoping he will triple up and then he may also be holding a high card as a kicker. Slim has a pair. It may be a little pair or a big pair. I know how he plays. He is just hoping to get the third one. I couldn't guess about the rest."

Everyone raised without any hesitation. The one construction stiff obviously didn't have his prayer answered and after much thought to the point of delaying the flow of the game, he wisely folded. There were two more rounds of betting and raises. That left only Slim and the two Shiny Shoes. The Shiny Shoes who had opened now folded.

"That's kind of strange, isn't it?" I said.

"What is so strange about that? It was predictable as geese flying south, " Tennessee said.

Slim's hand was finally called. He threw out a pair of tens with an ace as his high card. Certainly nothing to be staying in the game for. The Shiny Shoes threw out a pair of queens, which won the Pot. The Shiny Shoes who had opened threw out a pair of kings to show that he had openers, and scooped them up again a little too fast.

One of the construction workers wasn't paying close enough attention and asked to see the openers again.

"Pay attention my friend. I don't like to delay the game by showing openers over and over," the Shiny Shoes said. But he showed the two kings again.

"Did you see that? Did you see that?" Tennessee whispered. I had seen it. The first time he showed his pair of kings they were both black. The second time however, one of the kings was a red king.

"I don't get it. He had at least three kings in his hand. No one would've folded with a triple that big," I said. "He screwed up and no one noticed it at the table."

"He wasn't supposed to win. He was supposed to fold to keep Slim in the game. Slim didn't have a hand. They knew that and if the Shiny Shoes who opened stayed in, Slim would have certainly folded," Tennessee said. "That little move cost Slim about eight dollars, as near as I can tell."

"It doesn't make too much difference which Shiny Shoes, wins 'cause they will split the evenings earnings anyway. They have to work as a team to really clean up," Tennessee said.

"Deal me out on this hand. I got to take a leak," one of the Shiny Shoes said. "Let's all take a five-minute stretch," the other Shiny Shoes suggested. They all stood up and stretched.

"Say, where's the 'head' around here?" the Shiny Shoes asked.

Slim then said his only smart thing of the evening.

"The head? Right where it's always been."

"Oh sure." the Shiny Shoes said and headed off in the wrong direction. Slim looked over at us and winked again. At least Slim was enjoying himself. He walked nonchalantly over to us.

"Not doing too bad do you think? I damn near won that last hand."

Tennessee just shook his head but didn't say anything.

"Say Mac, do you have any extra cash on you?" I gave him the three dollars that I had planned to play on all night.

He looked surprised there wasn't more but he took it. Slim turned to Tennessee. "Do you want to get in on this action too?" Slim asked.

Tennessee spoke slowly. "I like to gamble a bit but letting you have money for that game is more like a gift. Those guys are not my favorite charity.

Slim misunderstood. "No, I wasn't asking for a gift. I will pay you right back."

"I think Tennessee meant it would be a gift to the Shiny Shoes," I said.

If Slim heard me he didn't pay any attention, as he was already returning to the table.

It was getting late and I had to go back to the room to get my gear, plus, I still had my lunch to fix. I caught Slim's attention and waved my pocket watch at him indicating that he only had forty five minutes before we had to catch the jitney to work. He waved back that he understood. I got his gear, made him a lunch, and motioned to a chair where I left his things. He waved to me again. So I left.

Slim didn't make it to work that night.

At lunch break Red asked me, "Where's Slim?"

"He missed the jitney," I said.

"No shit. I know that much," Red said.

"He probably got hung up at Nelson's," somebody said. Everyone laughed.

It was pay day and they let me pick up Slim's check for him.

Chapter 12

Nelson's Cat House

Slim was asleep when we got back after the shift. I slipped his check carefully under his pillow and headed for the shower room. When I returned to the room Red was in the room. Slim was sitting on the edge of the bed holding his head in his hands.

"I may have lost a little dough but I sure got it back from their bottle. It was real good stuff," Slim said.

"How much did you lose?" I asked. There was a pause. "Did you lose it all?"

"And then some," Red said.

"How could you lose more than you got?"

"They let me go 'light' on the last hand. It was their idea. I didn't ask them to. They said they trusted me and they knew, someway that last night was pay day. I really had a good hand too."

"Seventy dollars 'light', Red said.

I didn't even have to ask.

"I gotta meet them tonight at seven to give them their money," Slim said.

"They said they would let me in their game to give me a chance to win it back."

"I'll just bet they will," Tennessee had joined the conversation.

"You need a little diversion 'ol buddy," Red said. "Let's go cash our checks at Nelson's. Maybe that little redhead will make you forget your bad luck. I will swing by in an hour," he said. "That way the line will be shorter."

That wasn't the first time I had heard mention of "Nelson's". A mention of Nelson's, I had noticed, was usually followed by some laughter or some comment behind the back of a hand that you can't quite catch.

"What is Nelson's?" I asked.

Slim didn't answer right away, so I asked him again.

"Some of the fellows cash their checks at Nelson's," he said, finally. "You know you shouldn't leave your checks stuffed in your duffel bag like you do. If you lose a check you'll lose a whole weeks work."

"Should I get them cashed at this Nelson's place?" I asked.

"It's up to you," Slim said. "I can tell you, you will get your money's worth if you do."

"You mean it'll cost me something to get my check cashed?"

"Only twenty dollars."

"Twenty dollars?" I said. "Twenty dollars? That's :more than a day's wage. Nick's Tavern will cash them for nothing."

"Yeah, but all you get is a couple of beers. Don't be such a stick in the mud. Come on with us and I will show you the ropes. For two dollars more you can ask for your girl by name."

He could see I wasn't catching on.

"For Christ's sake, you know what a cat house is don't you? It's a whorehouse. Now don't try to tell me you don't know what a whorehouse is. Nelson's Cat House is a whorehouse on wheels. It's a trailer house fixed up real nice. Three of them to be exact."

"You cash your checks at a whorehouse?" I couldn't believe it. "And you have been there often enough to call them by their names?"

Slim started to say something but stopped. "Just come on with us today and you will have a surprise," Slim said.

"Let me think on it," I said. "You go ahead with Red and the others. Just leave me the keys to your car in case I come down later."

"You bet. I will give you your three dollars back when I see you. When you come down to Nelson's you probably won't see me, but just ask for Red."

"Why would I ask for Red?"

"Not our Red. I mean the redhead. She will be looking for you." Slim said. "You have to catch the line just right or you'll have to stand in the rain. I don't know why they didn't make the awnings longer."

"Thanks for the tip. I will try to remember that."

I sat on my bunk for a long time after they all left. There may be something to cashing your checks each week.

I remembered Dad never kept a check very long. Not that he ever had many checks.

I had three checks in my duffel. I had cashed only one check so far and that was at Nick's. My thoughts were interrupted by the entrance of Tennessee and none other than Whiskey Riley.

"If you ain't going to Nelson's Cat House, could you run us into Amboy? We need to get some money orders off to the hill country before they set the hounds on us," Tennessee said." We like to stop at the little bank, and then we usually have a boilermaker or two at Nick's, but just a couple."

Whiskey and Tennessee will never know how glad I was to have someone to talk to, and just to have something to do.

"Let's go," I said.

We drove out the service road that led to the gravel road to Amboy. At the intersection we saw the name in bright lights, NELSON'S CAT HOUSE.

"Can you imagine that they advertise so openly? I thought that sort of thing was against the law," I said.

"We are a long way from the nearest law up here," Whiskey said. "This is over the Clark County line by about mile. We're in Cowlitz County. The nearest 'real' law would be in Longview or Kelso and that's an hour and a half away from here."

I had to slow down as I made the turn toward Amboy.

"Looks like they're busy today," Whiskey said.

There was a line of at least thirty men standing in single file shuffling from one foot to the other waiting their turn to be called. It was raining very hard now and I smiled about that. Whiskey picked up on my curiosity.

"Ever been in a whorehouse son?"

"No."

I wanted to ask if he had, but I didn't dare. However, he read my mind.

"Not that it would be of any interest to you, but I ain't neither." Whiskey said. "I am sure Tennessee would go but he knows I would kill him if he did."

"Whiskey, you wouldn't kill me," Tennessee said. "You would just tell your baby sister and let her kill me."

They had a good laugh .

"Most of those hands just think it's a way to show that they're 'real' men," Whiskey said. "West Virginny men don't need to prove it to anyone. But don't be too quick to judge them, Mac. Not all those boys are bad ones. In fact there are some pretty good hands that let off just a little energy there at Nelson's."

We were going up Speelyai Hill by this time and it took all my concentration to shift down without stalling or spinning out on the hair pin curves. The steeper the curve the worse the washboards became. When we finally leveled off a bit Whiskey Riley had one more observation he wished to make.

"As I said, not all those hands are bad that goes to Nelson's. Do you agree?"

"I guess so,"I said.

"And not all them gals are moldy hay neither. We don't know their stories, and until we do, we shouldn't be too holier than thou."

We arrived at lower Amboy, Nick's, and the bank. The bank was across the road from Nick's Tavern.

"Let's do our business first. Then we can go to Nick's," Whiskey said. We all agreed to that plan.

I stepped up to cash my three checks while Whiskey and Tennessee were filling out their money orders. Tennessee seemed to be doing paper work for both of them. The man behind the glass window said, "It's none of my business young man but that's quite a bit of cash to have on you. Don't you have someone you could send some of it to?"

"No, not really," I said.

"Well, now that I have stuck my nose in where it probably isn't wanted," he said. "why not start a savings account with us? We pay two and a half percent interest, which is what you would get even in Vancouver. Your money will be safe and when you quit the job or are fired, you just come by and your money will be ready in ten minutes or less."

We just write you a check for what ever the balance is at that time."

"I could take it out whenever I want?"

"You bet you can. It's your money."

"I'll do it if you can give me cash when I want it rather than a check," I said.

"Like I say, you're the boss."

I kept ten dollars out and put $386.80 in the savings account. I walked off the porch with ten dollars in my pocket and a little red booklet showing I had more money than I had ever known. I felt pretty darn good. I hoped that Mr. Kilmer got his hay in before this rain hit. I really do. But I'm not sorry that I'm not there to help him.

I felt on top of the world as we strolled across the road to

Nick's. I would order an Oly and they wouldn't even ask my age. Slim and his activities were the furthest thing from my mind. We were an imposing sight and heads turned as we walked in. I'm six foot three, and Tennessee is about the same height and then there's Whiskey Riley who filled up the whole door way. I was glad I had my heavy jacket on so I wouldn't look so skinny. The place was full of loggers drinking beer. At the end of the bar an arm-wrestling match was just being decided. The winner looked around for his next victim. He spotted Whiskey Riley.

"Hey, big feller. You ever arm wrestle?" he asked.

"Can't say that I have. But I would sure like to watch you hands do it if I could," Whiskey Riley said.

"Oh come on," the big logger said. "It's all in fun."

"Well O.K., if you tell me a little about it first," Whiskey said. Whisky took off his jacket and revealed his huge biceps splitting out from his short sleeve shirt, which was too small for him. Even the logger was having a second thought.

Tennessee whispered to me, "This is going to be good. I ain't never seen Whiskey lose any kind of wrestling. Leg wrestling, arm wrestling, side holts, you name it. He will dump this stump jumper on his keister in about ten seconds. Just watch."

The big logger explained the elements of arm wrestling to Whiskey. Another logger squared them away. The two huge men strained and struggled, but slowly the logger started getting the upper hand, finally Whiskey went down, the back of his hand smashing into the countertop a bit harder than I thought necessary.

"So that's the way it's done," Whiskey said rubbing his arm. "I can see how that could be a good sport."

"You wanna try it again?" the logger asked.

"Why not?" Whiskey Riley said.

"Now watch this," Tennessee whispered again. "Whiskey

will break his arm off at the wrist and beat him over the head with the bloody stump. Just watch this."

The two giants squared up and started again. This time it took a little longer but the logger bested Whiskey again.

Tennessee just could not believe what he had witnessed.

"You're a good sport for a construction stiff," the big logger said.

"Uh-oh. Be ready to move," Tennessee whispered again. "It's coming for sure. That dumb guy made a bad mistake calling Whiskey Riley a 'stiff'."

"Could I buy you a drink?" the logger continued.

"Make that a boilermaker and you're on," Whiskey replied.

"You can relax, Mac," Tennessee said. "They're going to drink and not fight."

" I swear, I don't know how you could tell I worked in construction," Whiskey Riley said.

The big logger looked Whiskey right in the eye and started to laugh. Whiskey never blinked.

"But I tell you what little man," Whiskey said.

Tennessee slid off his stool. "Oh no, here it comes. It's going to happen."

"I'll promise not to call you a stump jumper or an apple knocker if you don't call me a construction stiff again," Whiskey said.

The pause that followed seemed to last forever. "Apple what?" the logger said. "Apple knocker? I ain't ever heard that before," and he started to laugh and Whiskey joined in, then everyone joined in, and the tension was off.

"Now let's have that drink," the big logger said.

"What do they call you?" Whiskey asked.

"Hell, you know me. You don't need to call me anything. We have met a thousand times in a thousand different places."

"I understand you," Whiskey Riley replied.

Before we left, everyone knew Whiskey Riley. Men who weren't even there later claimed to have known him.

Whiskey asked questions about their work in the woods. Good questions. They knew he was really interested. We got up to go and the big logger said," If you're in here next weekend I will give you another lesson in arm wrestling if you're game."

"Sounds like a good time to me," Whiskey said.

As soon as the door closed behind us, Tennessee grabbed Whiskey by the arm.

"Did he really beat you, Whiskey?"

"Look at it this way. I didn't get a busted jaw and I got three free boilermakers, and I met some pretty good ol' boys. Now does that sound like losing to you?"

"Yeah, I know Whiskey, but could you've beat him if you wanted to?"

"He is a strong one, that's for sure, but he ain't from the hills of West Virginny, now is he?" They put their arms around each other's shoulders and started to laugh.

"Well son, did you have more fun than going to Nelson's?" Whiskey asked me.

"Well, I don't rightly know," I said.

"If there'd been a fight, then it would have been more fun," Tennessee said. "Without a good fight, I think I'd rather go to Nelson's."

Whiskey shot out a big arm and wrapped it around the head of his good friend and brother-in-law.

"That does it Tennessee. I'm gonna write and tell little Carrie what you done said."

"You gonna write? It better be something you can draw, you big dumb hillbilly." They started to laugh again. They laughed and roared off and on all the way back to camp.

These are good men, I thought to myself. Mom would like them if she didn't know they drank a little.

I was, in truth, still more than a little curious about Nelson's Cat House, but I did have a darn good time that night after all.

Chapter 13

The Watch

I was tired when we got back from Amboy so I grabbed a bite to eat in the mess hall and went to bed. It was only 5 P.M. and the room was cool for good sleeping. The rain had never let up and the drumming of the raindrops on the thin shingle roof was music to put anyone to sleep. I didn't see Slim anywhere but I was not disappointed. At eight in the evening I woke up and went to the bathroom. To get to the bathroom it was necessary to walk through the day room. The poker games were in full operation. The same Shiny Shoes were there and so was Slim, right in the middle of the action. I nodded to him and asked him how he was doing.

"I could be having a little better luck," he said. "But I'm doing O.K."

I went back to bed.

Some time later, I don't know exactly what time, I woke up and felt a presence in the room. Perhaps I had heard something. The room was occupied by four of us, and we all came and went at different times, so to have someone in the room was not that unusual by itself. But there was something different this time.

I became aware that there was some motion in the room. The little wall light had been turned off for some reason. so the room was really dark. I turned ever so slowly, toward the rustling sound. I could barely make out the outline of someone going through my duffel bag at the foot of my bed.

Before I could shout out or grab the person or anything, a ray of light shown through the window from the headlights of a car turning in the parking lot. To my shock and disbelief I saw Slim.

He didn't know I was awake and had seen him. Perhaps I should have jumped up right then and confronted him, but instead I closed my eyes and didn't move until he had what he wanted and sneaked out.

"What the hell is happening?" I said to no one. Slim was closer to me than any brother could be. Yet he was trying to steal from me. He thought I had cashed my checks today. He thought I would cash them at Nelson's Cat House. He assumed I would stuff the cash in the bottom of my duffel bag where he knew I had kept the checks.

He didn't have to steal from me. He could have roused me out of bed and just said he needed some money. I would have given it to him. I had given him money many times without asking too many questions. All I had was about seven dollars, left from the ten I had kept when I cashed my checks. Whatever I had would have been his for the asking.

"I wonder if he checked my pants?"

I grabbed my jeans, which were in a heap on the floor near my duffel bag. I checked my pockets, and checked them again. The seven dollars, or whatever I had, was gone. Slim had skinned me out clean.

I laid back down on my cot, but now there was no going back to sleep. The seven dollars was not the issue but I thought how glad I was that the bank teller had explained a savings account to me. I laid on my cot and started turning the last few weeks over and over in my mind. Slim had changed a lot since we'd come to the dam. I guess I had changed too but not to the extent that I could lose all that my folks had taught me. Slim had begun drinking a lot soon after we got here. Then he started running down to Nelson's to meet bad women. And even though I remembered

Whiskey's comment that everyone at Nelson's was not bad,
men or women, you couldn't say they were "good" either.
I caught Slim in a number of little lies. Things that were not
important enough to lie about in the first place. And now
this heavy gambling. He was in way over his head with
the Shiny Shoes. I was convinced that when the summer
was over we would not be going off to college together as
we had planned from the very first.

It hit me that we had not followed the clear and simple
advice given to us by well intended people, "Stay together,"
they had said.

"You will do all right." We had not stayed together.

I had never felt so alone-in my life. Heck no, Slim didn't
have any money. He took a draw against his very first check
and had spent it all before pay day. I now know that twenty
dollars of that went to Nelson's Cat House. The gambling
losses had now put him in a hopeless situation. So bad in
his mind's eye that stealing was the only way out. I am
sure he thought he could outsmart the Shiny Shoes and
he'd be able to return the money, perhaps even before I
noticed it was gone.

The Shiny Shoes took him for the sucker he is.

He had betrayed me. It would never quite be the same
between us again. I had lost something tonight in the half
light of the room that was far more important than the
money. I had lost my best friend.

And I didn't know what I can do about it.

There was no use trying to get back to sleep, so I got
dressed without turning on the light. I went out the back
way, so I would not have to go through the day room where
I knew the poker games were in full swing. There was an
Oregon mist in the air. The old joke was that an Oregon
mist is a rain that missed Oregon and hit Washington.

I walked around the camp. It was probably still two hours
before we would catch the jitney to the tunnel, but just to
be sure of the time I reached down and pulled the leather

thong which tied my pocket watch to a beltloop on my jeans. The thong was there, but the watch was gone. The leather thong had been untied at the watch. My pocket watch was gone.

This watch was not just any old watch. It was a very special watch to me. My first impulse was to go into the day room, and grab Slim by the neck and squeeze until he coughed up my watch. In spite of all the bad thoughts I had toward Slim, I hesitated. This had to be a mistake. Slim might steal a little money from me, but he would never steal my watch. I must have misplaced it myself. I would probably find it in the morning. I felt a little better even though I knew in my heart I was probably lying to myself.

I was soaked to the skin and chilled. I sat down under the sheltering branches of a huge fir tree that had been left standing at the edge of the parking lot. I sat with my back against the trunk of the tree and cried. No one could have heard me sobbing over the steady beat of the rain. And no one cared anyway. I could have cried as loud as I wanted to and no one in the world would have known but I choked the sobs back until my chest ached.

The watch had been given to me by my brother. It was a very unusual watch. My brother said it was a navigator's watch. I'm not sure where he got it, since he wasn't a navigator. My brother had shown me how the watch had settings for temperature and altitude. The most interesting thing about this watch was that it had 22 jewels. Not 18 or 21 jewels like most watches, but 22 jewels. You could unscrew the stainless steel back and stamped right there for all to see was 22 JEWELS." I suppose I had shown that to just about everybody. My brother said I shouldn't take the back off that way because I could get dirt or dust in it, but I enjoyed showing the doubters that by golly this watch had one extra jewel in it some place.

The watch, since it was a military watch, had a 24-hour face. I found reading the 24-hour face easy, but many people had trouble understanding military time. My miner, Johnnie, had this routine of asking me for the time every night just before the jitney picked us up. This would make the time about 11:00 or so. Only on my watch it would say 23:00. So the routine went like this; Johnnie would say, "Mac, what time is it getting to be?", I would take out my watch, study it a bit, and then turn the face so he could see it and I would say, "There it is". Johnnie would always reply after a good long study, "Well, damn if it ain't." This routine went on almost every night. I never would tell him the time and he was too proud to admit that he had no idea what the watch said. Most of the crew was in on this little game and it was fun.

Tonight I decided I would try to avoid the usual chatter with anyone if I could. I waited until the jitney was practically loaded before I left the safety of the fir tree and swung aboard just as the door was closing. I had not fixed any lunch. Maybe I wouldn't be hungry. Slim was not on board. I don't know how many shifts a person could miss before they would get enough of it. Slim would have to be getting pretty darn close to that point.

"I am through worrying about Slim," I heard myself say aloud.

"I didn't hear you Mac. What did you say?"

"Nothing Tennessee. I didn't say anything."

If I could have found a way I would have gone home that night. I would have given anything to talk to my Mom that night. Not about a friendship gone sour. Certainly not about women working at Nelson's, or even about greed. I would ask Mom to tell me again how Granddad had cleared the land and how he had named the Valley. And where he had dug the clay for the brick that formed the foundations for most of the old barns in the Valley. I would ask her to tell me again exactly where the bear 'Wallow' had been located in the old days. And how my Dad had stood up to the W.P.A. boss even though he had a crew of men all ready to dig a drain ditch diagonally across our property instead of following the property line like they should, and won. Yes, if I could have, I would have gone home that night.

"Hey, are you gonna sit there all night?" Johnnie asked. He slid into the seat next to me. "Say kid, are you O.K.?"

"I just fell asleep a little," I said.

On the way into the tunnel I noticed Johnnie talking to Tennessee and then glancing at me. We were hitting fullstride in our nightly march to the portal when Whiskey Riley moved up beside me.

"Say Mac. I got another job for you tonight."

"You bet, Whiskey. Will it take very long? Johnnie will be needing me before long."

"Not tonight he won't. Tennessee, Red, and Easy Money will run the two drills tonight. Come on with me."

When we got some distance away from the noise he stopped me with a wave of his hand.

"Mac, I have told you all before, that when you go through the portal you have to think mining. If you don't you will get yourself killed, or worse, get somebody else killed. I don't know what's bothering you and I sure don't need to know. That's your business. But you ain't yourself. Until you are yourself, you stay the hell out of my tunnel."

I couldn't believe what he had just said. "You mean I'm fired?" I barely whispered it.

"Fired? Hell no, little man. You can work for me anytime, as long as you want. I like what I see in you. You will make a good hand someday. But you ain't got your mind on my tunnel tonight and I don't wanna be writing no young wife about how you got yourself killed."

"You know I haven't got a wife and I know you can't write. So what do I do tonight?"

"You clean the dry shack. And you better do it right by Gawd." He put his big arm around my shoulder. "Do this for me kid."

"O.K. If you need it cleaned."

"I do. If you need someone to talk to a bit, or if you need a short loan or something like that give us a chance to help. I mean it."

I swept the dry shack and straightened it up. It was warm and toasty by the potbellied stove. I did something I had never done since that first day. I stretched out and took a nap on company time. I heard the blast and it sounded like a-good one. I felt some better, and strolled down to the portal where the crew was eating their lunch while waiting for the air blowers to evacuate the fumes after the blast. I saw Whiskey and gave him the thumbs-up sign with a big grin. I was ready to work the second half of the shift. Unfortunately ,the night had one more turn to take.

Red, Slim's miner, came over where I was sitting a little ways apart from the rest of the men.

"Hey, Mac. Where's that lard ass friend of yours? Did he get hung up too tight with that little redhead Dee?"

In an instant I was on my feet and grabbed Red by his lapels, lifting him clear off the ground. I was surprised at my own strength.

"What did you say? Who did you say?" I demanded.

At once a circle of men gathered around us. Red's hand darted to his belt and produced a knife. I dropped him in a heap, but he was back up in a flash.

"No hardware, Red," Turk ordered. Red drew back and threw the knife hard enough to stick an inch into a rough timber at my feet.

"I don't need anything to handle this one," Red said. "But before I turn you every which way but loose, what in the hell are we fighting about?"

I could feel my knees shake. I wasn't afraid to fight. I wasn't afraid that Red could hurt me. My struggle wasn't with Red.

Red saw my hesitation and suddenly his face softened. He turned to the circle of men, "It's over," he said. "It's over."

He carefully took the intervening steps that separated us and put his arm around my shoulder. He took me a short distance away.

"Jesus, I thought you knew your friend was working at Nelson's. I would never have said anything if I thought you didn't know. Only don't ever put your hands on me. You're lucky I didn't slice you."

"So the one they call Dee is that your girl or something?"

"No, not really," I said. "She is just a girl I knew from the Valley where I was raised. I just never thought anything like that could ever happen to one of our girls."

"Maybe it's not the same girl," Red said.

"How many girls do you know who are redheaded and named DeDe?"

"Only one," Red said.

Whiskey Riley had observed the whole affair from beginning to the end. But I don't think he heard every word of our conversation, however.

"Are you sure you got that dry shack good and clean?" he asked me.

"Yes, everything is clean."

"Then it's time to get back to work." He turned away.

I turned back to Red. "DeDe was real smart. She was valedictorian of our class. That means she was the smartest. In fact she had everything going for her. She had good looks and a swell personality, everything. Why is she at a place like Nelsons's?"

"I don't know kid but you talk like she is dead. I think you've got to come to grips with the fact that this girl means more to you than you care to admit."

"No, that's not it," I said. "It's just that she is from my Valley. No one from the Valley ever amounted to much, but no one ever brought shame to it either."

"Don't go judging her too hard, Mac," Red advised. "It's not like she was a thief, or something really bad."

"So you would say that what she does is not as bad as stealing? Say stealing from a friend?"

"There is no comparison and no doubt in my mind which is worse. But what I think got your dander up Mac is the fact that you heard this from me instead of Slim telling you. I don't know why he didn't. You will have to take that up with him. I do know that he has known this since the first week you all were here. I can circulate the word around so no one will ask for her, if that's what you want, but I can tell you if that happens Nelson will let her go. As it is she has a good place to work."

"No. Oh God, no. Don't do that," I said. "If I know Deirdre she can make up her own mind as to what she wants to do. This just hasn't been a real good day for me. I need some time to think on all of this."

"Do your thinking in three hours from now. Right now we are thinking hard rock mining," Red said.

Whiskey Riley stood up. "Boys, let's get closer to it. All I want to see is assholes and elbows and both of them turned up."

Like a little band of Highlanders we followed our Chief to the battle ground. In those few steps to the entrance of the tunnel every man, if he was smart, was cleansing his mind of any and all exterior problems and worries.

Chapter 14

A Visit to Nelson's

It rained all through the night but by ten in the morning the sun broke through and everything was sparkling and clean. The salal and Oregon grape had lost their dusty grey appearance along the roadways as the rain washed them to bright green.

I knew what I wanted to do but I didn't know how to go about doing it. I started out by walking casually around the camp. This was not too unusual for me. This time however, I was on a secret mission and I wanted to be sure there was no one up and about that who might know me from the crew. I meandered over to the service road which was the main entry into the camp. I stopped and threw a few rocks at some crows cawing at me from the tops of some hemlock buggy whips. The crows were safe enough. I waited until there were no vehicles on the road and made sure that no one was paying any attention to me. I sprinted across the gravel road and into the brush on the other side. I moved fast, until I was fifty yards into the under growth. I stopped to catch my breath and look around. I was sure no one had seen me. I smiled to myself over my success. No one saw me and I can't imagine anyone would give a damn even if they knew what was on my mind.

I went deeper into the brush, which soon gave way to a nice stand of second-growth timber. The last thing I wanted was to be spotted by someone. Slipping through the timber from tree to tree brought back memories of my boyhood days with my brother. We used to play a game of sneaking up on each other, trying to see how close we could get without the other one knowing we were around. It is a miracle we didn't shoot each other. We always had our single shot .22's with us. My brother would always say, if he could hear me so could the deer.

And speaking of deer, I found myself following fresh deer tracks. The tracks had been made since the rain stopped. I followed the deer trail until it turned at right angles to the road and headed directly toward the river. They were probably headed for their early morning drink. In spite of all the blasting, truck traffic and other construction commotion I was glad the deer had not left the area.

I knew that I would have to make a decision in about a mile ,but I was in no hurry to reach that point. I stopped to listen. There are many sounds in the forest if you know what to listen for. I know people who say how quiet the woods are. That's because they aren't listening. When the woods are in fact, actually quiet, that's when you should really get concerned, because that's when you know you are not alone.

I could hear the blue jays passing on the word of my arrival to the next pair of jays down the line and to all who would pay attention. The blue jays are the self appointed sentinels of the forest and all the other creatures of the wild pay careful attention to their warnings. I stopped in a small burned-over meadow and helped my self to some wild strawberries. They were small of course but with a taste like nothing else in the world. The rain had not washed all the dust off the berries because the vines were too thick. The stump black berries weren't ripe yet but I noted that there would be enough for some easy pies when the time came. I missed my mom's pies.

I covered the mile to the intersecting country road in less time than I had wanted. I crouched in the brush, and picked me a spot on the other side that would get me into the brush as quickly as possible. I put my ear to the ground and satisfied myself that there wasn't any traffic near, and then dashed across the road and into the under growth on the far side of the road.

My objective was nestled in a little grove of second growth. There they were three trailer houses, each about forty feet long. They were much bigger than they looked from the road. They were placed to form a triangle. I circled carefully around. My goal was to get behind the buildings and to the top of a bluff to the rear of the site. From the top I figured I could peer down and see inside the triangle. I figured no one would be looking behind or above the trailer houses.

It wasn't that difficult to climb the bluff from the back side. When I approached the rim of the bluff I dropped to my stomach and squirmed and crawled the remaining distance just in case someone should look up.

It was going on eleven in the morning, and there was no activity below me. I'm not sure what I expected. I heard an occasional voice and a screen door bang several times. A female voice was trying to quiet a yapping dog. Nothing much was happening.

I told myself that I came here to see if I could make contact with DeDe. But now that I was here, I decided maybe that wasn't such a hot idea. Even if I saw her I decided not to show myself. What would I do? Would I say, Oh DeDe, I'm up here on this bluff spying on you? How has your day been DeDe? No, I had better stay under cover for now.

The sun was warm and the cool damp grass felt good. In fact too good and before long I was napping away. I didn't sleep long and woke up brushing red ants off me. I had sprawled out almost on top of the ant hill. The pungent smell of an ant hill is unmistakable yet I had lain down right in the middle of their throughway. I slipped back-wards off the rim of the bluff to where I could stand up, and pealed off my clothes to give them a good shaking.

Oh lordy, don't let anyone see me now with just my shoes and jockey shorts on. How could I ever explain being up behind a Cat House with nothing on but my shoes.

I was still brushing off real or imagined ants by the time I strolled nonchalantly back into camp. No one knew I had just paid my first visit to Nelson's Cat House. Yet, it seemed to me that every person I met looked at me as if they knew exactly where I had been.

I still wanted to see DeDe, but sneaking through the back-woods just wasn't the way to get the job done.

Chapter 15

A New Friend

I got in the habit of fishing about every other evening. In the beginning there were several of us, including Slim. We would hit the river a short distance up stream from the Yale Bridge at about six in the evening, and fish until dark. If we caught a ride to the bridge we could have our lines in the water in ten minutes. Even if we had to hike, it took no time at all. The hike was only a mile or so, and very easy.

The Yale Bridge is a beautiful high suspension bridge, which appears totally out of place in this remote corner of Southwest Washington. The bridge looked like pictures I had seen of the St. John's Bridge over the Willamette River where it enters the Columbia. The deck of the bridge was sixty feet above the water. This bridge formed the only link across the Lewis River for miles. I believe you would have to go all the way to Woodland to be able to cross the river by bridge. The view from the water level looking up at that bridge was a sight to see, particularly if the sky was clear. I mentioned this view to Slim.

"The most spectacular thing is the sky being clear," he said. Depending upon the weather at any particular time the water of the upper end of the Ariel Reservoir was either the deepest blue you can imagine or depending on the cloud cover, it would be black. At this time of the year the

sun sank below the horizon right into the water of the reservoir. I would have given anything to have had a boat to
explore the shoreline all the way to Ariel Dam.

The path down to the river hung on a rock out cropping,
then dipped gently down to the water. Once on the stream
conversation was difficult because of the noise of the river
moving through the gorge. The area had been logged but
the second growth firs were a hundred feet high. There were
many signs that the area had been burned at some time,
probably during the Yacolt Burn of 1902. Our best fishing
spot was a rolling rapid that went into a sweep against the
cliffs on the other side of the river. We would let our lines
drift to the end of the rapids, and if by that time we didn't
have a fish 'on,' then something was wrong. We started
out with worms for bait. But we soon discovered that tin
foil from chewing gum worked just as well and it sure saved
a lot of messing around. Think of it catching rainbow trout
fifteen and eighteen inches long on tin foil. I actually even
caught fish on a piece of maple leaf. These were practically
untouched waters. Very few fishermen had ventured this
far into the Cascade foothills, and we had it all to ourselves.
We could have brought the fish back to camp and the cook
would gladly fry them up for us, but we would most often
just show the fish off to each other and then release them.
Our boots came in handy, because the water was icy cold.
We had to pay attention to the time because when the sun
went down the gorge plummeted into darkness. There was
very little twilight time. We got caught several times and it
was a bit scary climbing out of the canyon in the dark.

Our fishing trips changed once the poker games started.
I found it harder and harder to interest anyone in a few
hours of fishing. Slim quickly lost all interest in fishing in
favor of gambling. It was not as much fun fishing by myself, so I stopped going too.

I was in the recreation room one evening untangling some
fishing poles and lines. It was just something to do. In the

recreation room that night was an older man. He was perhaps in his early forties. I had seen him with the survey
party that worked in the tunnel but since he wasn't a miner
I did not know him. The surveyors stayed by themselves
most of the time.

"Are you interested in fishing?" he asked. "My name is
Thomas Kyle. You're the one they call Mac, aren't you?"

"Some call me that," I said. I took his outstretched hand.
He wasn't a regular construction worker, that was for sure.
No one began a conversation with a stranger this way. But
his hand shake was strong and friendly enough.

"I'm the Chief of the tunnel survey party," he said. "I
guess I will be, for the rest of the summer at least. That Mr.
Riley is quite a foreman, isn't he?"

"He's the Shifter. He isn't a foreman," I said.

"You don't sound like the other tunnel men. You don't
seem to have a southern dialect," he said.

"Oh? Is that so?"

"I'm from Seattle myself. So I don't talk like the others
either."

"Oh? Is that so?" I said without looking up from the
tangled lines.

"Hey look, I'm sorry if I interrupted your concentration
with that mess of line. It is just that I get so anxious to talk
to someone that at times I guess I become intrusive."

"I'm sorry if I didn't appear too friendly, but I have had
some good teachers who speak against warming up too
fast. No offense intended," I said.

He was balancing a split bamboo rod in his hands. I had
always used a casting rod rather than a fly rod, simply because I had never even seen any fly fishing, let alone do
any.

"Do you fly fish, Mr. ah, ah?"

You can call me Tom, and yes I do fly fish," he said. "In
fact I'm fairly good at it."

"What's the main idea of it?" I asked.

"Take that rod over there, and let's go outside and I'll show you. That's about a forty dollar rod you have in your hand."

"Forty dollars? No fooling?"

"And that's not counting the reel," he added.

That conversation began a very interesting acquaintance and eventual friendship. He was a good fishing coach and before long I was laying the line out to given spots with some consistency.

"Well thanks for the lesson, Tom. I have to go see if I can get my partner out of a poker game before he loses his butt again."

"You have a partner?"

"Yeah, a buddy of mine came up here with me. We are the only two local guys in the tunnel. He likes to play cards."

"Would you like to go fishing tomorrow evening Mac? You have the basics down, now you need to practice. Would you try fly fishing?"

There was a strain to his voice, almost like panic.

"I don't know what we got planned for tomorrow evening but I'll see. Thanks again for the fly fishing lesson," I said.

"You bet Mac. I have enjoyed talking with you very much."

I smiled to myself. I had not said two dozen words in the hour since we met. He was obviously hungry for company.

The next day broke with a steady Oregon mist that was anything but fishing weather. I had forgotten all about Tom. Slim had taken another "draw" and the money was burning a hole in his pocket.

"Come on Mac," he said "Let's get into an early game. This is going to to be my lucky night. I can feel it."

"Go ahead Slim. I might join you later if it's just the construction men playing."

"My God, I hope there's bigger money in the game than just the local gang," Slim said.

"In that case I think I'll get some early sleep in while the rain is playing sweet lullabies on the shingles."

I had barely laid my head down when Slim came back into the room.

"Hey Mac, there's a guy out here running around calling your name. He's a strange duck if you ask me," Slim said.

Tom came into the bunk room right behind Slim as he was talking.

"There you are. Thank goodness. I thought I had missed you," Tom said.

"Missed me?" I asked.

"Aren't we going fishing?" Tom said softly.

"In this rain? I like it a little dryer myself."

He was obviously disappointed. "Look, how about going the first day it is half way-decent. Would that be O.K.?" I said.

"Sure would. You bet. Maybe we could get an early start right after the shift is over and go fish the Siouxon."

"Never heard of it."

"I spent last summer at the confluence of Siouxon Creek and the Lewis River," he said.

"You mean you were up here last summer?" I was amazed.

"Oh yes. I was the co-director of a significant archeological exploration of the Lewis River Valley."

"No fooling?"

"No, I'm not fooling. PP&L contracted the University of Washington to do archeological exploration of the basin that will eventually be covered by the water from the reservoir formed by the Yale dam. My real job is with the Washington State Museum at the University of Washington. I fell in love with this wild area, and when I had the chance to take the position as Chief of the tunnel survey party I jumped at it. I've been trained as a surveyor as well as an archeologist."

I could see that my chances for an early nap were over but that was all right by me. This guy was getting interesting.

"What is a P P and whatever you said?"

"PP&L. Stands for Pacific Power and Light Company. They own this site," Tom said.

"They own this dam?"

"It's their money that's paying your wages."

"I never thought about someone owning this place," I said. "I thought I was working for M&K."

"You are, but it's PP&L that is paying them. M&K are the general contractors."

"So this PP&L outfit owns the dam and they pay M&K to build it for them. Which one calls the shots?" I asked.

"Neither," Tom laughed. "Ebasco actually makes all the critical decisions, or calls the shots, as you say."

"Now who the hell is Fee ... ?"

"E-bas-co," Tom repeated. "Ebasco is the consulting engineering firm in New York City. They designed the dam. They are the men in the white helmets."

I had not noticed anyone in white helmets.

"It was the staff of Ebasco that convinced PP&L to change the design from a concrete arch dam to an earth-filled dam. The decision on the design of a dam is the most important decision of all. If the design is screwed up the project will have one delay after another. Yale Dam was originally supposed to look just like Ariel Dam. Ariel, or Merwin as they call it now, is a concrete arch dam. You have seen Ariel Dam haven't you?" Tom asked.

"No, as a matter of fact, I haven't."

"You would have driven right past it if you drove up from Woodland."

"We drove up from Woodland, but it was after dark and we didn't see much," I said.

"It's only about fifteen miles downstream from here. Do you want to go see it? I have a car. It's a beautiful dam."

His excitement was contagious. He obviously knew what he was talking about, and it would at least be dry in the car.

"Would we get back in time to go to work? I haven't missed a shift yet and I haven't been late either."

Tom was on his feet. "We will be there in forty-five minutes and I will see that you're back in plenty of time to keep your job commitments," he said. "It is a sight you'll never forget."

He was absolutely right. As we turned into the parking and viewing area I was dumbfounded. We sat there for a moment just mesmerized. Tom was pleased to see that I was really impressed.

"How could they make anything that big?" I finally said.

"It isn't so big as dams go. But she is a beauty isn't she?"

Ariel Dam bends gracefully across a deep gorge much like the gorge where we were working. White water poured down the spillway like a giant waterfall. The water looked whiter, I think, because the water in the reservoir which formed the backdrop was Crater Lake blue.

"The water coming over the spillway is actually wasted water, from the engineers' point of view, in terms of making electricity," Tom said. "As the other dams are built upstream, there will be less water going over the spillway because the water will be more efficiently stored in the reservoirs behind the new dams."

"I would think that the more water that goes over the spillway would mean more electricity is being generated," I said.

Tom smiled. "Do you think the juice is generated by water going over the dam? The water that turns the turbines, which is the modern day water wheel, is the water that flows through the dam, not over it.

Water drops through tunnels called penstocks to the turbines. The tunnel's openings are midway up the dam and
the outlets are down there at the powerhouse where the
turbines are located."

"This dam was built in 1931, twenty years ago, but they
planned even then for more water storage capacity upstream. They put in two more penstock tunnels than the
current capacity for the dam would require. At some time
in the future when the other dams are built they will open
the other penstock tunnels and double the generating capacity of the dam to make electricity for mere pennies,"
Tom said.

"About these penstock tunnels. Does that mean more
jobs for the miners?" I asked. I was thinking ahead to future summers.

"The penstock tunnels in a concrete dam are poured into
the dam itself, but in the case of rock filled or earth filled
dams you drill the penstock tunnels through solid rock on
the flanks of the mountains. The penstock tunnels at Yale
Dam will be 1500 feet long and each will be sixteen feet in
diameter. That is less than half the diameter of the diversion tunnel you are now working on. And yes, there will
be work for more miners and chucktenders."

The rain slacked off to a drizzle. We got out of the car
and walked a short distance to where we could see more of
the reservoir behind the dam.

"This place looks like a park," I said.

"It is a park. Look at the tables and outdoor grills. This
area was developed for the enjoyment of the public, and it
was all done with private money. This wasn't a WPA or
CCC project. Before this dam was built, I don't imagine
there would be a hundred people a year that would have
seen this country. But now, come up here when the weather
gets a little warmer, and if this damn rain stops, this place
will be crowded with picnickers and campers from Portland to Seattle. When the other dams are finished there will

be parks and campgrounds even beyond Cougar, Washington. There will be tens of thousands of visitors to this area every year."

"I find that hard to believe," I said. "I'm glad I am seeing it all now."

"How deep do you suppose the water is behind the dam?" I asked.

"The dam is over three hundred feet high from the level of the old river bed to the crest of the dam. I would say we're looking at about one hundred and fifty feet of the dam that's above the lake level on the upstream side. So that would give us around one hundred and ninety to two hundred feet of water," Tom explained.

"My God, isn't that something? How can an eggshell-thin dam like that hold back that much water? You wouldn't think it would be strong enough, would you?" I said.

"Not by looking at what we can see there. I would agree, but we are looking at only a small portion of the dam. I would say that if this dam is typical of most concrete dams, it will be as wide at the base as it is long across the crest. Most of the dam you can't see. It's under water."

"The sign says 1250 feet across the crest. You mean that the dam is 1250 feet wide down there at the bottom?" I asked.

"I would think that's about right. About a quarter of a mile."

"I knew it would have to be strong, but that is quite a plug in the gorge. Just think if the dam ever went out. You would have a wall of water 190 feet high crashing down this canyon. Of course I realize that could never happen with a structure this size," I said.

"There always remains the possibility of some disaster taking a dam out. There have been a number of concrete dams that have failed over the years. In fact there is a story that keeps going around that they thought Ariel Dam, this very dam, was in danger of going out in 1933 during a winter flood. I think it was 1933. Anyway the supervisor at the dam made a decision at midnight that in order to save the dam and prevent a gigantic wall of water from spilling down on sleeping Woodland and several other communities on the river that it would be better to open up the flood gates and send a series of twenty-foot tides down the canyon. The dam was saved, but Woodland got wet. There was a secret hearing about it all. The question was, did the man in charge unnecessarily flood Woodland or was he a hero?"

"What would you have done?" I asked. "If you were the man in charge?"

"Today, of course, you would get on the telephone or radio or jump in a helicopter, and warn the folks down stream before you opened the flood gates. In 1933 that was not possible. To answer your question, however, the man had to save the dam. That is not just a pro company decision to save their property but a humane decision. You can't let the water 'breach' the dam. Too many things can happen too fast when the water goes over the dam. No one has any control then".

As we talked about these most unlikely disasters we were slowly backing up to higher ground and found ourselves on the second level of the viewing area. We both realized what we had been doing and started to laugh.

"If that dam broke for any reason we could forget about outrunning the flood," Tom said.

"With each dam built upstream, as they are all integrated into a total network, each dam downstream becomes safer, at least in theory. When the entire Lewis River basin is harnessed, it will take one hell of a rain storm to flood it out. In fact the concern should not be from heavy rain or snow but rather water that is 'splashed'. What I mean is, if there ever is a major earthquake or earth slide that dumps half of that cliff over there into the reservoir, it could be a very real threat because it would generate a 'splash' effect, which causes water to breach the dam. Or if there were a volcanic eruption, say Mt. St.Helens or even some small cone like Tum Tum, or both at the same time, or..."

"O.K., O.K. So the world is a dangerous place. I'll sure be glad to get back in the tunnel tonight where it's safe," I said.

"Yeah safe. About as safe as an Englishman at an I.R.A. meeting," Tom laughed.

He continued talking nonstop, giving me interesting information about the area.

"The reservoir that Ariel Dam backs up is twelve miles long. When we fish at the Yale Bridge we are at the upper-extent of the lake. Yale Dam is being built a mile upstream from the bridge. The reservoir from the Yale Dam will extend another nine to ten miles. Eventually there will be a string of huge lakes totaling forty to fifty miles right up to the flanks of Mt. St.Helens.

"You think that Ariel Dam looks high and I agree, but Yale Dam will be thirty feet higher. And Yale will look much more massive since it will be an earth-filled dam," Tom said.

"I don't get it," I said. "How can they make a dam filled with dirt and expect it to hold? Why would they build a dam like that anyway? Another thing I'd like to know, why did they build Ariel Dam here and Yale Dam where it is being built and who decides these things?"

"I can answer some of your questions," Tom said. "You're the first person I've ever encountered on the job who asks any questions. I like that. The 'who' is a famous engineer contracted by PP&L in 1926, by the name of Lyman Griswold. He selected this site for Ariel Dam, the site for Yale Dam, a site further upstream where Swift Creek comes into the Lewis River, and a site where the Muddy River joins the Lewis."

"I've never even heard of those places," I said.

"Before last year I don't suppose that many had heard of those places. In 1949 less than two dozen people visited

Cougar, Washington or Ole Peterson's place. Ole's place is about where the next dam will be built after Yale Dam is finished. Have you ever heard of Ole Peterson?"

"No, can't say that I have."

"You should make a real effort while you're in this wilderness to meet Ole Peterson. I'm certainly going to try to meet him. In fact, I've written to him. I don't know if he will get my letter or not. His address is not precise. Ole is what you might call a recluse. But he is a true pioneer by any standard. He is reputed to live on a small tributary of the Lewis River three miles east of the community of Cougar, Washington.

The rain picked up again as the clouds dropped nearly to the ground The pounding rain on the big leaf maple muffled the roar of the water pouring over the spillway.

"I think I'd better have you get me back to camp," I said. "I still need some shuteye before the shift tonight."

"Sure thing. What time are you going to eat? Maybe I could eat with you if you don't mind."

"It's a free country. I'm not sure how long I will sleep so I wouldn't wait if I were you," I said.

We drove slowly in the 1949 Ford he had borrowed. He acted like he was afraid to get the car out of second gear. As we approached the gravel service road leading into the dam I could see that the usual line had formed at Nelson's Cat House. Some of the miners were standing in the rain with their diggers still on. Might as well stay dry while you wait, I thought.

"Do you know what they do at that place?" Tom asked.

"About what they do at any whorehouse."

"I wonder what it costs?" Tom asked.

"Twenty dollars."

"Twenty dollars?" Tom nearly ran off the road into the bar ditch.

"Of course most leave a five dollar tip if they like the

girl and I've never heard one man say he ever disliked the girls," I said.

Tom almost ditched us on the other side of the road. I knew he wanted to ask me if I had been to Nelson's, but he never asked.

I got out at the camp and I thanked Tom for an interesting morning and I meant it.

"I would like to go fly fishing on that creek where you dug for Indian things last summer and hear more about that," I said.

"You mean Siouxon Creek. Sure I will take you to the "digs" if you like. A year from now that area will all be covered by 100 feet of water so if you want to see the Indian diggings you will have to see them this summer."

"Thank you again," I said.

Chapter 16

Ole Peterson

We finished our breakfast, which really was our supper, and turned in for some shuteye before the room heated up. Working seven nights a week gets old before long, especially when you have to sleep a few hours in the morning and then try again for a few more hours in the early evening. It seemed like all we did was work, eat, and sleep.

Suddenly Tom Kyle burst into our room waving something in his hand. He had his trusty basket full of sandwiches in the other hand. I wished he would leave his damn basket out side.

"Look at this! Look what I got in the mail! Get dressed. We are going into Cougar," Tom announced.

"Has Cougar started a 'Place' where you can cash your checks?" Slim asked. "Has Nelson started 'a branch office in Cougar?" He thought that was very funny. Tom didn't pay any attention.

"Look at this postcard!"

I took the postcard that he was waving.

"The card went to Woodland and then back here to be delivered,'"Tom said. "I wrote him over three weeks ago."

The postcard read:

Kyle
Come up any time.
If I'm here, I'm here.
Ole.

"I wrote Ole Peterson and asked if he would show me the lava caves he has reported finding and any Indian campgrounds that he might be aware of in the area. This is quite an honor." Tom said.

"'Who the hell is Ole Peterson?" Slim asked.

"He is an old settler-hermit type. He has lived in this country forever," I said.

"Never heard of him," Slim said.

"Come on, Mac. This will be an experience you will tell your grandkids about. I've made a nice lunch."

"I just bet you did," Slim mocked.

Tom did not pick up the edge to Slim's comment.

"You boys run along and have a nice little picnic. I need a little rest before I get my check cashed," Slim said and winking at me. With that he rolled over and was asleep.

"Will you go with me?" Tom was almost pleading.

"Sure. What the heck. This sounds interesting."

Tom had borrowed a company pickup for the day. We were off down the gravel road to the intersection at Nelson's.

Instead of turning left toward Amboy we turned right to the Woodland-Cougar road. Nelson's was quiet. The line would form later. Before long we turned right on the road to Cougar which was due east. Five miles on this road and we were in Cougar, Washington. As towns go it wasn't much. Cougar consisted of a store that doubled as the post office and a scattering of other buildings in various stages of disrepair. Cougar made Amboy look like New York City.

"We will leave the pickup here in Cougar," Tom said. "There must be a way to drive in because Ole Peterson has driven in, but I don't want to get into some place I can't get out of with this borrowed truck."

"How far is it?" I asked.

"Only three and a half miles," Tom said. "I will carry the lunch basket."

"Three and a half miles? You mean both ways I hope," I said.

"No, just one way."

"Maybe we could drive a little of it," I suggested. But Tom was already hiking toward the outline of the deeper timber. It might be just as well, I thought. I did not have a high regard for Tom's driving skills.

Tom stopped where the trail entered the timber and pointed at a homemade sign nailed to a stump. The sign said:

GIVE MY REGARDS TO CIVILIZATION
OLE PETERSON

"A number of people have been amused by that sign but only a few have met the author of it," Tom said.

We followed a cord wood road for a mile. The truck could have bumped over the cord road if we would have gone slow enough, but the hike was not difficult. The cord road petered out to a trail following the river. Even when we could not see the river we could hear it. The stand of trees we were walking through would have been a logger's heaven. The trees were mostly old growth Douglas Fir, six to eight feet in diameter and over two hundred feet high. Mixed in with the fir was a scattering of Sitka Spruce and hemlock. I couldn't imagine how the old man ever drove a car in here. That story was just part of the 'legend', I suspect. The trail gained a little in elevation but it was generally flat. Just a pleasant walk. We came to a clearing where there had been a camp set up. In this area were huge cedar trees much larger in diameter than the fir but not as tall. Twelve to fifteen feet in diameter was common. The cedars were not as tall because they'd had their tops broken off in past windstorms. Several of these giants had been felled by someone.

"This is a shake cutter's camp," Tom explained. "They have cut 'bolts' of cedar and split them right here into shakes. How many roofs do you suppose came from that grand daddy lying over there?" Tom asked.

We sat down on a cedar bolt. Not that we were tired, it was just that the moss-covered chunks of cedar made an inviting chair. We didn't do much talking. We sat there and wondered. In the distance a woodpecker was drilling for his meal.

"Let's count the rings on that stump the one that hasn't mossed over yet," Tom suggested.

The stump was ten feet across. Certainly there were much larger trees but this was just the right size for the shake cutters to handle with their crosscut falling saws. The stump had notches about eight feet up where the cutters had placed their 'spring boards' which they stood on to cut it.

"Can you imagine trying to balance yourself on a spring board while you swing an axe for the undercut? Or while you pull your guts out on a two-man crosscut saw?" I said.

"They had to work above the taper of the tree where it comes down to meet the ground. The grain is not straight in the taper of the tree and therefore it's too hard to split for shakes. The loggers call that the 'bastard cut', I said. It required some agility on our part, but without too much trouble we were both standing on the top of the stump ten feet in the air. The space between the rings on this cedar were a half inch on the average. A tree grows one ring a year. We had counted the rings on trees as kids. With some careful counting of the rings you could come close to knowing the age of the tree at the time it fell. Tom was counting faster than I was. "I got two hundred and maybe a few more. This tree sprouted from a seed before our founding fathers were even a bit concerned over the tea tax," Tom said.

"This tree has probably had its top broken off a dozen times," Tom said. "The needles of a fir tree or spruce tree will tip in a wind storm letting the wind through . But in the case of a cedar tree the needles, that is, the scales, do not tip, but form a solid sail for the wind to catch. Consequently in a stiff wind the tops will snap off."

"Inspecting the rings of a tree can tell you more that just the age of the tree," Tom said. "Look here. Through this time span of the life of the tree something happened. See how close the rings are to each other? Here the rings are a half-inch apart, for ten rings, then here they are no wider than one-sixteenth of an inch, and here they go back to being a half-inch apart."

"Could it have been caused by a drought or a disease?" I asked.

"Perhaps. Let's count the rings again from the narrow rings to the last ring of the trees life. I wonder something," Tom said.

He didn't need to prompt me. I was already recounting the rings. This was just like a good mystery book. The clues are here if you know what to look for. "One hundred ten or so years ago what ever happened, happened, as near as I can count the rings," I said. "With simple arithmetic that would make the event some time in the early 1840's."

Tom swung down from our stump and literally ran to the next stump and pulled himself up to the flat top.

"I want to see if the years of slow growth are unique to that particular cedar or if this applies to all of them," he yelled.

His new stump was harder to read because it had a two inch mantel of moss on it that our first stump did not have.

But we found that the second cedar had the same narrow rings for the same period of time dating to the 1840's.

"Whatever happened appears to have affected all the cedar trees at least," Tom said. "Can you speculate what it might have been that caused the cedar trees to grow very slowly?" Tom asked.

"Like I said. Perhaps some insect invasion or a disease, but most likely a dry spell I would say. The trees didn't get enough water for some reason. But to tell you the truth I can't imagine a ten year dry spell in the foothills of the Cascade Mountains."

"I have a hypothesis," Tom said. "The last observed eruption of Mt. St.Helens was November 22, 1842. The eruption was sighted from Fort Vancouver which is about forty-five miles to the, south."

"Then that's it," I said. "The mountain erupting caused damage to the trees and stunted the growth for a decade."

"Hold on a minute," Tom said. "I'm a scientist remember. The volcanic eruption, as a cause for stunting the trees, is only a hypothesis. We can't treat it as a fact, not just yet."

I was intrigued. My imagination was in high gear.

"So can you prove or disprove the hypothesis in a scientific fashion?" I asked.

"Perhaps you never could. But for openers you would take a much broader sampling of trees than the two we have checked. Perhaps you would sample a hundred trees and they should not all be cedar trees. The stunting may have been unique to the cedar alone. Also I would think you would need to sample trees outside the region of volcanic action. If those trees showed stunting too you would know that it was not caused by volcanic action alone. You would rule out one by one all known reasons for trees to grow slowly. Also you could sample trees in other areas of known volcanic activity to see if the trees in those areas are also stunted. For example, you could study the pines on Mt. Lassen where we can pinpoint the dates of eruptions. And then... "

"O.K., O.K. Enough, enough. As far as I'm concerned the volcano hypothesis is the one I will tell people," I said.

"That is poor science but good conversation," Tom said.

"Think of the stories this cedar grove could tell," I went on. "Think of the elk that have grazed and rested under these trees and of the Indians that may have camped here, or hidden here, to hunt the elk. How many generations of blue jays have squawked out their warnings to the other animals and..."

"And how many woodpeckers found their noon meals in those trees? Which reminds me of how hungry I am," Tom interrupted.

"Let's have a sandwich and hit the trail. We have dropped too much time here."

We happily ate our sandwiches in silence.

The trail climbed to a bench on the other side of the cedar grove. We both sat down again. We had walked less than a hundred yards since eating our sandwiches but this was going to be the last spot on the trail where we could view the cedar grove.

"Makes you feel rather small and insignificant doesn't it?" Tom said.

We continued on. The trail was actually getting better. We crossed two small streams on logs that someone had placed to make a crude bridge. Nailed to a blazed tree was a hand lettered sign. It read;

THIS IS MY LAND
OLE PETERSON

"Oly likes to make signs doesn't he," I commented. "Tell me about this guy. Is he apt to be hostile for our coming on his land? Are we going to be looking down the business end of a shotgun?"

"I've never heard anyone say he was hostile to strangers. And besides he did invite me," Tom said. "I don't know too much about him except the stories I've heard. For example, he loves politics. But we need to be careful because I can't remember which party he hates."

"I'll be careful."

Nestled in a sheltered cove on a creek that ran into the Lewis River was Ole Peterson's cabin. It was much more than what you would normally think of as a "cabin" and a lot more than I had expected. The house was a two-story moss-covered wood framed house. The house had wood siding made of rough-cut lumber. It certainly was not a "log cabin." Scattered around were other buildings in various states of repair. This included the all-important 'out house' which was made of the same rough-cut lumber as the house.

Tom called,"Hello down there." There was no response so he called much louder. "Hello Mr. Peterson, it's Tom Kyle. Can we come down?"

"I don't care if you go down or not, but I wished you'd stop yelling about it." Ole Peterson had come right in behind us without making a sound.

"Mr. Peterson I am Tom Kyle, and this is my friend Mac McGowan."

I figured who you were. Glad to meet you. And you too McGowan," Ole Peterson said. "You boys ready for a cup of Ole's coffee? Come on down and sit a spell. It ain't much, but by God it's all mine and paid for."

On a post holding up one corner of the porch roof was still another of Ole's signs. This one read:

NO KORKS ALLOWED

"When did you come in this far, Mr. Peterson?" I asked.

"Mr. Peterson was my dad. He has been in the ground for many a year. I'm Oly. I left I-oway in 1892 when that Gawddamn Grover Cleveland caused us to lose all our money and our self-respect in the panic of that year. Had a stud farm and we lost it all." Ole went ahead of us into the house.

I whispered to Tom, "Was Cleveland a Democrat or a Republican?"

"I don't have the slightest idea," Tom whispered back.

"Come on in boys. I'm not bringing it to you." The doorway was a sudden flutter of chickens flying in every direction as Ole swatted at them. "Don't mind the birds," Ole said. "Just sit in the chair with the least in it."

Every nook and cranny that I could see was piled high with yellowed newspapers and old magazines. The question about Ole's political affiliation was clearly answered by another of his famous signs. This one was nailed to the wall above the table. It read:

NO DAMN DEMOCRATS ALLOWED

Tom nodded to the sign and I confirmed with a nod.

Ole Peterson was not a big man. It was hard to tell about his weight or general body configuration because he was wearing what looked like about four layers of clothing topped with what was left of an old worn red-and-black plaid wool macinaw. And this was summer remember. Later I asked Tom, "What do you suppose he wears in the winter when the snow is four feet deep up here?"

"Probably the very same clothes," Tom said.

Ole had a full beard but you could tell that some attempt had been made to give the beard a summer trim. I was struck by the man's eyes. They were piercing and more noticeable because they were deep set and very far apart. He wore his coat and shirt sleeves rolled up exposing the forearms of a man in his twenties rather than the arms of the old man that he was.

"Let's sit and chat a spell," Ole said. "What you got in the basket?" He didn't wait for Tom to answer he had already opened it.

"Thanks Tom. This is mighty white of you," Ole said as he took the sandwiches and apples out of the basket and put them all in a box that he had first tipped upside down to tap the dust out. Ole got two tin cups down from nails where they hung. His cup was on the table on top of more newspapers. He carefully blew real or imagined dust out of each cup before giving them to us. The coffee pot was an enormous cast iron affair that could hold several gallons. I learned later that Ole never threw the grounds out. He just added more coffee. The coffee pot was always on the iron cook stove and there was always a fire burning, night or day, summer or winter. The seasons would determine the size of the fire.

"Got to pour the java slow so as not to get too many shells," Ole said.

"Shells?" Tom asked.

"Egg shells. Improves the taste," Ole explained.

"You wanted to see the caves? Well, it's a bit late in the day to start to the caves. You will have to make that another time. I could show you where to get started, but if you ain't seen a 'tube' before you could walk right over the top of one and not know it. But that's another time. I've spent all morning looking for my bull and I'd rather sit and chat a bit," Ole said.

"That's fine with us," Tom said.

"There's thirty seven caves that I know of. I have named most of them. Let's see, there's Bat Cave, Spider Cave, Utterstrom Cave, and Dollar, Dime, Beaver, Flow, and the largest of all I modestly named Ole's Cave." He laughed at this and we joined in.

"I discovered the first cave just by fool's chance in 1895. A fellow in Woodland told me how they got here if you can believe it. This fellow says that when Mt. St.Helens erupted one time the lava flowed down this side of the mountain all the way to the Lewis River. Can you believe that? Anyway as the outside of the lava flow cooled the center which was still hot kept on flowing and pulled the lava into a hollow tube. The fellow kept calling them 'lava tubes' but I call them caves. They look like caves to me and that's why I call them caves. Besides I wouldn't like it so much if people said they were looking for Ole's Tube. Would you?"

"I see your point," Tom said.

"Do you have cattle up here? You mentioned a bull, "I said.

"Yep, I would have more if that dang bull was more

energetic. I accused him of getting all moon- eyed over a cow elk that comes through every three weeks. Rufus denied any real affection for the elk cow. But how much can you believe a bull anyway?" Ole laughed at the thought of it.

"Have another cup of java. I guess you want to hear my story. I guess you fellows ain't reporters but I bet you want to hear my story just the same. I've been interviewed by some of those reporters. Yes sireee. I think they were Democrats. Did I ask you if you wanted another cup of java?,

"No thanks, really. I am still working on this one. Thanks just the same," Tom said.

"Don't tell me it isn't strong enough for your taste," Ole said.

"No , the coffee is strong enough," I confirmed.

Ole took a long slurp of his famous coffee and wiped his bearded chin with the back of his hand. "Now where was I?"

"Oh yes, I was saying I never met a reporter that wasn't a damn Democrat. You boys vote regularly, do you?"

"I'm not old enough to register to vote," I said.

"I have never missed a vote," Tom said.

"Good, good. I vote Republican myself," Ole volunteered.

"I have voted Republican at times," Tom said.

"Good, good. Only you make it sound too much like a confession. I always vote for the best man. It just so happens that the best man has always been a Republican.I did fall for that Delano so-in-so the first time, I guess no one can have a perfect record."

"Do you have to travel to Woodland to vote?" I asked.

"I have. Yes siree. But usually we gather at Cougar and vote in the post office. One year I made my place the precinct. The Republicans got six votes that year."

"How many votes did the Democrats get?" I just had to ask that one.

"Nary a one. Nary a one."

The next obvious question was of course; how did you know the Democrats didn't get any votes? Neither Tom nor I asked.

"You fellers got any smoking tobacky?"

"Sorry, neither of us smoke," Tom said.

"You don't say." Ole lit a big pipe from a twig he had placed in the coals of the fire. "I grow my own tobacky but I like store-bought tobacky better."

"Six voters you say? Then there are others who live up in here?"Tom asked.

"You'd be surprised," Ole said. "None of them are as famous as I am I reckon, but there's folks up here."

"When I first came up here in 1893 I followed some miners in. We had to walk from Woodland. That's thirty-five miles to the west. Now they have a darn good highway all the way to Cougar. That's where it'll stop. Ain't no reason for anybody to come further up the river excepting to see me."

"You might be surprised where they will build roads in the near future," Tom offered.

"No. I just said, didn't I just say there's no reason for a body to go further up the river. Didn't I just say that? Weren't you listening?"

"Yes, and I am sure you are absolutely right about that," Tom said.

Ole looked sideways at Tom as if to say, if you aren't going to listen then I am through talking.

I decided to change-the subject and see if I could get the fire out of this old man's eyes.

"Do you go to Woodland very often?" I asked.

"Pretty often. I'm not one of those damn hermit fellers you know.

He still seemed to be a little testy.

"I went out in nineteen hundred. That's when I packed in ol' Betsy there."

He pointed at the cast iron cook stove.

"And again in nineteen and eleven. That's when I drove my first car in here."

"You drove a car in here in 1911?" Tom shook his head.

"You bet I did. I drove my second car in, in nineteen and sixteen, then I drove the Liberty in, in nineteen and twenty six. That was the year I went back to I-oway to bury my sainted Mother. God rest her. So you can see I ain't no damn hermit. I get out pretty often."

"Did you say you packed that stove all the way from Cougar on your back?" I asked.

"Hell no, not from Cougar. I packed it from Woodland. There wasn't even a road to Ariel then. It wasn't too bad packing once I put the sack of spuds inside the stove so it wouldn't bounce so much."

Tom and I looked at each other in total amazement.

"I have never heard of a 'Liberty' car. What did it look like?"

I hit on the right topic. The old man's eyes lit up with excitement.

"Would you like to see it? Come on down to the shed. Let me show her to you."

"You mean you still have it?" Tom asked.

"Of course. I got all my cars. By the time I run them in here they're almost out of gas and I never liked the idea of packing gas in here just to drive back out again. So I walk out light and buy another car in Woodland and load her up with everything I can stuff in it or tie on it and come back in. The folks in Woodland make quite a fuss over me when I go out to buy a new car."

"I bet they do," I said.

"Come on, let me show you my cars." He led us to one of the several out buildings that he called 'the shed'. The shed wasn't much of a building but one thing it did have was a roof in good repair. Neither Tom nor I was prepared for what we saw.

"Besides the Liberty touring car over there, I got that nineteen and eleven Hupmobile, a very good car. That one over there is a nineteen and twenty six Baby Grand, and then over there is a nineteen and twenty six Reo. That Reo is a story. Made in Lansing, Michigan. The great car designer and engineer Olds got in a tiff of some sort with the Oldsmobile Company that he had started himself. Dang people threw him out of his own company. So by Gawd, he started a another. He wanted to use his name because he was so well known he knew that his name alone would sell more cars. Well a bunch of those city-slicker lawyers said he couldn't use his own name. Can you believe that? Anyway, Olds full name was Ransom E. Olds so his initials were R.E.O. Get it? In any case he didn't do too good. He made too good a car. Way ahead of his time. Look here, the Reo had two wheel brakes, see, no hand brakes. Isn't she a good looking car? Six cylinders by Gawd. It was spendy in it's day."

"I wonder what a car like that would cost new?" I said.

"Hell, I can tell you exactly what it cost new. Don't you think I can remember what I paid for my own cars? The Reo cost $1550. Yes siree. But I brought you down here to see the Hupmobile."

He moved us to the other side of the shed. The cars were placed in the order he had driven them in.

"Have you ever in your life seen a better piece of equipment than the Hupmobile? Them's real carbide headlights and them's coal oil taillights. Ain't that something?"

"The car is a big one," Tom said.

"You bet. Nine feet two inches long. It had three speeds forward but only four cylinders. Built by the Hupp Motor Car Company of Detroit. I paid nine hundred for it brand spanking new.

"Now this little car here was a nice one. It was the famous Baby Grand made by Chevy. It was supposed to give the Model T Ford a run for it's money but old Henry was too smart for them. The Baby Grand is a five passenger touring car with an electric horn. And for sixty dollars on top of the sale price you could get electric lights, and get this, an electric starter. I don't suppose you boys have ever spun a crank before. The Baby Grand cost $490. They called it the 'four ninety'. Mine cost the extra sixty dollars but that was still a real good price I thought. It had a ventilating windshield and came with a jack and a tire pump."

"Ole, you have a fortune in old cars here," I said.

" 'Spect you're right. I was offered one thousand dollars for the Hupmobile and they would give me a new car. The new car had my interest, but what would I do with a thousand dollars? The damn Democrats would find a way to tax it all anyway."

"A thousand dollars is a lot of money, Ole," I said.

"You think I don't know what a thousand dollars is? Hell, I was offered one hundred thousand dollars for my seven hundred acres. Some damn fool thought they would log it some day. I didn't need the money, and besides, how could I take advantage of someone that ignorant?"

"No, I guess not, Tom said.

I sat gingerly down on the leather seat of the Hupmobile.

"Jees, the speedometer only has sixty-seven miles on it."

"I spun her around Woodland some before I drove her in. But it's got miles left in her," Ole assured us.

"I would think so," I shook my head, amazed.

It was mid-afternoon and although reluctant to leave, we knew we had to get started on the trail back to Cougar. The three-and-a-half miles was starting to loom longer in my mind. I was also afraid that my growling stomach could be heard.

"Now, about those Indian places you asked about," Ole said. "I ain't never come across what you could call a steady camping place. The Indians came through here but they didn't like Mt. St. Helens too much. It spooked them. I can tell you if it hadn't been for a band of Coweleske I wouldn't have made it the first winter. They showed me how to snag salmon. Then there was Indian Charlie. That's a good story for you. He was shot in the back of the head up beyond the Muddy River, they tell me. Someone thought he had led them to his gold mine. Anyway, I never thought he had a 'mine' as you would think of it. But come back another time and we can scout around a bit if you have any interest in gold."

"That would be great," I said. "I will look forward to it."

As we left, he shook hands with each of us with a grip that would shatter a diamond.

"Come back again. I talk too much. I know that, but I hope you fellers come back. I will show you where the caves are, real fast. And next time, if it's not too much trouble, could you bring me a couple of newspapers? It don't make no never mind if they're a little old."

"You bet," Tom said.

"And maybe some smoking tobacky too?"

"Sure, we can bring you some tobacco."

"Not any of that Velvet stuff. I like P.A."

"Prince Albert it is then," Tom assured him.

"Could you use another cup of java for the road? I have plenty."

"No thanks. I think we had better get hiking. But thank you just the same."

It was dark enough to turn on the truck lights by the time we got back to Cougar. Tom backed the car slowly out of the brush and on to the gravel road that Ole had described as a "good highway." As we turned, the headlights momentarily played on Ole's home made sign.

GIVE MY REGARDS TO CIVILIZATION
OLE PETERSON

Chapter 17

The Fight

On Saturday nights many of the construction workers went into Amboy to let off steam. They gravitated toward Nick's Tavern to do their serious drinking. If there were loggers in town they usually went to the Log Cabin Tavern, across the road from Nick's. The loggers didn't stay late as a rule since they started their day at three AM.

Nick's Tavern accommodated waves of men coming and going as the various shifts got off work. Men of the graveyard shift had to leave by ten thirty in the evening to get back over Speelyai Hill to be at the job by eleven thirty.

The day shift got into town about seven or eight in the evening depending on whether they spent much time at Nelson's before coming in. The day shift didn't have to get to work until the next morning so it was not uncommon for day shift folks to drink all night. Swing shift got into town about one thirty in the morning. By the time swing shift got started, the loggers were usually long gone, and the day shift would be half smackered and getting mean. Some pretty good brawls got started between shifts or crews. In the begining the miners made up the majority of the men, but as the project expanded to over a thousand men many different trades and professions were represented. My crew, on graveyard shift, missed out on most of the action because just as things warmed up we had to pull out and leave for work.

There was a group of Operating Engineers who worked days. Operating Engineers were anything but real engineers. This was a fancy title for cat skinners, crane jockeys, riggers, and the like. Anyway this group of five operators had the reputation of going into Amboy for the expressed purpose of starting a fight. It didn't matter to them who they fought or whether they won or lost. Fighting was their form of recreation. Some guys like to shoot pool; well, these guys liked to fight. When the five operators could not pick a fight with someone else they would choose up sides and fight each other. Since there were five of them one side would always be 'short'. People who watched them fight claimed that as one side was about to lose one of them would join the 'short' side so that the fight could continue longer. When the fighting was over they would drink beer together as if nothing had happened. Any loggers in the area stayed clear of this gang, and thought they were crazy.

When it became clear that the loggers were giving the construction workers in general, and this gang in particular, a wide berth, it was misinterpreted by some to be cowardice. But cowards they were not. The loggers just wanted a quick beer after a hard day's work in the woods. They wanted to relax, tell a few jokes, swap some tall tales, and go home. Most of them faced another several hours of doing chores on the small ranches they were trying to run. As individuals or as a group, they feared no man. They just wanted to be left alone.

A story circulated back to camp that some loggers had provoked some day shifters into a fight. The story had it that the loggers came over from the Log Cabin Tavern to drink beer at Nick's. If that was true, the loggers were looking for trouble and they sure got it. Apparently one of the loggers was hurt pretty bad and had to be taken to a doctor in Battle Ground, and then was transferred later to a hospital in Vancouver, Washington. The story had it that he was still unconscious when they took him away.

When I heard the story I thought, wow! that's taking the roughhousing too far. I bet the loggers will think twice before they leave the security of the Log Cabin Tavern looking for trouble. I put the story out of my mind.

The next Saturday night a bunch of us decided to run into Amboy after supper for a round or two of cold beer. It was Slim's idea and since I seldom saw him any more I looked forward to the evening. We had frankly forgotten the story about the 'brawl'with the loggers.

We got into town in the early evening. We played some shuffel board and shot some pool. Nick's was comparatively quiet.

There was a bearded fellow sitting by himself at a corner table, where he seemed to be watching everybody who came in. I knew by a glance at his clothes that he was a logger but I paid little attention to him.

Slim pulled up a stool and I was glad to see him.

"Don't you recognize Dave Swenson over there?" Slim asked.

"I don't believe I know a Dave Swenson."

"Hell, that's Butch Swenson's brother. You remember Butch."

Butch played for the Amboy Legion team in the summer but we played ball together during the school year. He was a year ahead of us. I respected him as a good shortstop.

"Come on over. I think you better hear Dave's story," Slim said.

We started over to the table where Dave Swenson was sitting but he nodded to the door and got up. We followed him outside.

"You're Jerry McGowan. I have seen you pitch some

pretty damn good country ball," Dave said. "Thanks. Slim said you had something I should hear."

Before the big logger could start Slim butted in. "It was Butch that got hurt in the fight the other night."

"I'm truly sorry to hear that. How is he doing?"

He is still in a coma. Going on the third day now," Dave said.

Slim interjected again. "There were five of them against Butch."

"I think it was the operators' gang from what Dave has told me."

"Boy, that's a different story than what circulated around camp at the dam."

"I don't doubt that," Dave said. "Butch had no business going into Nick's. We know that's trouble. We've pretty much left Nick's to the trailor trash and construction stiffs. But Butch had the Callahan girl with him and he knew Old Joe at the Log Cabin would never serve him or his girl. Hell, he won't serve no kids. They're only nineteen or so. Not old enough to drink, that's for damn sure. Anyway, they came over to Nick's and some fellow made some remark to Butch's girl and Butch decked him."

"He hit the guy?"

"That's the way the girl tells it," Dave said. "When Butch knocked him down he stood back to let him up. That's the way we were taught to fight. When you knock a man down you step back and give him a chance to get up. Then, if you have to, you knock him down again. Let me tell you boys, that's not the way the game is played by these guys. One of them sucker punched Butch in the kidneys from behind. That knocked the wind out of Butch and put him to his knees. He was slowly getting up thinking he had the time to get to his feet when the first, guy took his boots to Butch. It was no match from that time on."

"We heard it was a 'group' of loggers in the brawl," I said.

"A group of one," Slim said.

"Well, I'm going back inside to see if they show up here tonight," Dave Swenson said.

"You're not fixing to take on that gang of Operators by yourself are you?" I asked.

"Hell no. I may be a logger but I ain't that dumb."

"We'll go in with you,'" Slim said.

"If you boys didn't have anything to do with it, I would stay out of it," Dave said.

"What are you going to do," I asked.

"We asked the county Sheriff to arrest them but he said he only had one deputy for the North County and the Sheriff thought he was busy. So when I get these guys spotted I will pass the word to my falling crew, who will just by chance be passing through. If the others stay out of it, so will my crew, and I will take the main one in. I'll arrest him myself."

"Arrest him? You will never be able to pull that one off. You better let us help," I said.

"No. You have to work with this scum of the earth and you won't be able to watch your back all the time." Dave was adamant.

"It wasn't miners, Dave. It was a bunch of other construction workers. They're coming in from all over the world to work on the dam. We're with the miners and from what I have seen they wouldn't do something like this," I said.

"It's not the construction stiffs that worry me. It's old man Callahan. He has had a snoot full for two days now running around with a gun and someone not even involved may get killed."

"The girl was a bit embarrassed by the fight and all, I guess," Slim said.

"Embarrassed?" Dave's eyes narrowed. "The girl ran two miles home stark naked. They even took her shoes.

She ran, not because she was scared of that trash, but to tell her Daddy where they had left Butch for dead. Boys, that little girl saved Butch's life, of that I'm certain."

I hesitated to ask but, "Did they... did they hurt the girl?"

"She says no. But I don't rightly know. They held Butch while they stripped his girl. He wasn't hurt too bad at that point. But when he wouldn't stop struggling one of them broke a quart beer bottle over his head. The bottle was a full one. The Callahan girl said. Butch didn't move after that."

"Boys, I fought up and down Pork Chop Hill and we lost a brother when the First Marines 'advanced' from the reservoirs on the Yalu. We didn't do all that fighting just to come home here to America and let a bunch of outlaws take over our home town. We intend to arrest those bastards for what they did and take them into the County jail. If the Sheriff is too damn busy to send a deputy out here in the boondocks we will take the bastards to him."

"I lost a brother in Korea too. I'm staying Dave. If it's a fair fight I will stay out of it. If it's not fair, I want in," I said.

The Goddamn tears welled up in my eyes. Now why was that? Dave must have wondered if he needed a fighter with tears in his eyes. But he put his arm around my shoulder, "It's up to you," Dave said.

"Count me in on the same basis as Mac," Slim said.

As we were talking in the shadows, two pickups screeched to a halt in a cloud of dust in front of Nick's. Out swaggered five big and mean looking roundtops.

"That's them!" Slim said.

"The dumb bastards even wear their hardtops to town they're so damn proud of them. Are you sure that's them?" Dave asked.

"That's sure the Operators gang. I don't know if that's who mugged Butch and his girl or not."

"This is no time to make a mistake. I got my eye witness sitting right over there in the car. We'll see."

Dave went over and leaned in the window of the car. He came back shortly. "It's them all right. Cathy Callahan says she would know them anywhere."

"You boys go on back inside. I've got some business to attend to at the Log Cabin," Dave said.

We had barely settled down when the door flew open and in jostled Whiskey Riley, Turk, Tennessee, High Pockets, Red, and even Easy Money was with them. What an inopportune time for the miners to arrive.

"My God," Slim whispered. "We don't want our guys mixed up in this thing tonight. They might side with the Operators gang just because they are fellow construction workers."

I was afraid he might be right. I sauntered over to Tennessee.

"Why don't you and the crew drink up and make yourself a bit scarce around here? In a little bit this place will be crawling with loggers and they're in a very bad mood."

Whiskey Riley overheard the last of my comments.

"Hell, I'm not going to be chased out by no stump jumpers. There's enough beer to go around, ain't there?"

"Yes there is, but these guys have a pretty serious score to settle and they may not be able to tell the good guys from the bad."

"Do you know any of these local hands?" Whiskey asked. "Yes we do. Some of them at least."

"Do they have a legitimate beef coming?"

"I think they do."

"Does it involve any of my boys?" Whiskey asked.

"No it doesn't."

"What happened to get then so riled up?"

"It's a long story but five of those Operators put a young local in the hospital and stripped his girl naked and mauled her around some," I explained.

"No shit? My men are mostly mountain men from the hills of West Virginny and the coal fields. We don't treat women that way and we don't like them that does. It wouldn't be any of my boys that did that to this girl. We will just pick up our beer and retire to a quiet corner and see if these stump jumpers can fight when their women folk have been wronged."

While we were talking to Whiskey Riley, Dave strolled back in and sat down unobtrusively in the opposite corner from us. The place was filling up, which wasn't too good. The Operators gang was at the bar talking loudly and spilling beer. Others at the bar began moving away. These guys were so obnoxious that even the other day shift men didn't want to drink too close to them. A few more men came in. These men wore their jeans cut off at the tops of their fourteen inch boots. Their dress was a dead give- away that they were loggers, if anyone was paying any attention. The stage was just about set. A fifth logger came in but he didn't sit down. It was now five to five, and "high noon" was approaching. A sixth logger came in and stood by the open door.

Dave Swenson stood up to his full height and started slowly toward the bar. The man by the door reached over and closed it and turned the lock. We could see this all developing, but no one else seemed wise to it. The bartender, who we knew kept a baseball bat under the counter that he called "Big Bertha" did not even pick up on the fact that the mood in the bar was changing.

"My name is Dave Swenson" Dave announced. "And you five men, are under arrest for assault and battery, aggravated assault, and harassment." The other four loggers stepped forward and stood in place behind Dave. The sixth logger planted himself in front of the locked door.

It's amazing how quickly a bar can quiet down in a situation like this. I can tell you that bar was stone silent.

The Operators turned around on their stools to see who was speaking to whom. Then it dawned on them that Dave was addressing them. None of the five made a move to stand up. You could tell they were sizing up the situation. They had been here before.

"Under arrest? The hell you say. Are you some kind of cop or something? Her-assing you say? That's the only kind of assing we know. Do you know another kind of assing? They all broke out laughing, but no one else in the tavern saw the humor. The one doing the talking turned back around to nurse his beer but his eyes were fixed on the mirror behind the bar. The other four did not turn away.

Dave cleared his throat. Unfortunately his voice cracked a little and he had to clear his throat a second time.

"I am not a cop but I am making a citizen's arrest."

The spokesman for the gang was still watching Dave in the mirror with his back to him.

"We just come in here to have a nice quiet beer. Now if you stump jumpers will just relax and drink a cold one, or go on back across the street, and have several cold ones, everybody will be happy."

"A citizen's arrest means I hold you until the proper law arrives or I take you to the proper law," Dave said, "In this case, I'm taking you to Vancouver to the Clark County jail myself."

"Just how do you suppose to do that? Vancouver is two hours away."

The spokesman had never turned around. It looked like we were going into a jawing match. Dave relaxed some to go into more of his newfound legaleeze.

On some unspoken signal, the Operator at the end of the group of five grabbed the nearest logger, spun him around, and had both his arms pinned behind his back. The spokesman for the gang smashed a wine bottle and pressed the jagged edge savagely against the cheek of the pinned logger.

An enormous hand shot out from the side. That hand belonged to Whiskey Riley. With a sudden twist to the Operators wrist the broken bottle crashed to the floor with a shriek of pain.

"Now little man, don't you go carving up this one. I want to arm wrestle him again cause I've been practicing for a rematch, which he promised me. The logger who had his arms pinned in the sudden move was the same big man who had dumped Whiskey twice in arm wrestling.

Whiskey Riley had everyone's attention and, he went on. "Now boys, if that feller by the door stays out of this, it looks like we got a one-on-one situation here. I got no problem with a good old-fashioned mixer. Me and my boys will only be watching, unless someone shows steel or any other unmannerly item."

The gang of Operating Engineers were in heaven. This was their game. Their form of recreation. At least they wouldn't have to fight each other tonight, unless of course,this little action didn't take long enough to satisfy them.

But the loggers were not in a 'game'. A family member was hurt. They were defenders in their own land going against the invaders. The Operators were ready to play, but the loggers were ready to die. They had suffered enough at the hands of these outsiders. Now it was their turn to hurt those that had hurt their own.

To my surprise, and I think to the surprise of most of the onlookers, the fight didn't last long. The loggers were in top physical condition and sober. The Operators were neither in shape nor sober. The loggers could fight all right. Yes, they could fight. It was jab, jab, jab, and crash the right would fall like a sledgehammer. In most instances the Operators went down and stayed down. Dave Swenson wasn't even breathing hard.

Dave motioned to the guard at the door. "Go bring Cathy in."

Cathy was a perky and petite girl of seventeen or eighteen. She was dressed in new jeans and came walking right in. She shook her long hair to one side with a twist of her head. She walked right up to the gang members who were still sitting on the floor. She stopped in front of each man.

"He was one. He's one. That's the one who hit Butch with the bottle, and that's one too, and that's one."

"Are you certain Cathy?" Dave spoke softly.

"I'm very certain," the girl said in a remarkably strong voice.

"Get the ropes, men," Dave ordered.

"Oh my God," Slim whispered.

The miners rose to their feet in unison a half step behind their leader Whiskey Riley.

"Now boys, let's not get carried away here. We're not ready to see a lynching," Whiskey Riley warned.

"To tie them with. To tie them up," Dave explained.

The loggers tied the men's hands and feet and threw them none too carefully in the back of a waiting pickup truck. The loggers tied them all together and also to the truck bed.

"This way if we lose one of them we lose them all including the damn pickup," Dave said.

Some more loggers jumped in the back of the truck, and off they bounced, heading for Vancouver. A caravan of honking trucks, assorted cars, and even one logging truck tractor followed behind.

Whiskey called to the biggest logger, "Hey, apple knocker, when are you gonna let me get even in arm wrestling?"

The big logger slowly turned around. Once again I felt that 'room quieting' phenomenon that comes just before the storm.

"Oh no," Slim said. "Here we go again."

"Sir, I will give you the pleasure of a return match tomorrow night if you can come in, if you allow me to buy you and your men a round of beer."

"Make mine a boilermaker and you're on, apple knocker."

The whole tavern exploded in laughter. The logger raised his hand to silence the crowd. "This man can call me an apple knocker if he wants to but don't anybody else get in the habit."

"Jees, he called me Sir. I like that," Whiskey Riley said grinning.

Chapter 18

Indians Along The Siouxon

In a borrowed pickup we edged our way between the boulders on a cat road which had been cut through to a mile beyond the dam site. The cat trail ran at water level for the most part. The walls of the canyon reached so high, it gave the illusion of overhanging the river. The cliffs looked like the polished granite of a tombstone. Only this tombstone was over a hundred feet high. The cat road ended abruptly with a big mound of rubble shoved up at the end.

"How are we going to get across the river?" I asked Tom.

The water churned and tumbled as it tore through the gorge. A trip to the Siouxon was going to have more excitement than I had prepared for.

"There's a rope chair crossing that we used last summer to cross the river. I just hope it hasn't been torn down."

We found the rope chair contraption about a mile beyond where we had left the truck. The chair was tied down on our side of the river. Tom went first to show me how to sit on the thing and pull myself across. It wasn't too bad except my weight on the ropes caused my butt to swing only inches above the white water. If a person fell into this channel they wouldn't surface until they reached Japan. I was more than a little relieved when my feet were standing on rock on the South bank of the Lewis River. A short hike up the river and we saw our destination, the Siouxon. The Siouxon had cut a substantial canyon of its own but where it emptied into the Lewis River the water was relatively docile. In fact, Tom referred to the site as the Siouxon Bay. A bay was a good way to describe the confluence of the Siouxon and the Lewis. The beach was wide and sandy at this point. The Lewis River was much wider here, and quieter. It was as if the water was resting in this hidden bay, storing up energy for its sprint through the gorge.

With Tom leading the way we walked up the Siouxon for a hundred yards to the first of a series of benches. It was easy to see where the University of Washington's camp had been located by the fire rings, piles of cut wood, and most significantly where they had been systematically digging. The prehistoric residence was a "pit house" thirty to thirty five feet across and five feet deep.

"The Indians called this place Kathapootle," Tom said. "The Indians were Klickitats from the high plateau country near Mt. Adams. The Klickitat tribe had originally lived in Northern Oregon, but they got chased out by their arch enemies, the dreaded Cayuse. We found over fifty Indian artifacts at this site."

"Do you mean arrow heads?" I asked.

"Yes, we found arrow points and stone knives, scrapers, rubbing stones, a chipping hammer and a arrow shaft smoother, which is fairly rare."

"You didn't mention anything made of iron," I observed.

"Very good, Mac. The absence of 'trade goods' such as iron hatchets or glass beads indicated to us that the site had been abandoned before the 1800's. On the other hand this area is quite remote and it is possible that the Indians along the Siouxon had not come in contact with white men or with other bands of Indians who had traded with white men."

"That doesn't sound like a scientific conclusion to me." I enjoyed chiding him.

"We found a burial cairn. Had there been any trade goods in use we would have expected such items to have been buried with the owner. We found none."

"We wanted to do much more work here but our time ran out. Our contract with PP&L was just for the summer. We could have worked all winter but PP&L was not inclined to spot us any additional funds. What they didn't know was the team would have worked for nothing. PP&L couldn't comprehend that."

Tom grew animated as he told me the story of setting up camp, finding the first clues, and mapping the site. He was even excited telling me of the laborious tasks of screening and digging.

"If there would have been more time to have worked the site properly we would have dredged the creek right at the point where you see the creek narrowing down. That would be the most likely place to stand to spear fish. I am sure we would have found spear points and arrow points."

The stretch of water he was indicating was deep but unbelievably, clear. You could see every rock on the bottom, and just at that moment I caught sight of the largest trout I had ever seen.

"Those are sea run cutthroats returning to spawn," Tom said.

Tom showed me the layout of the pit house and told me about the daily activities of the Klickitats of so many years ago. The way he described it all made me feel I was right there watching the Indians spear the fish.

"McClellan made no note of any Indians inhabiting the Lewis River Valley when he came through in 1853. That was only ten years after the last eruption of Mt. St.Helens. The Indians were very superstitious about the whole region, probably because of the mountains erupting and the accompanying earthquakes. This fear of the area is reflected in the names they gave places. Names like Spirit Lake on Mt. St. Helens, and Yacolt, just south of here." I was familiar with the little logging town of Yacolt, Washington.

"What does Yacolt mean in Klickitat?"

"Yacolt, means, 'place abounding in evil spirits' or 'haunted place'. It shouldn't be too surprising to learn that the Lewis River Valley was essentially uninhabited.The Klickitat went toward the Columbia River for their trade.At a place like Celilo Falls on the Columbia, the Indians could catch salmon weighing fifty pounds or more as opposed to the cut throat, weighing only around ten pounds. The Cascades area of the Columbia was generally a place of peace. If a band of Indians didn't have the time or equipment to fish for salmon they could barter with a tribe like the Wishram or the Yakima."

Tom had filled his basket with food for our lunch. The basket was complete with a red-and-white lunch cloth which he carefully spread on the ground. He talked non-stop between bites of sandwich.

"A side reward of our work last summer was the discovery of the old trail blazes made by the McClellan survey party. Does the name McClellan ring a bell with you?"

"Not really."

"You probably have read of him in your history classes on the Civil War.Except by that time he was General McClellan. Now does it ring a bell?"

Fortunately he did not wait for my admission of ignorance.

"He was Captain McClellan when he came through here leading a survey party trying to select the best route for a railroad through the Cascade Mountains."

"This obviously was not the best pass," I observed.

"True. This particular pass would have been difficult but there were other passes that would have been more suitable. But poor Captain McClellan kept losing his men to gold discoveries."

"Gold?" Now that was more interesting. Ole Peterson had mentioned gold too.

"They ran a railroad from Vancouver, Washington to Yacolt. It was the dream of every businessman of the area that'rails' would go through to Yakima, which as the crow flies, is not all that far. If that could have happened the produce from the rich Yakima Valley would have been channeled through Yacolt on its way to the Portland markets and to the Lower Columbia ports. The produce would have been to the markets much faster."

"What happened? Why didn't they complete the line?"

"The military lost interest with the onslaught of the Civil War and then much later World War I came along and the nation decided they needed the rails more in other places. It was reputed that there were enough rails stock piled at Yacolt to push through to Yakima. But it was never completed and the line from Yacolt to Vancouver became primarily a logging train operation."

"Tell me more about the gold discoveries."

"There had been many small strikes all over the Cascades. I'm not a geologist, but it seems that where ever the overburden is removed or penetrated, they find mineral formations. Anyway, the Army lost hundreds of recruits to the gold strikes real and imagined. The soldiers would just up and desert. So McClellan always recruited local men when he could, preferably family men. His theory was that a man with a family was more likely to see the adventure through to the end and return to their families. On this survey of the Lewis River Valley there was a local settler by the name of Adolphus Lewis. His claim to fame was that he was the guide who led our Captain out of the wilderness after they had become hopelessly lost. His reward was to have the river named in his honor."

"I had always thought the Lewis River was named after Lewis of Lewis and Clark fame," I said.

"That is a common misconception. The Lewis River is named after Adolphus Lewis, guide to the McClellan party."

The day was getting on and we hadn't even gotten a line wet in the Siouxon. But it didn't really matter to me. I was having a heck of a good day. Tom stopped telling stories of the Lewis wilderness only long enough to pull himself across the river on the rope chair. He may have even kept talking then for all I know but I think the noise of the river spared me. As soon as we were back in the truck he continued the non-stop story telling.

I had enjoyed the day and I had learned a lot of new things. I was busting to tell Slim about the circular pit house, General McCellan, and all the rest. I hustled through the day room and scanned the tables of poker players, but Slim was not playing. That was a change but I was glad I hadn't found him in a game. He was gambling far too much. It wasn't a game with him anymore. I had watched his face as he 'played' and you could see it wasn't a mere game of poker to him. The expression on his face was one of pain or hate. I went on to the room in hopes of picking up a couple hours of sleep before I had to catch the rig down to the tunnel. Slim lay face down on my cot, and Red was on Slim's bed. The place smelled like a pig sty. It was obvious that they both had been drinking heavily. Slim stirred and rolled over to face me. He tried in vain to focus his eyes on me.

"Hi ol buddy," Slim managed. "Did you have a fine picnic with your good friend? He can sure make the cutest sandwiches to go in his little basket, can't he?"

" You are looped. Are you going to make shift tonight?"

"What do you care? Your not my ol lady."

"I do care, Slim. I hate to see you going to hell in a hand basket this way. And get your feet off my bed."

"I may be going to hell but I bet I don't go there with someone in lace shorts."

"You're drunk. I'll see you after the shift."

"Sure you got the time?" Slim said. Momentarily I remembered the watch and anger began to rise.

"And by the way Slim, that looks like my good shirt you're wearing. Get it off. I don't want you puking down the front of it."

He grabbed both sides of the shirt and began jerking. The buttons flew like shrapnel.

If I knew Slim, he would realize in the morning what he had done and feel real bad about the scene. He'd probably drive into Amboy and buy me a shirt worth twice the one he had, just ruined. That is, if he had any money left. It didn't matter too much it was only a shirt.

I shouldn't have let Slim's remarks about Tom get to me, but they did. I knew what he was insinuating. Tom had never done anything to offend me at any time. I didn't think the insinuations were true, yet maybe it didn't look good for Tom and me to be going off to so many places together all the time. It wouldn't be so bad if he didn't make those "little lunches" all the time and carry them in that damn basket. You don't make up a lunch when you go fishing. You just throw a sandwich or something in your pack. Another thing that was starting to bother me. I could never get out of his sight. He was always right next to me no matter if we were eating in the mess hall, playing pool in the recreation room, or doing anything anywhere. I felt smothered by him. I had already decided to put a little distance between us even before Slim had made his drunken remarks.

I managed to avoid Tom for several days. I just wasn't where he thought I would be. He finally caught up with me one day as we were waiting to catch the jitney.

"I tried to find you today. I thought we could do some fly fishing or go someplace," Tom said.

"Yeah, well I was busy doing stuff today."

"I looked for you yesterday too."

"I was busy then too."

"And tomorrow?" Tom asked.

"Yeah, as a matter of fact I am going into Amboy to cash my check and deposit what I can. Tomorrow is pay day you know. I have some stuff I should get. Then we're going over to Nick's to see what going on. I would ask you to come along with us but the car is already full."

"I could meet you at Nick's."

"We don't know for sure when we will get there and you could be waiting for nothing."

A strange look came over Tom's face.

"I guess I'm a little slow," Tom said, " I understand. I do understand. I get too overbearing." Tom said softly.

"No, that's not it Tom. I just had some things to do for awhile."

"You aren't the one that needs to apologize, Mac. I was hoping I wouldn't be so darn pushy this time." I started to make some lame reply but he raised his hand to quiet me.

"Thank you, Mac, for sharing some good times. I enjoyed your company. If you want to go fishing or anything look me up. Will you do that?"

"Sure. That would be great," I said.

I think he knew there wouldn't be any more trips.

I had a note from Tom a week later. He said he had to return to Seattle early. He had just been notified that he had been selected as the new Department Chairman. Now he had some work to organize before classes began in the fall. He said if I was ever in Seattle to look him up at the University.

But I never heard from Tom again.

Chapter 19

Timbering

Our crew had been making good time in the tunnel. We seldom missed our bonus level of production. We knew that the other crews were not doing nearly as well. From a collection of 'misfits' Whiskey Riley had turned the graveyard shift into the premiere drilling team on the dam.

They say that the Shift Boss on the other portal insisted on telling each of his miners where to collar their holes. It took them so long to get started that it was no wonder they weren't making any footage. The joke going around about day shift was that they needed three crews, one coming, one drilling, and one going. After our first shake down, Whiskey Riley had not let a man go. He had shifted one or two for good reasons that he could always explain to those involved, but as far as I knew no one had even come close to getting fired. I don't know why he put up with several of the guys that had drinking problems so bad that it would cause them to miss shifts, but I guess Whiskey Riley had his reasons and his limits. Slim and Red could be pushing their luck.

Whiskey Riley was always ready to jump in if someone needed help. It was easy for us to put out a special effort for him when he called for it because we had all seen him right in the muck with us.

Truckee was breaking in as an extra miner. After the jumbo was backed into place there wasn't too much for Truckee to do until time to move the jumbo again. Truckee always had a little mechanical checking to do on the jumbo, but as soon as he could he would come in and stand behind one of the miners. Usually the miner would let Truckee take the controls for a bit after the hole was collared. Whiskey Riley liked to see that kind of interest and encouraged it. Whiskey wanted everyone to know the other man's job. If there was a man sick or if one got 'tunnel frights' we could still drill out in good time, and stay on our bonus money.

There wasn't much on the job that Whiskey Riley couldn't do. There was one exception. He had never worked on a job that used a 'donkey engine' to pull the trucks loaded with muck out of the tunnel. On other jobs, Tennessee said they laid tracks and removed the muck with an electric train. Because of the size of the Yale tunnel they felt that the huge Euclid rock trucks could move the muck out faster. But you couldn't drive the trucks in the tunnel because of the carbon monoxide fumes. So they used a rig very similar to what is used in the woods to pull logs out, called a 'donkey'. It is a huge drum on which the cable turns with a series of pulleys; the power source is a D-9 engine stationed on a slab of concrete.

One day Whiskey Riley decided it was time for him to learn how to run the donkey engine. Blackie, the donkey operator, showed Whiskey the technique of how to brake the drum to keep the right tension on the cables, and then he turned Whiskey loose.

Whiskey Riley did not give up until three cables had been snapped.

"Anyone can do that job," Whiskey said. "Nothing to it. I broke those cables to give you boys some practice in cable splicing."

The crew horse-laughed Whiskey on that one. We lost our bonus that shift but no one grumbled because we could all see what he was trying to do.

His 'management style' would not be written up in professional journals, certainly not by Whiskey Riley. The only thing he could write and recognize was his own name. But here was a real leader of men who understood how to get the most out of a diverse group of people.

Years later, I realized this rough-and-tumble boss truly understood the concept of "cross training" before the term had been invented. He understood "empowerment" and "accountability" without ever hearing the words. To have tried to explain "successive approximation" as a method to reach a goal would have brought only a quizzical expression to this big man even though that's exactly the approach he utilized to solve everyday problems.

One day things were not going well at all. Turk asked Whiskey why he hadn't fired the whole crew when he had the chance.

"Heck, firing is easy. Training a crew to do what's right, now that takes something," Whiskey replied.

Whiskey could have selected the chucktender for each miner. It was certainly within his authority. Instead he had each miner pick their own chucktender. This gave each miner an investment in his teammate. The miner worked harder to help his chucktender succeed because, "he is my chucktender." Whiskey Riley had not written a procedural manual and had no forms to fill out. Perhaps not being able to read or write was a blessing. Whiskey had a rare quality of leadership and management that CEO's the world over would have paid a fortune for if it could have been packaged.

Can you imagine Whiskey Riley being interviewed by a graduate student in Personnel Management? The graduate student might say; "Mr. Riley, what techniques have you found to be most effective in motivating workers?" If Whiskey understood the question he might reply, "I just say, 'Let's get closer to it. And all I want to see is assholes and elbows and both of them turned up," and everyone goes to work to do their job." Can you imagine the grad student referring to his notes later and asking himself, " I wonder if assholes and elbows are new clinical terms?"

For several shifts the tunnel walls and ceiling took on a very different appearance after each blast. Instead of the walls and arch being smooth, with only the usual scars of the drilling steel visible, there would be large cubicles of rock broken out. The tunnel was taking on a ragged appearance and the arch was "squaring up.".Whiskey had told Turk and the other arch men early on,"Keep me an egg shaped arch and we might live to work another job." After one blast the south wall of the tunnel slanted off with an indent twenty feet off the intended course of the tunnel.

Until these changes in the rock started occurring Whiskey always had some of the miners do a "little barring down." This meant that several men under Turk's watchful eye would ride the top of the jumbo as it was backed into place. These men were equipped with a "bar" which was eight feet long. The bar had a point on one end and a prying wedge on the other. The men with these bars pried any loose rock from the ceiling of the tunnel and from the sides as the jumbo moved into place. Turk referred to this as "polishing up." In the past the men riding on top could get all the polishing done without holding up the placement of the jumbo, but recently because of the changing rock formations it took much longer to secure the ceiling.

While the arch crew would bar down, the rest of the crew would walk slowly behind waiting for Turk to give the arch his blessing. At this time the tunnel would be very quiet. The only sounds were the creaking of the jumbo, the sound of the diesel engine, and miners coughing. The miners barring down would tap a suspicious-looking rock and know by the sound emitted whether the rock was solid or loose.

If the rock was loose they would bar or "scale" the rock down. The miners enjoyed this function until now. Now it was no longer fun. It was nervous time. The barring down was taking much longer, the diesel engine on the jumbo was running way too long, and each rock scaled down seemed to produce another loose one right behind it.

"How do they know when all the loose rock has been pried down?" I asked Johnnie.

"The fact is, they never know for sure. You can't look behind the rock to see what it's holding."

"When a bar-down man puts the point of his bar into a small crack he doesn't know for sure if a two-inch slab of rock will peel off or if the whole damn mountain will come down. Once a miner starts to loosen a rock with his bar he can't leave it until the rock is down and the area is secure again. At least secure enough so we can drill the next round," Johnnie said.

Whiskey changed the procedure at this point. Only Whiskey and Turk, with one chucktender as a helper and a lookout rode the top of the jumbo now. He rotated chucktenders and excluded any chucktender who had a wife and kids, which meant I had to take my turn on top. The rest of the crew gathered in little knots of on-lookers watching the operation in silence, each thankful it wasn't his turn on top.

Even after the jumbo was finally in place and the drilling began it took much longer to collar a good hole. The rock was too badly fractured. Bonus money was out the window. As the jumbo went further and further under the fracture zone after each drillout the experienced miners became more and more uneasy and so did our fearless leader. We greenhorns could detect the growing tension but we did not fully understand or appreciate the seriousness of the situation.

One morning as we were riding out after our shift Tennessee pointed up to the mountain above the tunnel. "That's

what we are drilling through. That's why we are into rotten rock." He was pointing half way up the sheer cliff to a
point where the mountain came into a 'V' shape forming a
deep chasm some nine hundred feet above the tunnel we
were drilling. It looked like a substantial creek poured
through the V cut in the mountain. At one turn of the gravel
road you could see as many as four waterfalls. Each waterfall looked to be about ten feet high. I had admired this
particular scene from the first day on the job, and I never
failed to look up at this point on the trip out each morning.
The sun coming up over the river valley played directly on
the sparkling water cascading down the mini-falls.

There was one oddity that I had wondered about but
didn't have an answer for. Where did the water go? There
wasn't a stream or a creek crossing the road any place that
I could see.

The answer as to where the stream was going became
clearer with each drillout. The water was pouring through
cracks and fissures into the tunnel right through the tunnel
roof.

Typically the men working on the lifters, where I worked
would be in six to eight inches of water by the end of a
drillout. This water came from the drills themselves. With
one air pump going there had been no problem in keeping
the water under control, and the floor of the tunnel would
be dry again for the next round of drilling. Now however,
a single pump could not keep up. More pumps were
brought in. Eventually we had ten pumps in all. When the
pumps were all working right each threw a three-inch
stream of water. The pumps were driven by compressed
air and they kept 'freezing ' up. Solid ice would form
around each pump, reducing the pump's capacity to move
water. It kept the Nipper and Truckee busy beating on the
pumps with chuck wrenches to keep the ice broken off and
the pumps functioning. Even so, by the time we drilled out

the men who worked the lifters were in water above their knees. I never had it explained to me how frost and then ice could form around the air pumps when it was summer time. But that is exactly what happened.

The water pouring through the ceiling could always be handled some way. That was not what concerned Whiskey Riley and the other experienced miners. It was the "rotten rock," or unstable rock, that caused-the worried looks.

One night as we were about to begin our shift, Whiskey told us to stay put in the dry shack. Whiskey, Turk, and Easy Money took a walk into the tunnel by themselves.

A crap game started at once in the dry shack but it lacked the usual enthusiasm of the participants. Most of us sat around, talked softly, or ate a sandwich from our lunch pails.

Whiskey and the others came back to the dryshack in an hour. The crap game was over and the lunch pails snapped shut as we all gathered around our Shift Boss.

"Boys, we're gonna do some timbering," Whiskey began. "So if any of you hands have done spent the next two weeks of your bonus money, you shouldn't have. There ain't gonna be no bonus money for awhile."

There seemed to be an overwhelming sense of relief on the part of the experienced miners. "Praise the Lord," Tennessee said.

"Nipper, do you know how to make that telephone work? Get me the Walking Boss," Whiskey said.

After a few minutes the Nipper announced, "The Walking Boss is on the line," and he turned the phone over to Whiskey.

The dry shack became very quiet and we could all hear Whiskey's end of the conversation.

"Is this the Walking Boss?" Whiskey began. "O.K. Mr. Tory. This is Whiskey Riley. Mr. Riley."

Whiskey turned and winked to us over the use of the title "Mr."

"We're gonna need a load of timber down here... " Whiskey fell silent but we could hear a loud voice on the other end of the phone. Whiskey interjected every so often with a "but" or "I don't think you quite got the picture,... but ... I don't think... Whiskey handed the phone back to the Nipper. The Nipper cocked his ear to the receiver, "He's hung up."

Whiskey Riley turned to his crew and said his famous line.

"O.K. boys. Let's get closer to it. All I want to see ..."As he went out he kicked the screen door open with such force that it tore off the top hinge and left the screen door aslant.

Whiskey headed for the portal and we all fell in behind but without the usual jokes and bantering as we marched off to do our best.

I picked up my pace to come along side of Tennessee. "What is going on, Tennessee?" I asked.

"I suspect that Mr. Walking Boss told Whiskey to get his fanny into the tunnel and drill," Tennessee said. "It's a known fact that this crew is keeping the whole damn project on schedule and if we take the time to timber, schedules are going to get off whack and someone is going to lose some big money."

Whiskey Riley was walking ten feet ahead of the pack. As he came to the portal he suddenly stopped, still facing the opening to the tunnel, and threw out his huge arms to form a human barrier. Red had his head down so he didn't see Whiskey stop. He walked up on Whiskey Riley's heels.

"Jees Christ, Red, do I have to put a stoplight on my tail to keep you from running me down?"

"Sorry Whiskey. Sorry," Red sputtered. If this would have happened any other night it would have brought a roar of laughter.

Instead we gathered around our leader within the shadow of the portal. Whiskey rubbed his chin and spoke softer than I had ever heard him speak before.

"Boys, this ain't right. If ever there was a hole in the ground that needed to be timbered this is the one. I don't want to be the one to write a bunch of mothers and wives who are waiting in West Virginny that their worthless kinfolks ain't coming home except in pine boxes."

"Hell Whiskey, you ain't never wrote no letter in your life," Tennessee said. Everyone hooped it up at that one and the tension finally came down.

"And I'm not fixing to start now," Whiskey confirmed.

Then Whiskey spun around, and it was back to the dry shack again for all of us. Whiskey paced around like a caged gorilla.

"Nipper, can you make that telephone work again?" Whiskey finally said.

"Sure thing. Do you want Mr. Walking Boss again?"

"Hell no. Get me the Safety Miner."

Every tunnel job has a person they call the Safety Miner. This person is hired by the state. We had one but no one had ever remembered seeing him.

"The Safety Engineer has retired for the night," the Nipper reported.

"What the hell does that mean?" Whiskey demanded.

"I think it means he has gone to bed," the Nipper said.

"You explain to him that I don't know how to fill out the papers on the men that got themselves killed. You tell him I don't know what to put in the place where it asks how they got killed. You tell him that."

The Nipper repeated the message word for word and hung up the phone. "He says he will be down within the hour."

In forty five minutes a pickup came to a screeching stop right at the door of the dry shack. Out jumped Mr. Tory the Walking Boss. He was not in a good mood. "What kind of a Goddamn hillbilly move do you think you're pulling? No one goes over my head to call out the Safety Engineer," Tory said.

Whiskey was calm. "I didn't exactly call him out. I just was asking for some help on some paperwork that we will soon be doing."

The exchange was cut short by the arrival of a second pickup. The Walking Boss went quickly over to the truck and opened the door for the man inside.

"Good morning, Mr. Haley. I'm sorry you were disturbed so late at night. There really isn't any problem here. But I am glad you came down," Mr. Tory said.

Whiskey had edged over to the pickup. "Yes, we're all very glad you came down. Could we take a little stroll into the hole and take a look at the situation here?"

Mr. Haley was a small man in his mid-forties. He wore a hardtop that didn't fit right and suntan pants with a sharp crease in them. His hardtop sat too high on his head. No one had ever shown him that the liner was adjustable.

"You mean, go into the tunnel?" Haley's voice broke.

"Yeah, into the tunnel that's where we work."

"I forgot to bring a flashlight," Haley said apologetically

"That's no never mind," Whiskey Riley said. "The hole is light as day."

"For Christ's sake, can't you see the man needs a flash-light?" Tory said.

Turk produced a long flashlight from some place and shoved it into the man's belt none to carefully. The group went off toward the portal. When they got right to the entrance of the tunnel, Haley flashed the light inside. Every diversion tunnel is drilled in a big sweeping curve, so you can't see too far into the tunnel from the entrance. But here our Safety Engineer was, all crouched down, shining the light in circles from the outside . The man was afraid to go in. Even the Walking Boss was disgusted. Whiskey leaned over and said something to the man. Haley jumped back away from Whiskey and in the process his hardtop fell off into a puddle of smelly water. Whiskey leaned over and picked up the man's helmet, dumped the water out and handed it to him. Haley grabbed the hardtop and damn near ran all the way to his truck. The truck threw gravel all the way to the top of the grade.

"Now," the Walking Boss said. "You get this motley bunch of hillbillies back inside that tunnel and get to doing what we pay you to do or I will get someone in here who will."

I thought for a minute that Whiskey Riley was going to backhand this guy into the next county, but instead he grinned, "I got a pretty good idea what you mean by 'hillbilly' but what's a 'motley'?"

The Walking Boss got in his truck shaking his head.

"What do you want us to do, Whiskey?" Turk asked.

"Back to the dry shack boys. It must be about grub time."

Whiskey was half way through a triple-decker sandwich when he said, "Does anyone know how to make that phone work?"

The Nipper picked up the phone. "Who do you want this time?"

"I want G. Edward Murphey."

The Nipper hesitated. "Is that someone here on the site?"

"No, that would be in Boise, Idaho. Can you get that thing to go that far?"

"You want a G. Edward Murphey in Boise, Idaho, right? Just give me a few minutes and let me see what I can do," the Nipper said.

"Who is this feller?" Red asked.

"You mean Murphey? He's the guy whose name is on your paycheck. If I went any higher I would be talking to Mr. M or Mr. K. I guess you know who M&K are."

The Nipper dropped the phone and had to start all over with the operator at the other end of the line.

It wasn't all that long, less than a half an hour, when the Nipper shouted, "Get Whiskey. Murphey is coming to the phone."

Talk about a quiet room. You could have heard a fly land. Whiskey cleared his throat as he took the phone from the Nipper.

"This Ed? Whiskey Riley here."

We could all listen in again on Whiskey's end of the conversation. And I can tell you, listen we did.

"Thank you, thank you Ed. We are trying our best. Well that's mighty kind of you to say so. We are trying our best Ed. Well we seem to be having a bit of a problem getting any timber for the shaft.

Yeah, I think we need to. Yeah, that was my thought too. Tomorrow? Sure. We'll be looking for you. What? No, I wasn't going to send anybody home. Good. Who? Oh, he is as good as he will ever be and that's not much. I will tell him Ed. See you in the morning. What? Remember the difference in the time zones? Yeah, I guess. Good night Ed."

"Tennessee, Ed asked about you. I told him you were one of my top hands," Whiskey said winking at Turk.

"I heard what you said and I didn't hear you say any such thing as that," Tennessee whined. The place erupted with laughter.

"Now, I want this place dinged out. Nipper, take some hands and clean that jumbo so you could eat off it. Someone stack those barring down tools like we have some respect for them. The man is coming in the morning to see us and by Gawd this place is going to look good. He will land at a place called Pierson's airfield, wherever that is, and drive out. He says he will be leaving Boise within the hour."

Whiskey went outside to get some air. As he went out he kicked' the screen door off its last hinge. "Got to get somebody on that screen door right away," and he disappeared into the dark night.

A cheer went up that would wake the spirits of Indian Charlie.

Here we were, rough-and-tumble hard rock-miners cheering like school kids at a pep assembly. But we were impressed. Our-man knew the "big" man, well enough to call him by his first name.

Tennessee climbed up on the wooden table to address the multitudes. "Boys, you heard Whiskey. We got some sprucing up to do around here," he said in his squeaky voice. "All I want to see is...," and forty voices shouted in unison, "Assholes and elbows!" And where should they be turned?" "Up," shouted the crew.

G. Edward Murphey arrived on time. He greeted Whiskey Riley like a long lost brother. They toured the tunnel together for an hour then they went back to Murphey's car. Murphey must have said something very funny because they were both laughing real hard. As the car climbed up the grade from the portal, Murphey beeped his horn twice and Whiskey gave him a thumbs-up wave.

At lunch time the next day there was a huge vat of boiling water filled with the biggest and sweetest ears of corn I have ever seen. We had the best corn on the cob feast, with real butter, all compliments of G.Edward Murphey.

Two shifts later the first of the timber began arriving. The timber was 12x12-inch-rough-cut Douglas Fir. "Jap squares" they called them. The lengths varied from four feet to six feet, to eight feet. The ends were either cut square or at a predetermined angle. The trucks just kept coming in and unloading near the portal of the tunnel. One truck load was nothing but wooden wedges.

The timber was held in place by men standing on all levels of the jumbo. From the floor to the arch, across the arch, and down the other side men held the Jap squares in place until a man could drive wedges into critical joints, which would then tighten up the entire frame. Essentially that's what timbering does, it frames the tunnel. In between the big frames planking was placed, and all of this was also made secure by the use of wedges. It was necessary sometimes to drive a 20 penny spike but the use of spikes was scorned. It was a status item to secure an entire frame from rib to rib using only wedges. When a frame was completed we had a wooden roof over our heads and I felt a lot safer.

Timbering is slow and hard work. The Jap squares were cut from "green" timber, so besides being awkward to hold in place they were heavy.

You can't timber tight up to the face of the tunnel because if you went to shoot the next round, you would tear out the timber you had just installed. So we timbered up to within eight feet of the face. We were drilling only four-foot rounds so we could timber as close as possible. We would not get any bonus, because at four-foot rounds we could never make the minimum of eight feet and timber too. But what did that matter? We were finally working in relative safety.And just as important to all of us, we were being identified with the legend of our Shift Boss. Every time this story about Whiskey and G.Edward Murphey was repeated it became more elaborate.

To our surprise when we got our next checks there was bonus pay included. G.Edward Murphey had had the time keeper compute the average "B" money we had earned over the last month, and added that amount to each check from top to bottom. This continued as long as we were timbering.

"That was white of Murphey but Nelson's Cat House will be the only one to benefit from M&K's generosity," Tennessee said.

Chapter 20

The Fire

August, 1951, was unseasonably hot and dry as dry as June and July were wet.By the third week in August there was not a green blade of grass on the west side of the Cascade Mountains. The brush and ferns crackled underfoot if you got off the roads. A water wagon at the job spent it's time spraying water on the roads; otherwise the dust would have been intolerable. Some of the more heavily traveled roads and the parking lots were treated with diesel oil to control the dust. The parking lot at Nelson's Cat House was one of those heavily used areas that M&K decided to improve with diesel oil.

It was next to impossible to sleep during the day. The best time for us to sleep was early in the morning when we first got off shift. By ten in the morning the bunk house was too hot to sleep in. Each afternoon the temperatures soared into the high nineties, very hot for this country.

As the temperatures climbed each day an east wind would begin to blow. This stiff east wind came roaring through the many mountain passes, and the Lewis River Valley was no exception. This east wind phenomenon was created by the extreme barometric difference between an Eastern Oregon and Washington high and a low-pressure system sitting off the Pacific Coast. As the east wind slides downslope through the Cascade passes it increases in temperature. This wind is known throughout Clark, Skamania, and Cowlitz Counties of Southwest Washington as, 'the fire wind'. Conditions exactly like this preceded every major forest fire in western Oregon or Washington. Hearing mention of the Yacolt Burn and the Tillamook Burn still brings fear to every person in this vast forested region.

The Company was not unaware of the growing danger of fire. They had to know that if a fire developed they could not expect any outside help. Each community would have to fend for itself as best they could just as we would have to do at the dam.

Just in case, we had two pickup trucks which the Company took off-line and fitted for fire suppression emergencies. We also had two old pumper trucks that worked quite well as long as there was a source of water. The tanks on the pumpers would not last for any major conflagration without being recharged with water. We had the big water wagon that was being used to wet down the gravel roads and it was a good mobile source of water.

No smoking signs were posted throughout the area, so smoking was allowed only in very restricted areas. If you were caught smoking while traveling any of the many service roads on the project you would be fired immediately. I don't know for sure how they would enforce such a rule but it did cause the construction workers to think before lighting up.

Logging operations had started hoot-owling the last week in July and had since shut the woods down completely.

The loggers hated losing the time in their short season, but there was not a single complainer. These men knew what forest fires were like.

I had a lot of concern for DeDe. Nelson's was completely surrounded by timber and dry brush. A spark from any source such as a careless cigarette butt from a man going or coming and thinking about other things could torch the place in minutes.

We were at the portal but we had not gone to work yet
when word came down to us by telephone that Lower
Amboy was on fire. Lower Amboy was a group of old buildings mostly wood-framed with split shake roofs. This little
town was nestled on the banks of Cedar Creek. Upper
Amboy had newer buildings and was located a quarter of
a mile away and about two hundred feet higher off the
creek. But the word was it was Lower Amboy that was
burning.

If Amboy was burning, it presented a real and immediate threat not only to the dam site where we were, but to
the entire region. The east wind had already picked up and
could easily produce the most dreaded of all fire situations,
"a crown fire." When a forest fire "crowns", the fire shoots
into the tops of the trees some hundred to two hundred
feet in the air. The intense heat of a crown fire will soon
generate its own hurricane-force winds. The Yacolt Burn of
1902 was exactly that kind of a situation. People did not
lose their lives from being burned to death; instead the roaring overhead fire actually snuffed out the oxygen at ground
level. People, livestock, and unknown numbers of wildlife
suffocated. Make no mistake, a fire in Amboy was serious
business.

It took Whiskey Riley about one second to react. He
jumped up on a pile of timber and boomed at the top of his
voice.

"Gather up boys. Gather up. Amboy is burning. Someone has got to help them folks. I'm calling for volunteers to
go with me to fight the fire. If you don't want to go that's
O.K. too. Gather around if you're going with me."

Every mother's son rushed over to where Whiskey was
standing. Every single one. Whiskey asked no one in particular, "What do we need to fight fire?"

Slim and I shouted in unison, "Shovels."

"Load up those rigs with those shovels," Whiskey
shouted. "Can anyone operate that D-6" We had a D-6

Caterpillar tractor that was used to level some of the piles of muck coming out of the tunnel. A D-6 is not big as cats go but it is a wonderful firefighter.

Truckee went on the run to load the D-6 on a low-boy trailer nearby. Within a very short time, Whiskey had us organized.

Whiskey had the low-boy under way, the water wagon was filled, the two pumper trucks were filled, and a caravan of thirty assorted pickups and flat bed trucks came along too. Anything else that could move joined us all loaded with men on top, hanging to the sides, and stuffed inside.

"I'm going on in to tell the folks we're coming,"Whiskey shouted. The pickup he was in spun out and around the line of vehicles and disappeared in a cloud of dust.

I cannot fully describe the pride I felt with my miner friends who without any hesitation were willing to throw themselves into the task of saving this small rural community. Slim and I were "locals." It was expected of us to do what we could. But the rest of these men came from the South or God knows where. Maybe they assumed that we would do as much if their homes or towns were in jeopardy.

The water wagon spun out and high-centered on one of the curves going over Speelyai Hill. Unfortunately, it blocked the rest of the parade. The Cat was quickly unloaded, a line was put on the bumper of the tank truck, and they snaked it out. The rumpus had twisted the water valve and the truck was dumping water like it was the Lewis River itself. We left the Cat and the low-boy and stormed on with what we had. Whiskey would be wondering what had become of his crew.

We could see the orange glow in the sky several miles away and watched the sky turn to purple as we topped the last hill. It was a frightening sight. It looked like the entire town was ablaze. Flames were leaping sixty feet into the air as building after building exploded into flames. The local residents were trying their best to get their belongings out of the houses and into the middle of the gravel road. Midway in the area it looked like someone had gotten a pump and a fire hose into Cedar Creek, and they were doing some good with that effort.

Here we came over the rise into Amboy with every horn blaring and the men cheering. The cavalry had arrived. I stood as tall as I could in the pickup. I was hoping that some of the local fellows I had played ball with would see me and know that I was part of the rescue team.

Whiskey Riley was waiting for his forces to arrive. He was standing in the middle of the road at the north end of town where we came in. No one could mistake this giant standing there waving his men in and ready to take charge.

"Get to Nick's. Save Nick's," Whiskey bellowed.

The caravan of "saviors of the town" spun around the burning possessions being piled in the road, past the houses and stores already aflame or directly in the path of the flames, and on down to the south end of town to Nick's Tavern.

Whiskey directed the activities, still shouting, "Save Nick's."

"Get that line on the roof. Get that pump in the creek. Move that pump truck up to the porch. We got to save Nick's."

It may have been true that the fire was going to sweep the entire town anyway but it was the homes and belongings that needed to be saved. They didn't even try. In fact some of the actions of the construction men were at direct odds with protecting the town as a whole. For example, the pump dropped into Cedar Creek at Nick's could not get a large enough supply of water from the little creek. So the construction men did what they do best.They threw boulders across the creek to form a dam. This makeshift dam held back the water for the pump supplying water to Nick's but at the same time it dried up the creek and cut off all the water for the pump down stream being operated by the locals. The most depressing aspect of this entire debacle was watching the laughing and funning that went on during this tragedy.

Lower Amboy disappeared from the map of the State of Washington that hot August night, but Nick's was 'saved'.

The windows were all knocked out of Nick's early in the campaign due to the inexperience and just plain carelessness of the miners. Nick's never stopped serving during the entire drama. The beer continued to flow. Early in the event Nick's was pouring free drinks when it appeared that even the mighty efforts of the construction men would not save the tavern. Later however, when it looked like the battle was being won, Nick's suddenly switched and started charging again.

We started pulling out in small roving drunken bands after one hour of fighting the fire and three hours of drinking beer.

The town still smouldered. The saddest sight of all was seeing the piles of scorched household belongings that had caught on fire even after they were removed from the burning homes. We could have saved some of these cherished possessions, of that I was certain. Anyone of these small fires could still whip up into a raging inferno, and should be doused with water even now. But if the fire rekindled I imagine the locals would think twice before they put another call into the dam asking for help.

I was disgusted and ashamed, and slunk down in the bed of the truck for the ride home. Four hours earlier I had wanted everyone to know that I was with the crew coming in from the dam. Now I hoped that no one would recognize me.

The story that was published in the *Vancouver Columbian* describing the Amboy fire was the final act of irony. The newspaper story told how, "The volunteer unselfish miners risked their all to negotiate the treacherous Speelyai Hill in the dark of night to save what they could of Amboy." The story went on to say, "Unfortunately, by the time the men from the dam were able to arrive little could be done to save the town. What was saved was thanks to the miners from Yale Dam."

The reality was that all that was saved was what the miners wanted to save: one Goddamn tavern. It was not one of the crowning moments in the history of those who follow the construction industry. Relations were none too good between the construction workers and the local citizens before this incident. But after the fire, the locals were outright hostile.

The poor dumb miners could not understand why they were so poorly received in Yacolt, Battle Ground, Woodland, Cougar, and La Center, let alone in Amboy.

Maybe the town would have been lost anyway. Certainly, had the miners not responded at all, the town would have lost it's fight with the wind and the fire.

Tennessee perhaps summed it up the best. "I hope these stump jumpers have short memories. I hope we have no call to ask them for help of any sort. They might just tell us to go drill a hole in the ground."

Chapter 21

Whiskey Riley's Lunch Pail

There must be a thousand stories about pranks construction men pull on each other. The lunch pail is clearly the focal point of many of these 'tricks'. Every man's 'nose bag' is unique to the owner. The thermos bottle, which was very vulnerable, was not considered part of the lunch pail.

Some men painted their lunch pails strange colors to make for easy identification. The U.S. flag was a popular motif. Identification to avoid anyone taking the wrong pail was unnecessary because no one would dare take another man's pail. Mess it up a bit, play a prank with it yes, but never steal it. There is much superstition around the construction lunch pail. Often a man will take a new pail and beat it to smitherines just to make it look old. It was thought by some that it was bad luck to have a new lunch pail.

Every so often a crew would have a "dead boxer." A Dead Boxer is a person who waits for the word that someone has been killed. The Dead Boxer puts the grab on the dead man's lunch pail. The dead man won't be needing the pail, right? The lunch of the dead man will still be good, right? It doesn't matter if the Dead Boxer already has a full lunch. A man can eat two lunches once in a while can't he? The height of good fortune to a Dead Boxer is when a man gets killed before lunch.

Day shift and swing shift had both lost several men. We had not even had a man seriously injured. Both of the other shifts had a Dead Boxer. The one on day shift was a good miner and he wanted to transfer to our shift because we were the ones always on bonus money. Whiskey Riley reputedly informed the man that he should not put in for a transfer because if he did and if we should lose a man which could certainly happen, and if the Dead Boxer took the lunch pail of the fallen crew member that he might expect a bad accident to happen to him before another shift went by. I asked Tennessee if Whiskey was really serious.

"He damn well better be serious," Tennessee said. "Whiskey and I have a solemn pact that if one of us gets ourselves killed dead, and if there is a Dead Boxer around, the other one will kill him at the first good moment. Now I intend to follow my pledge and by God Whiskey better do the same or he'll never hear the last of it from me."

"How do you know we don't already have a Dead Boxer on our shift? We haven't had anyone killed yet," I said.

"The odds are we will find that out before the job is done because even as well trained and organized as Whiskey has this bunch we will lose a man or two before we 'bore thru.' That's just the way it is," Tennessee said.

Every man had something unique about his lunch pail. Quite a few had a large safety pin, like a horse blanket pin, for a fastener. I really wanted one of those pins but I never found out where they got them. I tied my lunch pail with a thin leather strap and I carried it over my shoulder. I was the only one who did that, and I thought it was keen.

Some of the pranks on a person's lunch bucket were funny but predictable, like the frog put inside, or the rock wrapped up like a cookie. That sort of thing. Some of the pranks were pretty disgusting. For example, someone rolled up a dog turd in wax paper to make it look like a fat frankfurter. Big Butch was the unsuspecting recipient of this 'joke'. When Big Butch unrolled the wax paper he must have known at a glance if not by smell what it was. Without a blink or a moment's hesitation he took a gusty chew on that dog turd. He swallowed, smacked his lips, and said to the world, "God that's mighty fine. But it needs a little salt."

At least five salt shakers came out of nearby lunch pails at once. Big Butch took one shaker and thanked the donor. He carefully shook on a little salt. Everyone on the crew was watching by this time. With lip smacking smug satisfaction he ate every last morsel of that dog droppings. You would have thought he had just eaten the finest fat frankfurter ever made.

Part of the fun of these tricks was to turn the tables in some manner on the prankster. By eating the disgusting item rather than recoiling, Butch had, in the eyes of the men, successfully turned the situation to his advantage.

One day Red opened his lunch pail expecting to find the sandwiches and fruit and things that he had packed for his lunch. Instead, his pail was full of lettuce, radishes,carrots, and more lettuce. Under all the vegetables and greenery was a note written in beautiful handwriting. It was obviously a woman's penmanship. The note said:

> Dearest Red,
> Here is your lunch. We assume you must eat like a rabbit too.
> The Girls at Nelson's

Everyone laughed until the tears came. What made this prank so funny was that Red never understood it and no one would explain to him.

The story I liked best was the trick played on Whiskey Riley. Whiskey had traded the flatbed truck that hauled us down to the portal each night for a beat up old bus. No one knew exactly how he did this, but it was greatly appreciated by the crew. When it rained, bouncing around in the back of a flatbed truck was miserable. When it didn't rain, the dust was unbearable. So the bus did a lot to improve our disposition as we went to work, and it was really welcomed in the early morning when we got off work. Even though it was summer by the calendar, the early mornings were darn chilly. The Truckee, who drove the bus, always had the old heater cranked up to full blast before we got on board, so the bus was warm and toasty. Whiskey liked to stretch out on the back seat and sleep going and coming each day. I don't know how he could sleep but at least he made a good pretext at sleeping. I don't know anyone who would have challenged Whiskey for the right to the back seat. If Whiskey Riley wanted the back seat he damn well could have it. But Whiskey had a strong sense of fair play. He never subscribed to,"rank having its privileges". So in order for him to have the back seat he would race for it at the end of each shift. If he got there first then he felt he had earned it fairly. Several times, different men, in sport, would challenge Whiskey in his sprint up the grade to where the Truckee was warming up the bus. The fact was that no man could outrun the big man up the hill.

Whiskey always left his lunch pail on a stack of 12 x 12 timber that we used for timbering in the shaft. With his lunch pail sitting on the end of the timber it was handy to grab it as he sprinted to the bus. He would snatch up his pail hitting it in full stride.

Some time during the second half of our shift one day someone had sneaked up to where Whiskey's pail was sitting and nailed it to the timber with 20 penny spikes. The word spread, and by quitting time every man on the crew was positioned so he could watch Whiskey Riley hit full stride to grab his pail only to have his arm jerked out of the socket when the pail refused to budge.

At last it was quitting time and true to form, off sprinted Whiskey, even faster it seemed than usual. He shot his hand down to the pail handle and to everyone's amazement he came up with the lunch pail and about twelve inches of the end of the timber hanging on to the bucket. Whiskey kept right on running. He never slowed down or looked back or even showed any sign that he knew he was packing a 12 x 12-inch piece of rough cut timber on the bottom of his lunch pail.

We found out later that Whiskey had figured out that something was up. Probably the way the men were all whispering and snickering had tipped him off. When he discovered his pail spiked down he had one of the carpenters saw off the section of the timber and carefully replace it just as it had been, except now of course it was cut loose. No one could tell without careful scrutiny that the timber was cut free. From where I was standing it looked like Whiskey Riley had broken the end right off that timber by brute strength alone.

I heard this story retold and demonstrated all over the camp and several times at Nick's in Amboy. But I was there and I saw it all. It was another page in the legend of this man called Whiskey Riley.

Chapter 22

The Cave In

We worked our way slowly through the area of "rotten rock" and the slow but necessary timbering that had accompanied it. The rock was hard again and we were back on bonus money. Morale was high as each drillout and blast was completed with precision. I myself had no way to compare, but the experienced miners knew we were good. Very good. I was making more money than I had ever thought possible. The figures in my little red savings account book were growing steadily. I knew I was liked by the miners and I knew Whiskey Riley had taken a special interest in me. "Give this hand some time behind the screw. I think he could be a miner soon," Whiskey said to Johnnie.

"If you were any kind of a Shift Boss you would know that Mac has already been behind the screw, and he even shows a little promise," Johnnie said.

"Sometimes having a lazy miner to work with has its advantages," Whiskey replied, with a wink at me.

If I got a machine, if one opened up for some reason, it would mean two dollars more a shift when we were working straight time. But the real difference would be in the additional "B" money that would be mine. I could operate the drill O.K., but I needed more experience in 'reading' the rock. You have to imagine some way what your drill is doing eight feet inside the solid rock wall. You need to know immediately if your drill bit hits a crack or a cleavage in the rock. You need to know what it means if the water running out of your bore suddenly turns muddy instead of being grey in color. You need to know how much pressure to put on the "screw," which determines the forward progress of the drill bit. If you try to go too fast you run the risk of plugging the bit, or worse yet, stick the bit fast in the rock. Sticking the bit is called "hanging a steel." If you hung a steel you were suppose to work away at it and try to dislodge it. Sometimes you could drill a hung steel out by using another steel and drilling it out. But more times than not you would end up with both steels "hung", Usually hung steel meant that the miner had misread the rock.

I had a tendency to have a too-heavy hand on the screw. If you tried to go too fast several problems could occur very fast. On the other hand, if you went too slow you were wasting time. It was a fine line that only time and experience could solve.

On this particular drillout there was an unusually large amount of gravel and rock left at the face of the tunnel, which the mucking machine could not pick up. When this happens it means hand mucking , with short-handled shovels. I didn't mind this back-breaking work because the cleaner you could get the face the better everything else would be that followed. For example, if the floor of the tunnel was clean, the jumbo could get up closer to the face. If the jumbo was close, it made the drillout much safer for the chucktenders who work on the lifters. Chucktenders must go out from under the cover of the jumbo for the short time it takes to change steel and to knock the chucks up or down. If the jumbo is up tight to the face the exposure time is minimal, but if the jumbo is sitting three or four feet away from the face the exposure time goes up dramatically. Thus the danger of getting clipped by rock slipping down the face from the drills above you increases.

In any case there are many reasons why you'd want a floor clear of rubble. Everybody pitches in to help but it is expected that the men on the lifters will do the lion's share of the handmucking because they are the ones who will benefit the most.

As it turned out there were five of us hand-mucking at the face on this particular shift. Interestingly, Slim was one of those helping. This was odd because Slim usually got out of the hand-mucking some way or other.

Slim and I had little in common anymore. We were cordial to each other but to say there was a strain in our relationship would have been an understatement. He had made several overtures toward reconciling but we had little to talk about. Besides, I wasn't quite ready to patch things up. If you were once a liar and a thief, I figured You would always be one. I knew Slim had stolen money out of my billfold to gamble with and he would have stolen more if I had not followed some good advice and put my money into a savings account in Amboy. I was certain in my own mind that Slim had taken my watch too, although I had not actually seen him take it. I assumed by now some professional gambler in Portland had the only tangible keepsake that I had of my brother. I think I would in time forgive Slim for the money, but never for the watch. I fully expected him to come up to me some day and say something like, " oh yes, here is that money I borrowed from you. You were asleep and I didn't want to disturb you at the time." But how could he ever return the watch? It wasn't that he didn't know what the watch meant to me. He knew.

Anyway, at this time we found ourselves shoveling loose muck together side by side. Suddenly, with no warning, there was a rumbling, rolling, and roar which reminded me of the crash of thunder when lighting strikes dangerously close. The lights blinked twice and went black. The thunder rolled again, echoed and bounced, and rolled again. Then there was silence. I had no idea what had happened. I sat right down where I had been standing. If you think you've been in the dark at some time I can tell you it isn't like being at the end of a tunnel when the lights go out. That is darkness. That is black. The eerie silence was intense. The dust that filled my lungs and caked my nostrils was the only sensation I can remember.

An eternity went by. At last I thought I probably wasn't going to suffocate. I could not get oriented to space. I reached out to feel the face of the tunnel to first see if there was still a face and then to try to determine which direction the tunnel ran. I was totally confused. I didn't know what had happened or what to do, so I remained sitting for what seemed like forever.

The first sound I became aware of was a thunk, thunk. Then I heard Easy Money's voice as calm as if he were in church.

"Boys, do you-hear that?" Once again I heard the thunking sound.

"That's me," Easy Money said. "I just knocked the handle out of a pick. I have this pick handle in my hands now," Easy Money continued. "I will kill the first son-of-a-bitch who lights up a cigarette or starts running around, or starts hollering. We are on the wrong side of a cave-in and the only chance you have is if you do what I say. If you don't do as I tell you, don't worry about getting out of the cave-in alive, because I will have already killed you. I will kill you with this pick-handle without batting an eye."

The quiet tone of his voice would have convinced anyone that he meant exactly what he said. Every word of it. His commands did not anger me at all, to the contrary, it gave me an overwhelming sense of relief. Someone had taken charge. I guess in most tough situations someone will step forward and assume leadership. In this case I thanked God we had Easy Money.

Time passed. I don't think it was, too long yet nothing seemed to be in the correct perspective. I reached out several times in that space of silence to touch the face of the tunnel. I found myself wondering if I had really heard Easy Money or anybody else. Maybe I had just imagined I heard his voice.

Easy Money's voice came again still firm and calm.

"Call out your name boys and tell me what shape you're in. One at a time."

"Tennessee here, Easy Money." Tennessee's voice was at least two pitches, higher than his usual squeaky voice. "And I'm O.K."

"Slim here, and I'm not hurt either" His voice sounded weak and trembling. "What are we going to do? What are we going to do?"

"Try to stay calm, Slim," Easy Money said. His voice was still firm but there was a quality of understanding and kindness as he tried to quiet Slim. "All I want right now is your name and condition. That's all," he said.

It seemed to be my turn. "Mac. I'm Mac, and I'm O.K. too. "

There was silence. No one else answered the roll call.

"Is there anyone else here?" Easy Money asked. Only silence.

"I feel someone else is here," Easy Money declared. "If there is someone who can't talk, pound a rock or something. "

I heard a slight rustle to my left.

"Easy Money , this is Mac. There is someone else here."

"Try to crawl or slide to him. Don't stand up. Crawl."

Before I had the time to react a voice responded from my left. "My name is Spade. I'm not hurt."

"Spade? I ain't heard of no hand on this job by that handle.When I tell you to sound off by damn, you do what I say," Easy Money said.

"I'm sorry sir. I'm not supposed to be here," the voice to my left said.

"Pipe down for now. We will get this all straightened out later."

Another very long period of absolute silence. Every so often I could hear rocks rattling nearby, like they were sliding down an incline. Other than that, total silence. I would guess that several hours elapsed, but that would only be an estimate.

"This is Easy Money again. I want everybody to push your nosebags over here to my feet."

I found my lunch pail and moved it to the right still staying seated. It may prove fortunate for us that we took our lunch pails into the face with us. Sometimes we did and sometimes we left them outside. It just depended on where we thought we would be in the drillout by lunch time When I moved my pail to Slim who was on my right, I brushed his arm. To my surprise he took my hand in his and squeezed it like we were shaking hands after meeting for the first time. You can't imagine how good that handshake felt. I squeezed his hand back. Easy Money's voice interrupted my thoughts.

"I have four nosebags counting mine. I want that fifth nosebag or this pick-handle goes to work." There was no response.

"Hey, Trowel, or Spade, or whatever the hell you call yourself, did you hear me?"

In a voice barely audible the latecomer said, "What's a nosebag sir?"

"I want your lunch pail, son."

There was no anger in Easy Money's voice. Anyone could tell that the newcomer, Spade, was not trying to fool us.

"At this point there is no way of telling how long we will be holed up in here. So I want all the lunches so I can ration the food out. So just pass your lunch over to Mac who will be on your right."

"I don't have a lunch, sir."

"That's O.K., son. When it is time you will have a share of ours."

More silence. I could not tell if I had my eyes open or not. I found myself rocking back and forth.This rocking seemed to make me feel better. I remember once seeing blind children in the School For The Blind in Vancouver rock back and forth. It's funny what comes to your mind. I remembered one football game when the lights went out just before half-time. I thought that night was dark. But this was true darkness. I smiled to myself as I remembered the score of the game. We would have been better off if they hadn't turned those lights back on.

Slim scooted a little to his left to where we were, back to back. We leaned against each other. I wanted to keep rocking but I stopped as I felt Slim's back against mine.

At last Easy Money spoke again. "You're doing real fine boys. Your folks would be proud of the way you're handling yourselves in this situation. Boys, Whiskey Riley would be pleased I can tell you. I won't know for sure for another hour or so but I think we're getting air."

I hadn't even thought about running out of oxygen. It was suffocating at first but that was from all the dust that must have been in the air following the cave-in. The dust must have settled some because I hadn't thought about air. The warning to not light up had to do with the concern over burning up the oxygen. My first thought had been that Easy Money feared gas.

Easy Money didn't wait an hour. "Boys, we are getting air. There is no doubt about that. If you want to light up go ahead."

Three cigarette lighters and a match crashed into existence. I was the only one who didn't light up since I'm not a smoker. The lights flooded our area bright as day. It reminded me of those huge searchlights that they used at the Castle Theatre in Vancouver when a big movie like "My Friend Flicka" was in town. I had never realized how much light comes off of one little match, but it is a lot.

From the light we could pretty much grasp our situation. The cave-in had occurred just beyond where we had timbered. It looked like the timbered section of the tunnel was all that was intact.

"That timber saved our butts," Tennessee said. "You're in charge Easy Money, but I suggest that we move in under the timber."

"Good-idea, Tennessee. We will go one at a time. I will light my lighter, which will give off just as much light as all four of us lighting up. I will bring up the rear. Go slow now we don't need a broken leg right now."

The floor of the tunnel was covered with boulders the size of T.V. sets, and several the size of a small car.

When we had all arrived under the timbered area Easy money said, "There may be more up there to come down. We will be much safer here if the arch collapses."

We could get a good look at the cave-in at this point. It looked like the bottom of the tunnel had come up to meet the ceiling rather than the roof caving in. The tunnel was clearly sealed by a slanting pile of muck and rubble from floor to arch. When we had all settled down again Easy Money took some wax paper from his lunch pail and twisted it into a torch. He lit the torch and moved over to where he could study Spade.

"Who the hell are you?" Easy Money asked. "I ain't never seen you before."

"I know," Spade said. "I just walked into the tunnel when a lot of men came in. I'm a fourth-year geology student at the Unversity of Washington."

Easy Money interrupted him. "We don't see many stargazers around here. What's your game?"

"No, I don't read the stars. I study rocks and rock formations. You know geology."

Easy Money had to think on that one. "I'll be damned. You go to a big school to study rocks?"

Slim interjected, "Hell, Easy Money, if you would've known that you would be a full professor by this time."

"I'll be damned," Easy Money said. "They actually study rocks? Now tell me again son, how did you get into this Gawdawful fix?"

"Well, I drove out from Vancouver to see the Peterson lava tubes. I had planned to map them. They tell me that some of the tubes have never been mapped. I heard that some of the lava tubes are being mapped secretly by a Boy Scout troop. Anyway, I heard about this tunnel being built, while I was eating at a tavern in Amboy. I just thought I would look it over while I was this close. No one stopped me or asked me any questions. I had my own hardtop. Then all of a sudden some great big man said something and everybody got up and walked into the tunnel. I just fell in with them. It is all really very interesting."

"Well I'm sure as hell glad we made it interesting for you," Slim said.

"When this all happened I thought it was some kind of a routine drill that you run every so often," Spade said. "It was not until Mr. Money threatened to kill me that I realized that this was not a drill."

"Good thinking son." Easy Money said.

"Mr. Money, would you really have belted me with the pick handle?"

Easy Money still had the pick-handle in his big hands. "I didn't say anything about belting you. I said I would kill you. And yes, I would have, without giving it a backward thought. I may still kill one or more of you before we see daylight again. And my handle is not Mr. Money. It is Easy Money."

The new guy from the university talked a bit more than he should have. "Well my name isn't really Spade either. I just made that up because I knew that everyone in construction has a nickname. You see in our course work at the University we take a lot of field trips where we shovel and pick rock. Actually it is not like the picks you may be familiar with. I mean a geology pick. A nick name like pick or shovel would sound funny. A spade is a type of shovel. Dr. James, who is my major professor, always felt..."

"Trowel, or Spade, or what ever in the hell you want to call yourself," Slim interjected," we don't give a damn what your major professor feels and we're getting a little tired of your jawing."

"Oh, I'm sorry," Spade said.

I suddenly remembered the advice given to us by the old man in the Vancouver Union Hall. "Don't tell your life story on the first shift." I know exactly what he meant, now.

"What do we do now, Easy Money?" I asked.

"We sit and wait. We got some food, we got lots of water, and we got air. We could wait this bump out for quite a spell."

"We don't start digging then?" Slim asked.

"No. That would be the wrong move at this point. We have the best "dig-out man" in the business out there and that's Turk. Between Whiskey Riley and Turk things are already organized and moving out there. You can be sure of that. We don't know if the whole dam mountain came down on us or if only part of the tunnel collapsed. We don't know if they will have to timber in to us or not. You know how that would slow the works down. We don't know if the jumbo escaped in one piece or not. If the jumbo is workable the first thing they will do is to drill a single hole in to us. They won't know if we got air or not. Getting air to us is their major worry right now."

"Another thing," Easy Money continued, "we may not be the only ones caught. As I remember it, the crew was just getting ready to move the jumbo into place when the 'bump' came down. If the cave-in caught the jumbo it could have taken half the damn crew."

"I hope for once that damn Whiskey Riley wasn't riding the jumbo in. But Jees you know that Turk would be on top," Tennessee said.

Easy Money just let us sit-there and think. Every hour or so Easy Money would light up a torch of some twisted wax paper. He would look us over real good and let the paper burn down to his fingers. On one of these light ups he gave each of us a quarter of a sandwich. I got mostly bread, but it couldn't have tasted better.

As the wax torch faded I saw Easy Money out of the corner of my eye arranging some small rocks into a line. I knew he wasn't playing marbles, so I watched carefully at the next light-up. The row of little rocks were covered by water. He started another row about six inches higher up the rubble pile. I moved over closer to Easy Money where only he could hear.

"Do we have a problem here?" I asked, nodding to the row of new rocks already being covered by rising water.

"Could have. I will watch it another time. Don't need to mention it yet. If their butts get wet I guess they will move higher up the rubble pile."

In the next two hours I moved to higher ground twice. No one else said anything. We obviously had water coming in and it was not draining on out. Perhaps, I thought, when the water reaches a certain level it will begin to drain on through the cave-in. Or perhaps the water would stop coming in at some point.

Easy Money gave us all a quarter of a cup of coffee at the next light up. We continued to move up the rubble pile to keep out of the water. If anyone else was aware of the encroaching water they were not mentioning it.

Slim and I started chatting softly to each other. We talked about ball games we had played in together and about friends and what they would be doing this summer. He never once mentioned DeDe and I was glad. To tell you the truth, she had been on my mind a great deal lately. When I got out of this mess I decided I wanted to figure out some way to see her. Some way other than the obvious one.

Spade had not said a single word since Slim had chopped him off. At least the greenhorn caught on fast.

Tennessee hummed the Red River Valley or some representation of it. Everybody was aware of the water now. We all would scoot up the rubble pile in unison.

At each light-up I noticed that all eyes went to the ceiling first. We had some space yet to go before this situation got real serious. I reasoned that, as the water crept higher up the rubble pile it would be spreading out more and therefore start to slow down in the vertical direction. However it wasn't working that way. The water was coming in noticeably faster. I could imagine men starving to death in a cave-in or even perish from lack of oxygen, but I had never thought about drowning in a cave-in. I was thinking about it now.

Easy Money was the first to speak on the obvious.

"Boys we got a situation developing here as you can all see. Does anyone have any ideas?"

"Do we try digging now?" Tennessee said. "We still got our shovels."

Spade spoke for the first time in hours. "Mr. Money, or I mean Mr. Easy, at the last lightup I noticed a big pipe hanging on the tunnel wall. What is that for?"

"Good thinking, son. But I ruled the blow pipe out several hours ago. That's the blower pipe. That's the way they pump fresh air into us when we are drilling, and then it reverses to pull the fumes out after a blast. But look at the end of the pipe."

Easy Money lit another torch and all eyes went to the end of the blower pipe.

"The end that is exposed is pinched down to only half its normal size. Even if a person could squeeze through the opening some way, and there is no way, how would you know that it isn't cut in half or completely caved in a hundred feet or so down the line ?"

"I don't think it is closed off. That's where our air is coming from," Spade said.

"How the hell do you know that?" Tennessee demanded.

"The smoke from Mr. Money's torches goes across the top of the tunnel and then it is swept away from the mouth of that pipe. There is air coming in through that pipe."

Easy Money had another twisted wax torch going within a second. The black smut and smoke rose at once to the crown and just as Spade had predicted it swept away from the opening to the pipe.

"I think I can crawl through that opening if I can get up to it," Spade said.

The pipe which should have been thirty inches in diameter was crimped to half the normal size. The blower pipe hung on the wall near the top of the tunnel but it was only about eight feet above our heads from where we had retreated up the rubble pile. If we were on the floor of the tunnel the pipe by contrast would be thirty feet above us. We had evacuated that far up the inclined pile of muck.

"It's a long-shot, boys. What do you say we go down with a fight? If the kid is willing to squirm through that opening let's get him up to it. Get those planks the ones floating over there. Get the shovels working men. By damn, we're gonna build a platform up to that pipe."

Interestingly enough, we had all kept our shovels. All except for Easy Money. All he had was a worthless pick-handle but he became the official torch man.

It took us three hours of rolling boulders, shovelling gravel, and inserting planks but finally we had a platform that reached to the pipe. Time was running out. The water was already over the base of our elevated platform. But the pipe was within reach. Spade took a rock and began tapping on the pipe.

"What are you doing that for?" Slim asked.

"Morse Code. Maybe someone will hear it and recognize code."

"You can tap out words?" Easy Money asked with open amazement.

"Now ain't that something," Tennessee said. "Did they teach you that in rock school?"

"No, Sea Scouts."

As good as the idea was we received no response.

"Should we wait a bit more?" I asked. "They could be drilling for us right now."

"If they were drilling, how close would they have to get before we could feel some vibration?" Spade asked.

" Fifty or sixty feet I suppose. Christ, I don't know," Easy money said.

Spade laid his head against the pipe, and we all spread our hands against the loose rock and prayed we would feel something remotely like the vibration of a drill. We did not.

"Where would they start the hole if they were drilling for us?" Spade asked.

"What do you mean, where would they start the hole?"

"I was wondering if they would start at the-floor level of the tunnel, because if they do, that is at least twenty-five feet below where we are now."

"Hot damn! You may have a point there. They'll be drilling a hole into a lake," Easy Money said.

Tennessee, who had been quiet during all this discussion started to laugh.

"Tennessee, Don't you go getting goosey on us now, " Easy Money pleaded.

"I'm not getting goosey. I was just thinking, I hope that big dumb hillbilly Whiskey Riley puts his eye to the hole when they bore through to the lake. God, I would like to see that."

It is strange what will strike your funny button in a situation like this. We roared with laughter. All except Spade who was still practicing his Morse Code on the pipe. But then he didn't know Whiskey Riley like we did.

As we laughed we all moved onto the platform which would just accomodate the five of us.

"If you don't mind, Sir, I think the time has arrived to try the pipe. I'm the smallest built, and so I nominate myself."

"Well son if you're game for it, we are fast losing other options."

Easy Money gave us all another quarter sandwich and a sip of coffee a piece. Except he gave Spade a half sandwich.

"Wait, I got a half sandwich," Spade said. "I got too much."

"If you're hungry eat it," Easy Money said. "It ain't no mistake. If you're not hungry then leave it. Does anyone have a problem with that?"

"I sure as hell have no problem with that," Tennessee said. Slim and I concurred. Spade ate the half sandwich.

Spade took off his hardtop and set it carefully on the edge of the water, rim up, so it would float He pulled off his outer heavy coat and he indicated he was ready for us to boost him up to the pipe.

"I wish I had time to give you a crash course in Morse Code so we could communicate as I go along. I will take a short handled shovel and push it ahead of me. I will bang on the pipe with the shovel about every three minutes. If I can go further in the pipe I will bang three times. If I bang twice it means I can't go any further and that I am coming back or that I am in trouble."

He stood on one foot with the other one in Slim's cupped hand. He pulled his foot out of Slim's stirrup and turned around to face us. My first thought was that he was going to back out. I couldn't blame him if he had second thoughts. That wasn't it. He stood on the platform of rocks with his face lit by a new wax paper torch. There was no fear in his eyes, only excitement. He reached into the back pocket of his jeans and handed Easy Money his billfold.

"So you guys know my name is not Spade. My name and my folks' name are in my billfold. If you get out and I don't, I would appreciate it if you would give them my billfold. If I don't bring a relief party, which means I didn't make it, and if it begins to look like you won't make it out either, please put my billfold in a place where you think it will be found. No one in the world knows that I'm in this tunnel. No one will ever look for me in here let alone inside an air pipe."

Easy Money took the billfold and put it inside his shirt pocket.

"Son, I will take some pleasure in giving you back your billfold in person."

"When you get on the other side you will have to bang on the inside of the pipe like hell or no one will know you're in there." Tennessee said, matter-of-factly. "There will be lots of noise outside. If they've started to drill for us just save your energy until there is a lull in the drilling because no one on God's green earth will ever hear you while they're drilling."

"What will I find when I get to the other end? How will I know I'm at the end?" Spade asked.

"Son, I have no idea," Easy Money said.

His foot went back in to the cupped hand stirrup.

"So long then. Anything you want me to tell your folks if it comes to that?" Spade said.

"I ain't got no folks," Easy Money said.

"Whiskey Riley will make up a good story for me," Tennessee said.

He glanced at me. I shook my head no. Slim at first shook his head, no, but then changed his mind.

"Yeah. You look up Mrs. Mary Elizabeth McGowan and tell her that Mac, or I mean Jerry, was a good boy."

He was serious. "Done," Spade said.

With parting handshakes all around Spade threw a shovel into the pipe, and with Slim hoisting and others steadying him, he twisted sideways past the crimped end of the pipe and was gone from sight. We could hear him scooting and struggling along. Each tap, tap, tap, was greeted with a cheer and I would tap back to him. We could bear him proceeding for over an hour but after that we weren't positive we could hear him. We all stood right next to the pipe during all this time and no one had paid too much attention to the water for some time.

I was very tired and sat down. This was between light-ups. To my surprise and dismay I was sitting in water above my waist. The water had risen dramatically during the time we were getting Spade on his way.

At the next light-up I calculated that if the water continued rising at this pace we would have two more hours at the most.

The most discouraging thing was it appeared that the accumulation of water was accelerating. I had the thought that perhaps we had somehow tapped into the river itself.

"Shall we dig?" Tennessee asked.

"We can pull more rocks over to make the platform wider and a bit higher but as far as serious digging goes I think we are fresh out of time," Easy Money said. "Hell, boys I'm hungry. I don't see much point in saving the rest of the grub."

We all silently agreed. We could barely build the platform faster than the water was rising. one by one we just stopped rolling rocks around. The platform was as high as the opening of the pipe.

"Boys, we got a decision to make and I will not make it by myself," Easy Money said. Before much longer the water will be high enough to run into the blower pipe. We will still have a little space left to us when that time comes. The water running into the pipe might be enough of a safety valve to keep up with the incoming water. Then again it may not keep up with the rising water. But one thing is for sure if the kid is still in the pipe when the water starts to run into it his goose will be cooked. On the other hand it has been a long time since he's left; he may be dead anyway."

Easy Money reached out with his pick handle and fished in Spade's floating helmet.

"Do any of you hands got any change on you?"

We all reached into our pockets and gave Easy Money what we had.

"I got four pennies here and four silvers, three quarters and a dime."

Everyone take a copper and a silver. Between now and the next light-up I want each of you to make up your own mind. If you want to take the chance on the pipe carrying away enough water to keep us alive place your silver piece in Spade's hard top. If you vote to dam up the pipe so that the water can't flow into the pipe, put in a penny. Do you all understand? It will take three pennies or three silvers to make the decision. If it's two to two, I will vote again. Any questions? Oh, one more thing. Don't anyone ever ask me how I voted. With God as my witness I will never say how I voted and I will never be asking you how you voted. In about twenty minutes, I will give you fair warning, and I will light up again. Have your vote in the helmet by that time. You will have plenty of time to think on it."

The hardtop was placed within easy reach of us all and the wax torch blinked out leaving us in total darkness again.

In less than a minute, less than sixty seconds, I heard four coins clink into the hardtop and slide to the center of the hat.

"I guess you boys make up your minds fast when you do it in the dark," Easy Money said. "I'm not waiting for the next twenty minutes to go by. If you have made up your minds let's count the votes. I'm lighting up now."

In the center of Spade's up-turned hard top shone four shiny copper pennies.

"So be it," Easy Money said. He pulled off his rubber-ized jacket.

"This rubber coat will make a dam for the end of the pipe. We will stop the water from entering the pipe if we can, for as long as we can. I'm not saying yet that I'm going to die in this God forsaken spot, but if I do, I will be with some damn fine company."

Slim and I began talking to each other again, just low, and about nothing in particular. Tennessee tried to break the tension with a story. "At least this ain't like one bump I was in. It was in a West Virginny coal mine. Let's see that would be in January, 1940. I remember it was cold. We lost 92 men in that bump. It was at a place called Bortley."

"How was it different?" Slim asked.

"We didn't have no water and I can tell you a man will do some pretty disgusting things when he gets thirsty enough. I can remember..."

"Tennessee, for Christ sake, we don't appreciate your stories just now," Easy Money interrupted.

"How long have we been in here do you suppose?" Slim asked.

"The cave-in happened before lunch time which would make it before two thirty in the morning. It is now 11:30 the next day," Easy Money said.

"The next day? That was two days ago. It didn't happen just yesterday morning. Is it 11:30 day or night?"

"Does it make any difference?" Tennessee said.

"How long has the kid been gone?" Easy Money mused.

"What difference does it make ?" Tennessee said again.

"I hope he got out." I said.

Slim and I draped ourselves over the pipe where we could hang on to a bolt on the far side of the pipe. The water was up to my chest but it was over Easy Money's shoulders. The cold water had long since numbed my legs and body and I wasn't all that uncomfortable anymore. I found myself getting so sleepy. I guess we dozed off.

I don't know for sure how long I slept but we were all awakened by a strange-looking mop of red hair peering sideways out of the crimped end of the pipe.

"Well now if that's not the saddest collection of shit I've ever seen." It was Red. It really was. It was Red.

"Give me a few tries with this hydraulic jack and I will spring this opening wider. Whiskey said to send lardass out last. Be ready to go. Whiskey says to tell you to move it cause this overtime is getting ridiculous."

In spite of our situation that brought a good laugh from us all.

"Mac, you go first, then Tennessee, then I will go, and Lardass must be you, Slim. You're last." Easy Money was still in charge.

Tennessee was getting panicky. "Jees, Easy Money, let me go last," Tennessee pleaded.

"No,' I want Lardo to go last, Tennessee. If someone gets stuck it will be him and I don't want others stuck behind him. Slim understands. He is not complaining."

"You don't understand, Easy Money," Tennessee whined. "I'm goosey. If I get in that pipe and know that there is someone behind me I will go crazy. I could hurt someone. I know what I'm doing. Let me go last. Please, I got to go last."

"It's done then."

"If it makes you feel any better Tennessee, I am not about to get stuck in any Goddamn blow pipe," Slim said.

Tennessee relaxed at once. "If you do get your lardass stuck Slim, I will chew about forty pounds right off it."

We emerged into floodlights that made the area bright as mid day. Once our eyes adjusted to the lights I could see many people milling around. Whiskey Riley was there to greet each man as we climbed down the ladder that had been placed up to the blower pipe. Whiskey wrapped his big arms around Tennessee in a bear hug probably more life threatening than the cave-in. Tears ran down both of their faces and they made no attempt to hide it.

"Does this mean I won't have to support my baby sister?" Whiskey Riley shouted to his brother-in-law loud enough for everyone to hear. Someone shoved a cup of steaming hot coffee into my hand. Nothing ever tasted better.

The hero, Spade, was being interviewed by the Portland *Oregonian*. It was hard to imagine how a big city paper like that had even heard about the cave-in, let alone sent a reporter and a photographer all the way out here from Portland.

Tennessee, who was the last to emerge, was given special celebrity attention because he was the last. A newspaper man cornered him at once and was about to give him a full bore interview much to Tennessee's delight. Unfortunately, at that precise moment, somebody with a warped sense of humor goosed Tennessee. Tennessee flew into the poor reporter knocking him down, shouting all the time, "Goddamn it. Goddamn it." Needless to say, Tennessee's tenure as a celebrity was over.

Two ambulances were waved back to where others were trying to get us onto stretchers. It was mass confusion, and more than a little bit embarrassing since we could certainly walk on our own. We had lost some hide off our elbows and knees from scooting through the blow pipe but other than that we weren't hurt. We were told it was company policy to take us by ambulance to the nearest hospital for "observation.".So we were going to Longview, Washington to a hospital. Well what the heck. Why not?

Tennessee and Easy Money wanted no part of the ambulance and were prepared to put up quite a rumpus when Whiskey Riley stepped in and volunteered to take the two himself. Whiskey to the rescue again. (I speculated that most of the "observation" would be done at Nick's in Amboy.) In the chaos, Slim had been dumped off his stretcher and was complaining about his knee getting hurt.

Finally the stretchers got underway again headed for the waiting ambulances. Just as my stretcher was carried past a crowd of people a woman came out of the crowd and bent over me.

"Are you O.K. Jerry?"

Her make-up was smeared and her eyes were swollen and red. I blinked my eyes and wondered for a-moment if I was still on this earth.

"DeDe, how are you? Hey, Slim, it's DeDe. You are the most beautiful sight I have seen in months. What are you doing here? How did you get here? DeDe is it really you?"

"Are you O.K.?" she repeated.

"If I wasn't before, I sure am now," I managed to say. "You are sure a beautiful sight for these tired eyes."

"And never trust the words of a silver tongued Irishman," DeDe replied.

They had picked up the stretcher and were under way again. DeDe ran along side of the swaying stretcher and shoved a piece of paper into my hand.

"Give me a call, Jer. Please, give me a call."

"I will. I will." I shouted.

Some big faceless miner in a high falsetto voice parroted, "Are you O.K. Jer? Give me a call, Jer."

I feigned a kick at him. Voices all around me in high falsetto voices were chorusing, "Are you O.K. Jer.? Come back
soon Jer." and on and on.

In spite of the harrowing experience of the last few days
I felt warm and very happy. I was looking forward to giving DeDe a call.

Chapter 23

Returning To Work

Spade was the only one who could sleep at night. Slim and I had gotten used to sleeping in the day time so we were having some adjustments to make in the hospital. But we enjoyed our short stay in Longview.

We were getting lots of attention and all three lapped it up. Slim called his brother and asked him to drive over to tell Mom that I was O.K. It turns out she had not even heard yet, that anything had happened in the first place. Isn't that something?

"The whole rest of the world is reading and hearing about our 'big escape' from certain death and the word hasn't even reached The Valley yet. Does that tell you something about our Valley?" I said.

We only had one visitor from the crew. Easy Money drove out once to see us at Longview. He stayed a grand total of fifteen minutes. He was obviously uncomfortable all the time, short as it was. Tennessee and Easy Money never did check into the hospital. Which didn't surprise us. Many of the Hill People still think that hospitals are places you go to die and they didn't want any part of it.

He did stay long enough to give Spade a little white box. Spade opened the box and between layers of white cotton was a silver necklace. The necklace had four silver rings attached to the chain. Each silver ring encased a mint-bright 1951 copper penny. Spade held the necklace in his hand probably wondering what he would do with a ladies necklace.

"It's not for you Spade," Easy Money said. "It's for your Mother. It's the crew's way of thanking her for raising such a fine son. I don't know if it means anything to you or not but there's more than one child in West Virginny who has added 'Spade' to the list of people they thank God for each night. Our women folk in the hills don't have a notion of where Yale Dam is and they may never know, but they all know the name of 'Spade'. Slim and Mac will tell you why the four pennies. I've got to go now. See you later." And he was gone.

I explained to Spade how we had voted with pennies while he was in the pipe.

"I'm glad there are four pennies then, instead of four silver pieces," Spade said.

"If there had been four pieces of silver rather than the copper tossed into your hardbonnet we wouldn't even be here talking about it," Slim pointed out.

The next day Slim's brother drove up to see us. I could tell something was bothering Slim. Most of the time since we had been in the hospital I had spent talking to Spade. I couldn't hear enough about the University of Washington.

With Spade and me holed up all the time it did not give Slim anyone to talk to. So I was glad to see Slim's brother show up.

Spade didn't seem to mind my endless questions about college. I was particularly interested in their medical school.

Spade didn't have as many specifics as I would have liked but he knew a lot about such things as the library or should I say, libraries. And he knew more than I needed to know about the fraternity houses.

"Are you really interested in going to medical school?" Spade asked me.

"No, I want to study law, with maybe an in-between step as a school teacher and coach. I have a friend who wanted to study medicine at one time. The information is actually for her."

He told me about classes of unbelievably large size. Classes larger than our total high school.

Spade and I were in the day room talking but I could see Slim and his brother down the hall in a deep discussion of their own. I smiled as I saw Slim's brother reluctantly reach into his billfold and give Slim several bills. Slim had probably found a game somewhere and needed a grub stake to get in it. Before long they strolled down to where we were talking. We all chatted a bit and then Slim said, "I wonder if I could talk with you alone, Mac?" Slim's brother picked up the slack at once by saying to Spade, "Come on. Let's find the coffee shop in this hotel. Let me buy you a cup of java."

"You're on," Spade said, and off they went.

Slim stood looking out the window of the day room for a few minutes.

"I haven't been a good friend to you have I?" Slim opened.

"Oh, I don't know about that. We have gone different ways here recently but that happens."

"No. I have let you down time and time again."

"I felt maybe there in the cave-in we were getting back together a little," I said.

"Your the best friend I have ever had and I couldn't leave it that way."

"My God. You sound like you're going to die or something."

"No its not that, but I have decided not to go back to the tunnel."

"Why?" I could hear the desperation in my voice.

"I start shaking all over every time I think about the job. I can't go back," Slim said.

"Hey, it will take them two weeks to clean up the mess. We will be on the payroll all that time before we even have to think about going under-ground again. By that time you won't mind it so much."

"I just can't go back. I am going home with my brother today when he leaves. I just wanted to say that I am sorry that I let you and myself down so much."

"Aw, forget it. I don't know what you're talking about, Slim."

"Yes you do.I should have told you myself about Deidre working in Nelson's Cat House. You shouldn't have had to hear it from someone else," Slim said.

"DeDe doesn't mean anything to me, "I lied." She can do what she wants."

"Maybe. But I should have told you. You know it was DeDe who got us our place in the bunkhouse, don't you?" Slim said.

"She what?"

Slim started to laugh. "I guess she told Old Man Nelson to get us in out of the rain or she was going to pack up her tail and go into Amboy. She would have, too. Nelson believed her. He could see it in her eyes."

"So Nelson threw those two guys out to make room for us? Incredible," I said. "We owe her a lot for that one."

"I don't think we could have lasted much longer eating and sleeping the way we were," Slim said.

"I had no idea why he put us in the bunkhouse until now. Thank you for telling me."

"You say that DeDe isn't anything to you and maybe she isn't but I can tell you she has always had a soft spot for you. Do you know they say that within an hour of the cave-in she was down at the portal. I don't know how she got there but she did. She was serving coffee to the workers and stuff like that and she wouldn't leave until we got out.

She wasn't there because she was worried about me or any of the others although I'm sure she was concerned about the rest of us. It was you she was crying for."

Slim's story caught me off base. I would have to think about it some. I blew my nose. Then a thought struck me.

"You mean to say that in less than an hour after the cave-in someone got the word to Nelson's Cat House? That while we were in that hole, not knowing if we would ever see daylight again, some sad sack raced up to Nelson's to relieve their concern over our fate? I hope the line wasn't too long ! " We started chuckling as we pictured the scene. "Here's my twenty dollars and oh, yes, did you hear there was a cave-in at the tunnel and some guys got trapped. But don't worry they're probably dead."

My mind switched back to the conversation. I tried one more desperate approach to get him to change his mind about not going back. I couldn't think what it would be like without him.

"What about college? Do you have enough saved yet?" I pretty much knew the answer.

"I have less than thirty dollars back at the shack. Do you think that might do it? I started the summer with more money than I have now. Isn't that a corker?" Slim laughed sadly.

"Look, there is still time to earn some more, and I have this idea which I should have shared with you by now. If we work it right the first two years won't cost us too much if my plan hits you right." That stopped him for a moment. I could tell he was interested. "I have more than enough saved for the two of us," I said.

"No, I couldn't do that. I would just throw away your money trying to double it. Oh, yes before I forget it. Here are the three dollars I borrowed from you some time ago."

I took the three crumpled bills, which I knew had been in his brother's billfold only a short time earlier. He didn't say anything about the other seven dollars be stole out of my jeans that night, and neither did I.

Spade and Slim's brother came back into the room. But they could see we had a little more talking to do so they stayed out of earshot.

I wanted one more try at convincing him to come back with me to the tunnel.

"Don't feel so bad about being afraid of going back under ground," I said. "Do you remember how scared we were the first night when we found out we were not going to work in the mess hall?" That memory of so long ago started us both laughing."Christ, I still get goosebumps at times.You think I wasn't scared in that cave-in?"

"We were scared at first because we didn't know anything. But now I know and I can't get over being scared. Now *I know*. I just can't go back." Beads of sweat popped out on his forehead and I felt very sorry. No man should do anything that scares him that much.

" You will always be my best friend," Slim said. "I wish you could know how much I have always wanted to be just like you but I'm different. I will never measure up to you. I just hope you won't let our differences change our being friends. That would really get me."

I held out my hand and he took it with a look of relief on his face.

"Good friends have differences, and even an occasional falling out I guess, but if they are good friends they come back together again. Don't they? As for me Slim, I'm looking forward to many more fallings out with you. Goodbye Slim. I'll look out after your gear until you can get back up for it or I'll bring your stuff out with me when I come out in the fall."

"Thanks. I will have to go back to get my car. Unless you want to buy my car? Do you have any cash on you?"

That did it. We both let out belly laughs until Spade and Slim's brother walked down to see what was so funny.

"My God, Slim, you would try to skin me right up to the end wouldn't you?"

I walked with them to the parking lot and shook hands with Slim's brother and again with Slim. The car started rolling slowly. Slim leaned his head out the window and turned back to me.

"By the way, Mac, did you ever find out who took your watch?"

"Not for sure, not until right this second. You see I never told a living soul about my watch."

If Slim had a reply I never heard it, as the car pulled away. I have wished a thousand times since that I would have kept my mouth shut. But I didn't. It was a hell of a way to part.

As it turned out, that was the last time I saw Slim. That was the very last conversation we ever had.

Chapter 24

The Investigation

Things got back to normal in the tunnel. It took ten shifts to muck out the cave-in and extend the timbering beyond the area of the cave-in. I would not say that the whole incident was forgotten but the collapse of the tunnel was certainly put to rest and, the job went on.

We had been too busy and I was too tired after each shift for me to think much about Slim not coming back to the job. The rest of the crew seemed to understand and did not pass judgment one way or the other.

Since I thought the cave-in was history I was surprised to receive a letter from Mr.D. M. Nelson, Personnel Director. The letter was waiting for me when I got off work Tuesday morning. It read:

> Dear Mr. J. McGowan,
> B. Rosen with our insurance carrier will be at the work site on Wednesday.The purpose of this visit is to interview individuals who may have knowledge of the minor rock slide that occurred in the diversion tunnel now under construction. Please make yourself available to B. Rosen Wednesday afternoon. The interviews will be conducted in the office of the Personnel Director beginning at 3:30 P.M.
> Personnel Director,
> D. M. Nelson

I took my letter with me to work that night. Half of the crew had received identical letters. Whiskey Riley stood on the table in the dry shack and waved the letter to get our attention.

"I don't know what this means but it looks like we are going to have an 'investigation' of some sort. This is very common after a bump like we had. It seems they are sending a lawyer fellow out from Portland to ask us some questions. Some fellow by the name of..."

"Rosen," Tennessee said. "Rosen," repeated Whiskey.

"You know Whiskey, Portland is the city of Roses," Tennessee said. "There is Rosenbloom, Rosenblatt, Rosenstein, and..."

Everyone roared. I wasn't sure I knew what they were laughing about but I joined in the laughter too.

"Whiskey?" I said. "My letter calls it a 'minor rock slide'. Is that what we call a cave-in?"

"Well it sure was a rock slide all right and it damn near killed some miners so I guess you could call it a *miner* rock slide."

It sure wasn't a carpenter's slide." Again everyone roared with laughter. Whiskey continued, "Tell him what you know not what you think you know. And no one has anything to be worried about. If the interviews last a half-hour you will get a full hour's pay. So talk slow. That should make up for any lost time. Don't worry, I will be there."

I walked into the Personnel Office right on time. The outer room was filled with the crew from my shift. Mr. Nelson gave us all time to get a cup of coffee. "This won't take very long men, Miss Rosen has just a few questions. I think." Mr. Nelson was all smiles. It was the first time that I had seen him in a suit and tie, and it looked like he had a fresh haircut.

"Miss Rosen? Did you say Miss?" Whiskey said. "This should be interesting."

"Miss Rosen wants to chat with me a little first. So just make yourself comfortable," Nelson said to us.

Nelson went into the back office and they talked for over an hour. Nelson finally appeared at the door. He didn't look too cheerful.

Nelson waved at Whiskey Riley. "Come on in Riley. She wants to interrogate you for awhile." He leaned over as Whiskey walked past and whispered, "This is not going well at all. Be damn careful what you say to this little lawyer bitch" Then in a voice with normal volume Nelson said, "Go right on in Mr. Riley. Miss Rosen is waiting for you." Then he dropped his voice to the whisper again but loud enough for us all to hear. "I have got to have a cup of coffee. Don't let her make a gelding out of you until I can get in to watch."

"Do I have to go in, Nelson?" Whiskey asked. "I don't do too good talking to women."

"She isn't a woman, she's a lawyer. And it will be worse if you don't talk with her," Nelson said, as he pushed Whiskey toward the door of the office. After forty five minutes Whiskey Riley stormed out followed by a small woman dressed in a suit. "I am not through with my questioning of you, Mr. Riley." There was a menacing tone to the woman's voice. She set my teeth on edge.

"I believe you lady," Whiskey said trying to control his voice. "Only lady, you are asking the wrong person. I'm only the Shift Boss."

"Are you the one in charge or not," she spiked back.

"I'm in charge of the drilling on one shift. I will take the full heat that comes down on the drilling but I ain't the Walking Boss and I darn sure ain't the Project Engineer. But I will tell you what I am. I am through jawing with you about it. Lady I'm. tired and I'm hungry and so are my boys you've kept waiting here. I ain't et since 2:30 this morning. So if you don't mind, I'm done". And Whiskey stomped out.

Miss Rosen called after him "I will get back to you Mr. Riley."

She glanced at her wrist watch. "Mr. Nelson, may I see you for a moment?" After only a minute or two, she was right back in and announced: "I would like the following men to remain, McCormack, Curtin, Wagoner, McGowan, and Roscoe. The rest of you can come back at nine in the morning. Thank you all for waiting and being so patient. I did not realize it was so late." She had slightly mellowed.

No one had to be told twice. The door sprung open and the room emptied, except for the ones she had called. McCormack was our hero, the one we called Spade. I knew that. Curtin was Slim, and he never came back to the job. I was McGowan of course, so that left Easy Money and Tennessee.

"Are you Wagoner or Roscoe?" I asked.

"I'm Roscoe," Tennessee said. "Percy Roscoe."

That struck Easy Money as the funniest thing he had ever heard.

"Can I call you Percy?"

"If you do, I will make your ol lady a widow," Tennessee screeched.

"If I had a name like Percy I guess I would be goosey too," Easy Money said. We were all chuckling, even Tennessee, when Miss Rosen and Mr. Nelson returned to the room. Nelson had a worried look on his face. "Miss Rosen, has gone to freshen up. Which means she had to go to the john," Mr. Nelson said. "But I have a little request of one you hands. It is something like 'for the good of the order sort of thing.' I hate to ask one of you to volunteer after you dropped so much time here this afternoon but..."

Tennessee was the first to speak."My Momma didn't raise any fool to volunteer for anything."

Mr. Nelson ignored his comment and went on. "Miss Rosen needs to have someone drive her to Woodland yet tonight. You see, her driver quit right after they got here this afternoon."

"I can't imagine why the driver would refuse to drive such a nice lady like that one," Easy Money said.

"I don't know why he quit but he did," Nelson continued. "I would have bunched it too," Tennessee said. "Can you imagine being with that sour puss with no way to get away from her?"

"Anyway, I sort of mentioned that I would be glad to get someone to drive her to Woodland so... I don't think it will hurt our cause any and our cause needs a little help right now."

"Then I got an idea," Easy money said. "You drive her. Anyway, I ain't got no driver's license."

This gave Tennessee the out he was looking for too. Driver's license? Damn, I always intended to get one of those.

Well that's a shame cause you sure need someone what's got a driver's license."

All eyes turned to me. "Would I have to drive her back yet tonight?"

"Oh no." Mr. Nelson said. They had their sucker. "She said she wouldn't need to be back until nine in the morning."

"Do you mean I would drop her off someplace and drive back here tonight and then go get her in the morning in time to get her back by nine? Jees, when will I get my shut-eye? I've got to go to work yet tonight you know."

"Take a room in Woodland. Don't worry about your shift tonight. We will cover you," Nelson said.

He could still see my hesitation. "Do this for me kid, and I will make it right by you. Charge your room to the Company."

"I haven't eaten yet."

"Buy yourself a steak dinner in Woodland. On me. Hell, have a steak for breakfast too if you want."

He was almost pleading. He wanted the negotiations to end before the lady returned. "I don't know. It's almost six-thirty now, we won't even get to Woodland until ten. That's like double shifting."

"O.K., O.K., you damn bandit. You're on the payroll from now until you get back," Nelson said.

"Straight time? Or... I wondered how far I could milk this.

"Put down anything. Just get this little bitch out of here."

He was so busy trying to wrap up the deal that be didn't notice that Miss Rosen had walked in behind him. I am sure she heard him call her a 'bitch' but she did not let on that she had heard.

I stepped forward and politely extended my hand. "Miss Rosen, it would be a pleasure to see you safely to Woodland and return you in the morning in time for your meetings. What are you driving?"

She did not take my outstretched hand. "Thank you. I hope you are more competent than my last driver. The rented car is in the parking lot. Here are the keys. Mr. Nelson will you help me in carrying the recorder and my papers to the car. I wouldn't want to leave my notes here of course."

"Of course."

"It will take us a few minutes. Perhaps that would give the driver time to put on a clean shirt."

Nelson came very close to getting his deal cancelled right then.

Tennessee, Easy Money, and I walked out into the parking lot. There were only two cars left in the lot. A Company car and a big black one.

"Hey, Mac, that's a brand new Caddie. A 1951 Caddie."

"Does it drive like any other car?"

"You bet, only better. Look, it's got the wrap-around windshield."

"I have never seen a windshield in one piece," I said.

"I guess not," Tennessee said. "The 1951 Cad. is the first to have one. But you better get a move on. Do you own a decent shirt? Never mind, I have a real nice western cut I've been saving. It will fit you O.K. if you roll the sleeves up a bit."

"I have some good-smelling stuff you can use," Easy Money offered. "Come on, let's get you fixed up a little."

"Can we watch you drive off in that big boat?" mused Tennessee. "I wonder, will she sit in the back or in the front?"

Chapter 25

Woodland, Washington

S he returned for another load of papers. This gave Tennessee and Easy Money the opportunity to show me where the ignition switch was because I didn't have the slightest idea. They showed me where to turn on the lights and how to adjust the sideview mirrors. When the lights were on, all the other accessories had a low light behind them, like the windshield swipers and so forth. I was glad to get things like the swipers located because a light mist was beginning to fall. It was quite a sensation to sit on real leather seats. This was some difference compared to coming up the Woodland-Cougar road in Slim's old Chevy.

She got in the front seat and we were off with an embarrassing jerk and a jump. I could see Easy Money and Tennessee in my sideview mirror slapping each other on the back and bending over in laughter. I would get used to this wagon in a bit.

"How fast do you want me to drive Ma'am?"

"Use your own judgment."

As we passed the last floodlight in the parking lot I stole a sideways glance at B. Rosen. I'm not too good a judge on age, but I would guess she was thirty, maybe a little less.

Not too bad a looker either, or she could be. She was dressed in a woman's suit that looked like a man's suit with a white blouse that showed at the throat. She had on a ridiculous hat that looked like a man's felt hat. I don't know why she wore such a dumb thing at least not inside the car, but she did. Because of the hat I could tell only that her hair was dark. I would keep quiet and just drive. I didn't want her to think I was a talker.

I turned right at Nelson's. The sign was on and it looked like there was some business tonight. It was early. I hoped she wouldn't see the sign and make any connection with the name and our Personnel Director. She didn't seem to notice. I must give DeDe a call. We soon made our turn west onto the Woodland-Cougar road and I settled in for a very long, dark ride.

When I saw the lights bathing Merwin Dam I couldn't stand the silence any longer. "This is truly a spectacular drive down the Lewis River. It's too bad it's too dark to see much. Those lights on our left are the lights at Merwin Dam," I ventured. "Merwin Dam is a concrete arch dam."

"The dam is certainly well lighted," she replied. "I am looking forward to the morning drive. My previous driver made me so nervous that I did not enjoy the ride at all."

"The mornings are especially nice because at this time of the year the sun comes up right out of the river, or so it seems. The river flows west right out of the rising sun. "

"You don't sound like your miner colleagues. You are not from the South, are you?"

"No, I'm a local. In fact I'm the only local left in the tunnel. My friend came up here with me but he left awhile back. So that makes me the only local on the job." Now why did I say all of that, I wondered to myself?

"Where did you get your training to be a miner?"

"I'm not a miner. I'm a chucktender."

She thought a bit on that. "Is it your goal to be a miner?"

"Not really. I don't think so. I'm just trying to earn enough money to go to college this fall."

"Oh really? What do you plan to take up in college?"

I slowed to negotiate a curve. "I want to be a lawyer." She was only one of a handful of people I had mentioned that to, and I had no good reason to mention it to her.

"Would that be Stanford then? Stanford is about the only school in the West with much of a reputation. I went to the University of Chicago myself."

"I thought they said you were from Portland."

"Heavens no. I flew out to Portland from the home office in Chicago. Have you been accepted to Stanford?"

"Accepted? I don't have it all figured out yet, but I won't be going directly to a big school like that. I'm going to have to get into something I can make a living at while I save money to go on to law school."

"That would be different," she said. "Selecting the 'right' college for you is very important if you are going to make law your field. In fact, the school, is the second most important aspect. You already have the most important qualification."

I stepped right in to it. "What's that?"

"You are a man. But let's talk a little more about your job in the tunnel."

"Am I being interviewed?"

"Only if you don't have any objections. I can ask you the very same questions tomorrow and then you will be obligated to answer. So if you prefer to wait..."

"I don't mind one way or the other, so fire away."

"For example, I don't have a good grasp on your training and qualifications to work in the tunnel."

"My qualifications? I needed a job. I wanted to get money to go to college this fall and there was nothing in the little valley where I was raised except working in the hay fields. I knew I would never make it that way. After Whiskey Riley arrived he trained us all. He just shut the job down until we knew what we were doing. Whiskey Riley would have made one heck of a teacher. I'm a chucktender but Whiskey saw to it that I learned more than that. I can drill if the rock is good."

"So you would describe your training as 'on-the-job'. Is Mr. Riley an alcoholic?"

"I wouldn't know. I never asked him."

"Why do you suppose they call Mr. Riley, 'Whiskey' Riley?" she asked.

"Never gave it too much thought."

"Do you know why he was late in reporting to the Yale job site?"

"No, I never asked him."

"He left a court-mandated treatment program early or he wouldn't be here yet," she said. "If I would have been in that D.A. office I would have hauled him back and he would be in jail today."

"Oh? Is that so? In that case I would have met you or some other insurance lawyer much earlier. Cause there would have been more business for you if things would have continued as they were going before Whiskey got here."

"That's interesting. You make it sound like Mr. Riley had concern for safety. The record would not support that conclusion."

"I know he would not send a man in where he wouldn't go himself."

"And did you know that the company was willing and prepared to hire men especially trained with explosives, but your Mr. Riley insisted on his own men, none of whom had received any formal training with explosives, to manage their own blasting?"

There was nothing but scorn in her voice.

"All I know is how relieved the experienced miners were when Whiskey told us we would be doing our own loading and shooting. Do you know how many 'rabbit holes' we have left?"

"How many what?"

"A rabbit hole is a 'round' that only partially goes off. When that happens you have to redrill between the old holes which are still loaded to the hilt. Well, we have not had a serious rabbit hole situation since Whiskey explained his Rabbit hole rule. Rabbit holes are common when the men who load and shoot are not the same men that drill.

Whiskey Riley told the crew that if we didn't load and wire right and we had rabbit holes he would make the miner who was responsible redrill by themselves while the rest of us waited out side the tunnel. That way only the ones responsible would be killed. Do you know that we had three rabbit hole situations before whiskey Riley came and none since."

"How would Mr. Riley enforce such an unusual rule as that?" she asked.

"He said he would kill any man who did not redrill a rabbit hole. So a person who was responsible might just as well take his chances drilling between loaded holes as with Whiskey Riley. In case you're wondering, after a blast it is not hard to determine which miner messed up. There is no guess work as to who is responsible."

I should have stopped talking long ago. I should never have mentioned that Whiskey said he would "kill" somebody.

"Then the men who work for this Riley are frightened and intimidated by him."

"Not if you do your job."

"But you did say that he managed by fear of physical assault."

"Whiskey Riley is not a mean guy like you make him him out to be. Heck, Whiskey is a big pussy cat. A man like Whiskey Riley doesn't have to be mean. He is so big and he knows his stuff so well that we all have respect for him."

"But you did say or at least implied, that Mr. Riley would resort to force on occasion. Is that what you said?"

"I didn't mean it that way. If you challenge his experience or size, you would be too dumb to work in the tunnel anyway."

Let's leave your Mr. Riley for a bit and talk more about you."

"There's not much to talk about."

"Perhaps not, but frankly I am confused after reading your personnel jacket," she said.

"I got a personnel jacket?"

"Everyone has a personnel folder. Yours is brief. But it has your birth date as October,1933. Is that a correct birth date?"

"Yes."

"I believe that would make you under the age of eighteen. You are only seventeen years old. You are not supposed to even be on the job. You shouldn't have been in the cave-in because you were not supposed to be there in the first place. Who was responsible for that? Does Riley know how old you are? Or should I say, how young you are?"

I felt trapped. "Look Miss Rosen, Whiskey has no idea how old I am. To him it's a question of how good a hand you are, and I am a good worker. The lady at the Union Hall was misled and she jumped to the conclusion that I was eighteen. Whiskey had nothing to do with it."

I can accept that you willfully misrepresented your self at the point of employment but that does not excuse a basic management responsibility to read the personnel jackets of the men under your supervision. Now does it? That is certainly the minimum expectation."

"Miss Rosen, Whiskey couldn't do that."

"You mean he didn't. He didn't take the time, or perhaps you mean he knew of it but continued your employment in direct opposition to state and federal labor law because he thought you were a 'good hand'. In other words you were someone he could exploit. And slow down! You are driving faster and faster. Slow this car down!"

I let up on the accelerator. She was right on that point. I was driving much too fast for the road and weather conditions.

"No, I mean Whiskey couldn't read the files but not for the reasons you think. Whiskey can't read."

"He can't what? Riley doesn't know how to read? Oh God, do we have an illiterate in charge of a major construction project?"

"I said he couldn't read. I didn't say he was dumb,"I retorted. "Whiskey came from the backwoods and followed his father and brothers into the coal mines of West Virginia. He was big and he got started young..."

"Just like you?" she interrupted. But are you saying that he has not been trained in management or engineering, or anything?"

" I doubt it. But Miss Rosen, he is a born leader. He knows how to do everything in the tunnel and he takes care of his men."

"Do you think 'taking care of your men' means keeping a man on the payroll who has an obvious and uncontrollable nervous condition? Or paying men full salary even when they have expressed a fear of going to work on any given occasion? Is this your idea of 'taking care of people'?"

"You don't understand Miss Rosen. It is not uncommon for men with years in the tunnels to have a 'bad' feeling on any given night and freeze up at the portal. If that happens Whiskey doesn't make a big thing of it but gives the man some work to do out side for the shift. If it happened again and again I suppose Whiskey would let him go."

"Have you ever been so afraid that you 'froze up'?"

"No, not eactly. But if I did I know that Whiskey Riley would give me a little time to get myself squared away," I said.

"Were you frightened during the cave-in?"

"Lady, I was scared shitless. I'm sorry I didn't mean to put it just that way."

"Don't apologize for a stupid question," she said. "We just won't consider that a judicial term." For the first time she laughed. It was actually a nice laugh. I was going to suggest to her that she should laugh more that it probably would not hurt her in her climb up the professional ladder. I thought better of that idea.

The road skirted closer to the river at this point. "It looks like a black velvet ribbon, doesn't it," I said. "Just think of the stories it could tell. That water you see down there, Miss Rosen, started as snow or rain high on the slopes of Mt. Adams and Mt. St.Helens. The Lewis River is in an endless race to catch the mighty Columbia at the appointed place at Woodland, Washington. This is a lonely strip of road. Have we met more than two or three cars since we left the dam?"

She turned her head and faced me directly until we had eye contact.

"I would appreciate your poetical skills more if I thought you were not trying to divert the conversation," she said.

"Even the Lewis River must be diverted at times in order to allow the main part of the job to be accomplished," I said.

"Am I driving slow enough for you now? I could back off another five miles or so." She didn't reply.

Ten more miles of twisting river road went by before she spoke.

"You think quite highly of Mr. Riley don't you?"

"Yes, I surely do."

"That is all fine but now I know that there have been Labor Law infractions, both federal and state. I can't just ignore that."

"No, I don't suppose you could do that and still do your job, Miss Rosen."

I knew at that moment I was out of work as soon as her report got turned in. She said something I didn't quite catch.

"I'm sorry, I wasn't listening. I was doing a little mental arithmetic. I was trying to figure out how much money I have saved so far. What was your question again?"

"Do you have enough saved?"

"It will be close. But I don't think that was your question".

"The question was, at the time of the cave-in was there an established chain of command?"

"I don't understand what you mean?"

"Well, everybody knows that Mr. Riley is the boss. When the cave-in occurred Mr. Riley was on the outside, the other side of the cave-in. Who was in charge of the men caught at the end of the tunnel behind the cave-in?"

"Oh, that was Easy Money," I replied.

"That would be Mr. Wagoner?"

"Yes, We know him as Easy Money."

"O.K., so this Easy Money was in charge."

"He sure was."

"What I am getting at is, was that a predetermined chain of command? In other words, how did you know that he was the responsible supervisor in charge at that time?"

"Because he had the pick-handle."

"I'm sorry but I don't understand," she said.

"He knocked the handle out of a pick and said he would brain the first person who didn't do as he said. That made him in charge. I figured he took charge to try to save us all if he could."

"Do you think this Easy Money would have actually struck you with this club if you would have disobeyed him?"

"If he could have found us in the dark, which he couldn't, I am sure he would have done exactly what he said he would do."

"And that being?"

"He said he would kill the first man who lit up before he told us we could," I said.

She stared out into the rainy night and talking to herself she said, "What kind of Neanderthals do we have working for us?"

"Damn it, lady. Someone had to take charge." I was getting a little warm under the collar with this babe. "If there had been gas in that pocket, lighting up could have blown us all to hell, excuse my language again,or even if there weren't gas, he didn't want an ounce of oxygen to be burned up by some damn smoker. And another thing, when you described someone as having a nervous condition, I let it go by. But are you talking about Tennessee?"

"I was referring to Mr. Percy Roscoe."

"Yeh, Tennessee. Well he may be a bit goosey but he is a good man. I mean a really good person."

"I am not challenging how 'good' or 'bad' he might be but only if he is a safety factor." She could see I was getting hot.

"I don't see how being a little goosey had anything to do with the cave-in."

"It may not directly have anything to do with the cave-in, but his vicious assault on members of the-press certainly increases the Company's exposure to litigation."

"Tennessee didn't mean to hurt the guy, and anyway all he lost was a little dignity for being knocked on his can," I said.

"He knocked down two reporters," she corrected me. "And the fact that Mr. Roscoe was not disciplined had nothing to do with a little matter of patronage I suppose."

"I don't know what you mean."

"I mean that Mr. Riley and Tennessee, I mean Mr. Roscoe, are related are they not? Had Mr. Roscoe not been a relative, would Mr. Riley have been so understanding?" she asked.

"Whiskey Riley would always be fair even if it was his mother. Which doesn't mean that be would deal with everyone the same."

"How can you be 'fair'without treating everyone equally?"

"If you can't see that, then all your fancy education missed something along the way," I said.

"Jerry, you don't seem to understand. I must be sure I make a complete report. This is a very important assignment for my career."

It was the first time she had called me by name. "I'm known as Mac," I said. "Is this what it's really all about? Your career? I know by the nature of your questions that you feel you will have to hang this on somebody. It doesn't matter if I lose my job. I'll make out all right, but don't go walking on people like Tennessee or Whiskey Riley to make your name. Please, don't do that."

"But what if one of those people turns around and sues the Company? What then?"

"Look Miss Rosen, Whiskey Riley is not going to sue anyone. Neither will guys like Easy Money, or Slim, or me. I don't know Spade all that well, but he doesn't seem like the type either."

"Spade? Who is Spade?"

God damn it. She didn't miss a thing. I'm talking again when I should've been listening.

"There is no one on my list to interview by the name of Mr. Spade. Tell me who he is," she demanded.

"He was just one of the guys."

"A guy where? I am supposed to have a complete list of all the men involved." She was almost in a panic. "Tell me who Mr. Spade is or I will ask you again tomorrow and then you will have to say."

"Spade was kinda the hero. He's the one who went through the air blower pipe that got us all out or we would've drowned. He is a student at the University of Washington. I don't know much more about him than that except he has guts. I can tell you that."

"Are you saying he wasn't even a proper worker on the job?"

"I guess you could say that."

"This is incredible. I don't know what I will do with all of this but I do believe you have been telling me the truth. Perhaps not the whole truth but no one could make this all up."

"I'm not a liar, if that's what you think."

"No, you're not, Mac. In fact you are a very remarkable and interesting man of rare character."

She did call me a 'man,' not a seventeen-year-old boy. I may have been a seventeen-year-old kid when I arrived at the dam but I wasn't a kid anymore.

The lights of Woodland greeted us as we rounded the final curve.

"There seems to be a little life in town," I said. I spotted the Shell station on the other side of the street, the one Slim and I had stopped at on the way up to the dam on that first night.

"I think we should get some gas, if you don't mind."

"There's a Texaco station just ahead," she said, peering through the rain.

"I think I will try that Shell station." I cranked a hard U turn before she could protest. I recognized the service station man who came out to serve us.

"Do you remember me?" I asked him. He looked me over carefully.

"No, I can't rightly say that I do. Should I?"

"Me and my partner stopped here for gas in late May."

"No, I don't think so. I would remember a car like this."

"We weren't driving a Cadillac then. We had an old Chevy."

The man stepped closer and took a better look. "You do look familiar but there's a lot of folks that stop here and I'm sorry but I can't say that I know you. Why?" the station man asked.

"I was just curious if that Del Monte check we left you, that you didn't want to take, was any good or not."

He stopped with the nozzle still in his hand. "You had the old Chev that had the wipers that wouldn't work. Yeah, now I remember you. Do you want gas or what?"

"You bet I do."

"Well, how much?" He bounced the nozzle into the gas tank.

"Be careful with that nozzle my good man. I don't want the paint chipped on my car."

"How much?" he repeated.

"Give me a dollar's worth if it won't run you short." I gave him four quarters. Not another word was spoken while he splashed the gas into the tank.

"What is this all about?" Miss Rosen asked.

"Oh, nothing much." I spun away throwing gravel over the pumps. I took another U-turn and pulled into the Texaco station across the street from the Shell station while the Shell manager watched with his hands on his hips.

"Fill her up. If you please." I leaned over toward Miss Rosen and announced, "I paid for the last gas. How about you paying for this stop?"

"Certainly, but what is going on here?"

"Nothing to speak of but I wish Slim could have been here. There is an old saying in my valley which says, you should be nice to everyone, 'cause you may end up working for them."

"I don't think I get it," she said.

We pulled into the parking lot of the only motel with its lights on. The Timbers Motel, the sign said, daily and weekly rates.

"Is this it?" she asked incredulously.

"There ain't too many motels in this area," I said.

"This will be fine, I'm sure, "she said.

As I stopped the car she turned in her seat. "You know, I rather envy Whiskey Riley. I would give anything to be able to command the respect and loyalty that he does."

"It's not a one-way street either, Miss. Rosen. Whiskey Riley respects the men who work for him just like they respect him. Loyalty comes easy when men respect each other. Some day I think I will be leading people, and I hope to pattern myself after Whiskey Riley. "

"I wouldn't be surprised, Mac."

Chapter 26

Things That Go Bump In The Night

She let me do the talking. "We would like a couple rooms."

"Only got one left. Take it or leave it." The manager, or owner, or whatever he was, sat behind a slowly moving fan reading a comic book. He obviously did not want to be distracted from his heavy reading.

"Could we see it?" I asked.

"It's the only one we got. Take it or leave it," he said, without looking up. "Or, you could go sleep in the parking lot at the old Finn Hall."

"We will take it," she said.

The manager reluctantly turned the corner on the page he was on and spun the registration form around for us to sign. Miss Rosen signed the form.

"That your car out there?" the manager asked.

"Yes, it is," I said. "Is there a problem?"

"No there isn't a problem, yet, but if you park that Christmas tree back where the room is going to be there will be a problem in the morning when you find the hubcaps gone."

"What would you suggest?" Miss Rosen asked.

"If it were mine, I would park it right under that light, where I can keep an eye on it for you. I'm on all night."

"What would that cost extra?" I asked.

The man looked wounded to the quick. "Have you priced hubcaps? The only place I know that would even carry hubcaps for a brand new Caddie would not be open until morning. You could take a chance, I guess."

"How much?" I repeated.

He rubbed his unshaven chin. "For a buck I could almost guarantee that your car will be O.K."

"That is extortion," Miss Rosen exclaimed.

"Pay it," I suggested.

"The room is six dollars in advance and can we keep the buck separate? It just mixes up the bookkeeping."

"Of course," Miss Rosen said with resignation. She produced a twenty-dollar bill.

"And here is your change good-looking," the man said. Miss Rosen ignored the comment but in the light of the office I got another good look at her. The manager was right, she was good looking when she wasn't asking questions.

"It's number seventeen. The last one down the line. The number is off the door but it's the last one in the string. See ya later," he said. He pretended to go back to his comic book but he was running his eye up and down Miss Rosen.

"I am glad you're with me Mac. That crook gives me the creeps."

"He was just selling insurance. Just another insurance salesman," I said. She should have understood that.

"I wonder if we had to buy our hubcaps back in the morning if he would have washed the Lewis River mud off them first," she said.

I held the door for her. The door opened up into a small room with a single bed, a table with cigarette burns on it, a lamp, and a chair. Another door went into a bathroom shower combination. I tried the lamp. It didn't work. I threw the wall switch and a single light bulb that hung from the ceiling partially illuminated the place. The shades over the windows were heavy. That was at least one good thing.

"I have seen better motel rooms," she said. I hadn't seen better ones. This was the first motel room I had ever been in. I carried her things in which took three trips. She had two large suitcases, which I put on the bed. I didn't know where else to put them. Her recorder and papers I put on the table between the cigarette burns. She was sitting in the only chair when I finished.

"We have an awkward situation here," she said.

"I don't think so," I said. "Don't give it another thought. I will just sleep in the car if that's all right with you. It won't be the first time I have slept in a car. If you're hungry I will go try to find something for us to eat. I think I can get us a sandwich or something like that. We won't find a regular restaurant open at this time."

"As a matter of fact I am famished," she said. She looked very relieved that the sleeping arrangements were taken care of.

"If there is a choice do you have any druthers for the kind of sandwich?"

"Anything you can get will be fine. Do you have any money?"

"A little. Mr. Nelson said to charge things to the Company but that won't work for sandwiches in Woodland at this time of night."

She pulled out another twenty-dollar bill from her leather billfold.

"That's a lot more than I need," I stammered.

"I hope it is more than you will need. But don't worry I will add what ever you spend to my bill to the Company."

During this conversation over the food and money she was standing with her back to the closed door. I was facing her. Suddenly with no warning there was an unmistakable noise at the door. I could hear the outside door knob slowly turn. Miss Rosen jumped about six inches in the air and before I could take a step backward she was clinging to me for dear life.

"Somebody is trying to get in!" she whispered.

I raised my finger to my lips to quiet her. I pried her loose from me as gently as I could and motioned to her to get on the other side of the bed. The door rattled again, more determined and louder. I cast about for something I could swing or throw. There was nothing. The door was pushed on this time. Whoever it was wasn't going away.

"What will we do? I'm afraid," she whispered.

I whispered back, "I don't like this either. Get behind the bed I'm going to need a little room to operate in if he comes through the door."

There was another rattle of the door handle, then silence. I motioned to her that the person outside had not left the door. We did not hear any retreating steps. I positioned myself to where I hoped I could get in the first lump by surprise. After that we would just have to see what happens. She kneeled down behind the bed with just the top of her head and two wide eyes showing.

In reality, I thought we probably had a confused drunk out there who probably just thought he was at his own room. However, fear is very contagious and I could feel my hands damp with sweat.

There was no further noise from outside for a long period of time. She crept out from behind the bed but she still stood behind me. She held my right arm with both of her small hands as if my arm was giving her strength or courage.

We both heard the footstep on the door sill. There was no mistaking the sound. Whoever was out there had been listening all this time. She spun around me and flung herself into my arms shaking like a leaf in a spring storm. To tell the truth, it felt good to have her cling to me that way. This was a new experience for me. I wanted to just hold her and smell her hair but I didn't know just what to do. So, I patted her on the shoulder like you would in calming a young colt. I didn't know what I was doing, but it was calming her down. She stopped shaking some but she kept her head buried in my chest. The top of her head came only to my chin. On an impulse I laid my cheek against the top of her head and just kept patting her shoulder. She didn't seem to object.

The intruder mumbled something that we didn't understand and walked away. We waited. It was no ruse, he had definitely given up. I walked her over to the chair and sat her down.

"I think it's over," I said. "I don't think we have anything to worry about now." I tried to sound as confident as I could.

"I'm going out now to get some food," I finally said. "Lock the door behind me and put the chair against the door knob." I showed her how I meant. "When I come back I will knock four times and say my name. Don't unlock the door for anyone for any reason unless you know it's me. You got it? Are you O.K.?"

"Yes, but I'm not hungry now. Do you have to go out?"

"I'm hungrier than ever," I said. "I'll be back as soon as I can. Lock the door at once and you'll be O.K. I won't be long. "

I stepped out of the door and promptly stepped in a pot-hole full of rain water which poured over the top of my shoe. The rain was bouncing off the blacktop and I didn't have a hat or jacket. I ducked into the motel office. The manager was still reading his comic book.

"What can I do for you?" he asked.

"Is there a place where a guy could get something to eat at this hour?"

"Sure. The bar across the street can fix a pretty mean hamburger. if that's what you want," he said.

"Thanks," I said and turned to go.

"Hey, wait a minute mister. Where are you going to bounce your head tonight?"

"Why?"

"It doesn't make me any difference but if you share the room with the dolly it will cost you another two dollars."

"I'm not sure where I will be sleeping but go ahead and put the two dollars on the bill cause I might sleep in the chair."

"In the chair, in the bed, it don't make me a damn bit of difference, but if it's in the room it's two more bucks. And there ain't no putting it on the bill."

I dumped two wadded up dollar bills on the counter and turned again to leave.

"You need anything else mister?" he asked.

"Like what?"

"Oh, I don't know. I have both short and long jugs of real good booze just as an example."

"No, I don't think so," I said and left.

At the little bar I ordered four 'super' hamburgers, a couple small bags of potato chips, a couple of Babe Ruth bars, and two Cokes on ice. My entire shopping list came to $3.61 including the sales tax for the Governor. I gave the girl the 39c I got in change. She seemed very pleased.

The manager was still busy with his literary challenges. I ducked into his ring of light as though I needed a moment to get out of the rain.

"Say, how good is that hootch you were talking about?" I asked.

"It's the best. It's Canadian Club. If you know good stuff then you would agree. It goes down real smooth."

"How much is a pint?"

"Only ten dollars."

"Isn't that a little expensive?"

"Not for this time of night it's not mister."

"O.K. give me a pint."

"Whatever you say. Is there anything else that you're going to need?" he asked.

I wanted to ask, "like what," but I didn't. I stopped in the door way with a thought that surprised me. On an impulse I returned to the counter.

"There is one thing you could do," I said. "In about an hour come by the room and shake the door knob good and hard and pound on the door a bit."

"Oh, I don't know if I can leave the front desk or not," he said I put a dollar bill on the counter.

"In an hour," he confirmed.

I knocked four times and identified myself. The door opened crack and then sprung open the rest of the way. She had been waiting right by the door. I slipped inside and brushed off some of the rain.

"Has it been quiet?" I asked.

"Yes, but you certainly took your time." Her tone was more relieved than angry.

"I got us some groceries," I said, and began to spread our supper on the table. The candy bars can be a snack in the morning," I suggested. "Would you want something to wash the hamburgers down with besides the Coke?" I asked with a little hesitation.

"My God C.C.," she said. "That's the best Chicago could offer, let alone Woodland." She didn't ask me where I got it or how much I paid for it. I got the total supply of two glasses but I didn't pour them. "I'll just take my hamburgers and go out to the car and let you get some rest. I will see you in the morning."

She let me get all the way to opening the door, and I thought I would have to go on out, when she spoke.

"If you would prefer, I guess you could sleep in the chair just as well as in the car."

"To be honest with you sleeping in the car is going to be chilly tonight and I'm pretty wet. So, if you really wouldn't mind I would appreciate being able to stay inside tonight. But only if you are sure it would be no bother for you."

"Please, do stay inside. You won't be any trouble at all."

"Well, I can tell you I do appreciate it." I poured each of us two inches of C.C., as she called it.

The hamburgers were as good as I have ever eaten, or maybe it was just that hunger was a good cook. The booze slipped down without a ripple. A sense of boldness came over me which surprised me.

It may have been the good stuff. I don't know. Anyway, the next bright idea just jumped out of my brain and out of my mouth.

"Miss Rosen, would you object greatly if I grabbed a quick shower? I haven't had the time since I got off work many hours ago to get cleaned up and this has been a long day."

There wasn't the slightest hesitation. "Help yourself. While you do that I will have the opportunity to retire."

"I won't take long and thank you for letting me use your facility."

The water was only lukewarm but it did feel good. I stayed in the shower longer than I had planned. I had just finished drying off some and had wrapped the towel around my waist when I heard a loud banging on the motel door.

Jees, I had forgotten my unholy pact with the motel manager. I had let the hour slip by and here I was in the bathroom with just a towel on. I didn't have time to decide, what now? The bathroom door flew open and there was Miss Rosen in my arms again. She had only a thin-tan colored night gown sort of thing on. To my embarrassment, my towel came loose in the back where I had only loosely cinched it, and it fell to the floor. I didn't know what to do, so I just kept holding her tightly to me and whispered to her to keep very still.

The manager really did a number on that door. For a moment I thought he was going to get carried away and really knock the door in. But then we heard him walk a few steps away and stop, and then he came quickly back and splattered the door with the flat of his hand one last time.

There I was, naked as a jay bird, but still comforting this poor frightened woman. She stepped quickly backwards out of my arms and to my surprise took a long and interested look at me. The front of her nightgown was all wet. Her garment clung to her like a piece of cellophane. She gave a low laugh and came back into my arms and hugged me again but this time it was a different hug. This was not a hug of fright.

This was great, but now what do I do? I didn't have long to worry about it. She looked intently into my eyes and took me gently by one hand and led me to the bed. I mumbled something about not having much experience in these things, or something like that.

"Good. Let's learn together," she said.

And we did.

The next morning we went for a late breakfast. I ordered that steak Mr. Nelson had promised. We chatted about this and that and everything. Finally, I said, "Do I have to keep calling you Miss Rosen?"

She laughed. "My first name is Bernice. Bernice Rosen."

"Bernice? What a nice name, "I said.

"It is really Bernice Rosenstein, but my grandfather changed it to Rosen when he came to America."

"Some of my ancestors changed their name too but it was while they were still in Ireland. Anyone with a "Mc" or an "0" before their name was outlawed by the English. So some of my kin changed their name to Gowan and some changed to Smith but my Grandfather refused to change his name. He left and came to America for many reasons, but one reason was to keep our name. I wouldn't change my name for anything I guess."

How did they get Smith out of McGowan?"

"Gowan means blacksmith in Celtic. McGowan means the son of the blacksmith. But the real reason for choosing Smith, according to my grandfather, was that Smith just so happened to be the most common English last name."

I stayed on this topic too long. "I can't imagine anyone changing their name I repeated, feeling akward."

"You aren't a Jew either," she said.

"Are you a Jew? Well I'll be darned. Are all Jewish girls this good looking?"

"Absolutely," she laughed. "You have never known a Jew before?"

"Not to my knowledge. I guess there are some in Portland but there never were any in the Valley where I grew up." I recalled the comment that caused all the miners to laugh about Portland being the city of 'Roses'. Now I understood their joke. I didn't think it was very funny now, however.

"It doesn't bother you to be seen in public with me?" she asked.

"Bernice, I have never been more honored in my life. I mean that."

"Well for your information you are just as 'big' but not nearly as 'dumb' as I have always been told that the Irish are. And I like being with you too."

"I don't think I need any more information for my report. Is there a way you can get back to the dam and I can get this car back to Portland?"

"Sure. I could drive you to Vancouver, where you could catch a bus to Portland, and I could catch the Yacolt Stage Line to Yacolt. I know I could get somebody to drive over from Amboy to pick me up there. I would drive you on into Portland but I have never driven in a big city like that, and to tell you the truth I'm a little leery."

"Let's do it. I won't take the bus however, I'll just call for someone at the Portland office to come pick me up. I will call Mr. Nelson to tell him of the change of plans and have him send someone to this Yacolt place for you, if you wish," she said. "We don't have to be out of the motel room until eleven. Would you like to go back to the room?"

"Yes I would."

When the Yacolt Stage stopped at Marble's Store I was only one mile from my home. Roy McKee, the owner and operator of the bus line asked, "Are you getting off Jerry?"

"No Roy, I'm going to the end of the line with you."

"Glad to have the company. Sometimes this is a lonely, dark run. How's your Mom doing?"

"She is just fine. I haven't seen her this summer but she's doing fine."

Tennessee and Easy Money met me at Yacolt, so I didn't have to worry about getting back to the dam.

"Do you want to stop at Nick's for a beer?" Easy Money asked.

"I would really rather get back to camp. I'm awful tired."

They knew that something was different but they had the good sense, not to ask about it.

It was ten days later that Mr. Nelson received a letter from The Industrial Insurance Company of America (IICA). The letter was signed by B. Rosen. Mr. Nelson was waiting at the dry shack to show us the letter when we arrived at the tunnel at the beginning of the shift. We knew it was an occasion because Nelson, like most of the brass, did not come down to the portal any more often than they felt they had to, especially to meet the graveyard shift.

Nelson gathered us around and read the letter to us. The letter said:

> Mr. D. M. Nelson, Personnel Director
> M&K
> Yale Dam Project

Dear Mr. Nelson

Attached is my full report regarding the displacement of material from the ceiling of the diversion
tunnel now under construction at the Yale Dam site
in Southwest Washington. In brief, and in summary,
the conclusion of IICA based in part upon exten-
sive interviews and on on-site observation, was that
this incident was both unavoidable and unpredict-
able, and as such no measure could have been taken
to have prevented the occurrence. No liability on the
Company nor on any individual has been established. IICA considers this a closed file unless
new or conflicting information is forthcoming. I was
particularly impressed with the management style
and organizational structure developed and executed by Mr. Riley. Please extend my personal ap-
preciation to Mr. J. McGowan for the assistance he
rendered toward the timely completion of
this report.

Sincerely,
B. Rosen, Legal Dept. IICA

"What's she saying? What's she saying?" Whiskey Riley
wanted to know.

"She is saying that the cave-in was an act of God and no
one is at fault," Mr. Nelson said.

"Hell, I could've told her that, if that's all she wanted to
know."

"Is a displacement of material anything like a cave-in?"
Tennessee asked.

"Just about the same," Nelson said.

"Hey that little lady said I had style," Whiskey beamed.
Whiskey was obviously very pleased with that revelation
even if he wasn't too sure what she meant.

"Don't crow too much, Whiskey," Nelson said."Look right here, she says that you executed whatever style you might have had. That means you killed it. That's what execute means." Everyone but Whiskey Riley had a good laugh. Nelson was having the time of his life.

Whiskey grabbed the letter and pretended to be reading it. "I still like what the little lady said." As his eyes proceeded to the bottom of the letter he recognized his own name. She done wrote my name. See Tennessee, it says Whiskey Riley."

"It says Mr. Riley, and yes I can see it."

"Oh yes, Mr. Riley," Whiskey corrected himself after pretending to 'reread' the line.

"Boys, this calls for a corn on the cob feed tomorrow at the end of your shift. I will personally arrange for it," Mr. Nelson said.

I had remained in the background of the circle of men who had gathered around Nelson to hear the good news. Nelson waved me forward and put his arm around my shoulder.

"Mac, I don't know what kind of a number you did on that lady lawyer but what ever it was you did a damn good job of it."

I could feel my face getting hot and my reply was far too defensive.

"I didn't do any number on her. I just answered her questions. I answered them the best I could."

"Didn't mean to imply anything but a job well done, Mac. You did us all a good turn because when she left here she had tight jaws," Nelson said. "But tell me how in the hell did you manage that little matter of Whiskey throwing the State Safety Inspector out on his butt?"

"Bernice... I mean Miss Rosen didn't ask, and I didn't mention it"

"Bernice?" It sounded like two hundred voices said it at one time. How could I have slipped up? The fact was I had thought quite a bit about Bernice Rosen in the past few days.

The crew finally stopped laughing .These guys don't miss much. They gave me knowing grins.

"By the way, I haven't received any expense account from you yet. Didn't you have some out-of-pocket expenses?" Nelson asked.

"I didn't have much in the way of expenses." Every one roared again. Everything I said seemed to bring the house down. "Let's just forget about the expenses." That broke everyone up again" I'm glad everything worked out so well." And everyone went into another fit of laughter.

That was not the last I heard of B. Rosen. Five weeks later, during my last week on the job, I received a note from her. The note came from Chicago, Illinois. She said she was going to be in Boise, Idaho at M&K's head office the second week in October. She said that Boise didn't seem too far from Portland, and if I could get a free weekend to meet her in either Portland or Boise she would wire me the money for a plane fare. She said she would look forward to hearing from me. She enclosed a business card with her business address and telephone number on it. On the back of the card she had written her home address and phone number.

I didn't write or call her back. It would have been my first airplane ride too. If I had thought I could afford the air fare and the other expenses of a weekend in Boise, I might have taken her up on the invitation. I really would have liked to have seen her again. But I didn't feel I could put out the money, and to have her pick up the tab instead would have changed everything. In Woodland I didn't mind if she picked up the bills because she was charging them to the Company.

I have thought of her many times and wondered if she ever thought of me and of that rainy night in a little out-of-the-way corner of the world in Woodland, Washington.

Chapter 27

How Do You Build a Dam?

"You want to do what?"

"I heard that you had a model of the dam. I was just wondering if I could see it?" I said.

"Are you some kind of an engineering intern or something?"

"No, I just have some questions ," I said.

"Do you work here?"

"Yes, I'm a chucktender. I work in the diversion tunnel."

"I know where chucktenders work, for Christ's, sake. Are you somebody's kid?"

"Sure, I am the son of Mary Elizabeth McGowan. I am Jerry McGowan. They call me Mac."

"No, no, I mean is your old man somebody ? A boss or something?"

"My Dad is dead."

"Now tell me again. What is it you want?"

I just want to see what the dam will look like when it's finished. I heard that you had a model made, and I've got some questions to ask somebody who might know something but it doesn't look like you're the fellow. So..."

"I never saw a chucktender smart enough to ask a decent question. Besides, the engineer's office is off limits. You can't just barge in here and expect staff to sit down and explain something you wouldn't comprehend anyway.

I can't take the time with every construction stiff who is working in the tunnel," he said.

"I'm not just working in the tunnel. I'm helping to build a dam," I said.

Unnoticed by the two of us a grey-haired man had poked his head around the corner of a partition, and was listening to our conversation.

"What's the confrontation all about, Jenkins?"

"Nothing Mr. Henderson. I think I have handled it now."

Mr. Henderson came around the counter where Jenkins was standing. He extended his hand to me. "My name is George Henderson, I am the Project Engineer for Ebasco. Ebasco is the consulting engineers' firm for Pacific Power and Light. What was it you just said?"

"I said I would like to see the model of the dam."

"No, what did you just say? You said you were not just working in a tunnel..."

"I said I was building a dam. Only I would like to know more about what I'm building."

How old are you son?" Mr. Henderson asked.

"I'm seventeen. No I mean I'm eighteen, Sir." Henderson did not miss my slip-up.

"Jenkins here would be glad to spend some time with you. I think starting with the model would be an excellent way to begin, don't you think so Jenkins?"

"That would be a good place to begin Mr. Henderson, only I have some work ahead of me and..."

"I know you do Jenkins," Mr. Henderson interrupted. "And I appreciate that fact. But right now, I don't think you have anything more important than to talk with this chucktender, who is working in the tunnel, that will divert the river, so we can build this contraption, so engineers like us will have something to do, so that Truman won't draft us."

"You bet Mr. Henderson, I agree. But how much time should I spend with him?"

"As long as Mac McGowan asks intelligent questions you will have the time to give intelligent answers."

Mr. Henderson took a battered notepad out of his inside pocket.

"Do you spell that with a Mac or just Mc?" Mr. Henderson asked.

"It's Mc," I said

"Jerry 'Mac' McGowan. I want to remember the name. Here is my business card. Look me up some time, will you?"

Wow! I was getting a collection of business cards. "Thank you Mr. Henderson."

"Call me George."

"I'll do that."

"Nice meeting you Mac."

"Nice meeting you George."

With a wave of his hand he went back inside his office. I turned to Jenkins, who was absolutely pale. "You know Jenkins, maybe you should go to the john unless it's already too late."

That broke the ice. Jenkins laid his head back and howled with laughter. "Nice meeting you George," Jenkins parroted, and roared again. "Nice meeting you George," he said again and shook his head. "Come on Chucktender Mac we got a session in the chart room."

The model was a work of art. It was mounted on a four-by-eight sheet of birch plywood. "The relief is to scale," Jenkins said. "The river goes east to west. See here. Here is Merwin Dam. Here is the Merwin reservoir behind Merwin Dam. The lake is twelve miles long. Here is the Yale Bridge."

The tiny wires representing the cables on the suspension bridge were made of silver wires with rust painted on exactly like the cables on the real bridge. The detail was perfect in every respect.

"Now coming upstream is Yale Dam. There she is. Isn't she a beauty?" Jenkins said.

"Frankly, it's kind of plain compared to Merwin Dam."

"Well that's the way she'll look. Plain to some but an engineering wonder to others. The reservoir from Yale Dam will go all the way to where the blue narrows down to the river channel again. That will be about nine or ten miles. The darker the shade of blue, the deeper the water. Over there is Mt. Adams, almost due east. Over there is Mt St.Helens. The headwaters of the Lewis River is in the Mt. Adams country, not St.Helens. Some day there will be another dam up stream from Yale dam. See, they locate a dam just downstream from a major tributary. The reservoir will fill the canyon of the tributary as well as the gorge of the Lewis. This will greatly increase the amount of water impounded. Look here. Yale Dam is just downstream from the confluence of the Siouxon and the Lewis River. The lake will back up the Siouxon canyon and see how blue the water is? That means, like I said, the water will be very deep."

"I have been to the Siouxon," I said.

"The heck you have." There was more respect in his voice when I told him that.

"So Yale has the Siouxon. The next dam will fill up Swift Creek canyon, right here. Now, you tell me where would you locate the next dam after Swift Creek?"

I looked carefully at the huge relief model. "Maybe about here, so this valley here could be flooded by the reservoir." I was pointing all the time I was talking.

"Right you are, chucktender Mac. That's the Muddy River your pointing at and that may be another dam site."

"But why the Lewis River?" I asked.

"Good question," he said. "There are certainly many rivers in the Northwest. Why the Lewis River? The main reason is that the Lewis River watershed complements the larger hydroelectric plants on the Columbia River such as Bonneville Dam and the Grand Coulee Dam. By that I mean, the dams and the reservoirs on the Lewis will be at full capacity in the months when production is way down on the Columbia. The Lewis River is a winter stream, and the Columbia is a spring and summer stream. There are other reasons too. For example, the Lewis River is not 'flashy.'

"Flashy?"

"Yeah, the Lewis River does not have a record of flash flooding. The Lewis will flood to be sure, but the water comes up steadily and it is predictable. The 120 inches a year rainfall is spread over many months."

"You can say that again. Like spread out over every month. This country has two main seasons, wet and rainy"

"But any location considered as an adequate site for a hydro station must have two things, 'head' and 'flow.' Head means pressure and flow means volume. The height of a dam will give the 'head' and the capacity of the reservoir assures us the 'flow'."

"How many feet high will Yale Dam be?" I asked.

"Yale Dam will be 323 feet high. That is more than the length of a football field stood on end. Now look here. This will be a 'secondary' dam. It will only be 45 feet high, but look what it will do. This forty-five-foot dam, which looks more like a dike in comparison to the main dam, will impound the water in all this area here. This secondary dam is called the 'Saddle Dam'because the area of water it will back up reminded someone of the shape of a saddle. See, look at the relief map carefully. There is a low spot in the natural terrain. Without the Saddle Dam the water from the new reservoir would spill over, right here.

"The Saddle Dam will be fifteen hundred feet long and three hundred feet thick at its base. Like I say, we call it a 'secondary'dam but let me tell you, it's a major dam in its own right." He stopped to let the proportions sink in a bit.

"If the Saddle Dam is three hundred feet thick, it will be about as thick as the main dam is tall," I observed.

"That's exactly right. Which brings up an interesting point. Most dams are about as wide at the base as they are long at the crest. For example, the main dam, or Yale Dam, will be fifteen hundred feet long and twelve hundred feet thick at the base. Or going back to using a football field for comparison, think of the main dam as being five football fields long, four football fields thick, and one football field high. But now look at the Saddle Dam. The proportions are not the same. The Saddle Dam will be fifteen hundred feet long, as I have said, but a mere three hundred feet thick. You see it is out of proportion to most dams. Why do you suppose that is?"

"It looks to me that the engineers don't expect the pressure to come to bear on the Saddle Dam like they think it will on the main dam. It looks like the Saddle Dam just fills up a low spot."

"You have the picture, chucktender Mac. You have the picture.But taken all together this is a major plant. A major project."

"Why isn't Yale Dam a concrete dam like Ariel Dam just downstream?" I asked.

"You mean Merwin Dam?"

"They call it Merwin Dam now but it used to be called Ariel Dam," I said. "A friend of mine told me that Yale Dam was originally designed to be a concrete arch dam too."

"I don't know where you heard that but it's true. Not too many people know that. But that was before we got involved. My firm recommended that Yale be an earth-filled dam because the materials needed were readily available on-site, and therefore the project can be finished and on line much faster. And while there is some economy in this method, speed was the most important factor. Time is critical. This dam is a major defense effort. Did your friend tell you that? An important factor in PP&L getting their federal license so fast was the need for power in this area to maintain the aluminum industry which is a key aspect in the defense policy of our nation."

"My friend did not mention that."

"Good, that is reassuring. Before we are through I would like to hear a little more about this friend. Anyway, the Pacific Northwest is power hungry primarily because of the 'Aluminum Triangle', which is the area from Vancouver, Washington to Longview, Washington where most of the nation's aluminum is smelted. This industry is critical to our defense needs, and it sucks up one hell of a lot of energy. And here we have the Lewis River hydro-electric plants sitting right in the center of the triangle. So, with the Lewis River dams on line to complement the Columbia River projects, the pot lines in the aluminum plants will never have to shut down from lack of power as they do now."

"I never thought of this as a defense thing," I said.

"Well, it is. Do you think that business in Korea is the big show? Hell, it doesn't amount to anything. It's Berlin. That's the prize. Hell, those dumb G.I.'s in Korea are dying for nothing but to buy us a little more time. The big show will be in Europe when the Ruskies decide it's time to over run Berlin and all of Western Europe."

"My brother was lost in Korea," I said.

"Yeah, well I'm sorry about that. MacArthur is right you know. The minute the Chinks came in, we should have used the bomb. God, I hope MacArthur runs for president. Truman is no music critic and he sure as hell is no general. Now don't get me started on politics. Senator Joe McCarthy knows the score. There are commies all around. I bet we have our share right here on the project. Christ our security is lousy. Do you know they let a couple of Greeks, who were so called engineers, come right in here with their cameras and look the whole place over from top to bottom. They're going to the Cabinet Gorge project in Idaho next.

Can you imagine letting a couple Greek commies, right in here?"

"Maybe we could get back to the dam," I said. I didn't want to push this guy too far because he could end up turning Tom Kyle or me into some 'Unamerican Activity Committee."

"Sure, you want information about dams. Earth filled dams are not a new idea. Hell, there was one built in Ceylon five hundred years before Christ. I would like to have seen that one. It was only seventy feet high but it was eleven miles long. Just think about that. Eleven miles. That's like from here to Amboy. In the gold fields of California, over a hundred years ago, rock filled dams were common. The rock filled dam is the first cousin to the earth filled dam. By the late 1930's the soil mechanics had pretty much been worked out by engineers like Tergaghi and Cassagrande. Tergaghi and Cassagrande had done a lot of work to establish the principles of 'piping' and 'seeping' through dams. Hey, does any of this interest you?"

"You bet it does. And I'm trying to follow you," I said. "It's a lot more educational than your politics." Jenkins roared at that..

"Well then, by 1940 most of the problems had been worked out such as slope and slip, compaction, and so forth. There are some minor problems still to be worked out. The spillway must be very broad to prevent water from cutting the dam on the downstream side. The downstream slope must be very gradual this requires the slope to be protected from 'rain drop' erosion and so forth. Once the significance of the forces developed within the earth-filled dam, such as percolating--that is water percolating through the dam was well understood, and the principles of the laying of materials and compaction were known, and once we knew it was all subject to laws and principles of science, we could work all these factors into the design. They didn't always understand these principles in the recent past. If they would have, would Fort Peck Dam have slipped in 1938?"

I thought I should say something to show I was listening.

"What happened at Fort Peck Dam?"

"That wasn't our project I can tell you that. At Fort Peck, on the Missouri River in Montana, they moved the fill material, hydraulically."

"I don't understand what that means."

"They delivered the fill material to the dam in a 'slurry' form. Liquified. It is economical of course to move materials through pipes like you would water, but you had better apply basic science to the operation or you will have one hell of a mess. Now Fort Peck is the granddaddy of the earth-filled dams. To give you a comparison, Fort Peck required 125 million cubic yards of fill material. Here at Yale we estimate it will take about three million cubic yards. So Fort Peck is a big one. It is the largest earth-filled dam in the world by sheer bulk. It is 250 feet high, which is not as high as Yale will be, but Fort Peck is over 21,000 feet long. That's almost four miles. Anyway, in 1938 a major portion of Fort Peck Dam 'slipped' or collapsed. It caused a completion delay of a year as I hear it. There never has been an earth-filled dam lost using the design that we're using here at Yale Dam. Never."

He continued non-stop. "In this design you start with a 'core' of fine material. Clay in our case here at Yale. You then add layer after layer of progressively larger material compacting each layer with D-8 Cats pulling a 'Devils foot'. One of the remaining controversies is whether the devil's foot works better than oversized rubber tires to pack it down. The final layers of rock will be bigger than automobiles, this gives the dam its bulk. We have found a local source of clay but we can't use it until it's time. We must divert the river first. That's your job, chucktender Mac. Get that damn river flowing through the mountain. They are working the clay right now. It's just like the farmers do when they're preparing a field to plant corn. Maybe you've seen the cloud of dust raising every day just beyond camp. We have six D-8 Cats that chase each other around that sixty-acre field all day long. Each D-8 pulls a specially designed pulverizer. The farm boys call them disks. The clay is getting so fine that the Cats sink in up to the top of their tracks in the dust.

"Now this next part is interesting. It's not likely that we can get the clay in place and compacted before the fall rains start again and we want the clay as dry as possible when we compact it. So do you know what we will do? We will lay a cover of black top four inches thick over the entire field just to keep it dry. That will be more blacktop than all the roads in this whole backwoods have ever known. All of this is being done because the material for the 'core' is so important."

Jenkins stopped for a drink of coffee. He had been going continuously for over an hour. I thought this could be my chance to slip in some other questions.

"My friend who works on the survey crew in the tunnel says that one reason the design of this dam is earth-filled is because the area is not stable. He told me that an earth-filled dam can buck and roll but it will finally settle back in place once the action is over," I said.

"That's nonsense," Jenkins said. "But I have heard that stuff too. Nothing to it. It is true that an earth-filled dam would withstand an earthquake, for example, better than a more brittle concrete dam but what are the chances of a major earthquake in this area?"

"Less than three years ago we had quite a shaker in this area. It came right at noon. I can remember the trees moved like buggy whips."

"You don't say?" Jenkins seemed surprised.

"Or what if one these mountains erupt?"

"Now I know you're kidding," Jenkins said. "The nearest mountain is Mt. St.Helens. Does it look to you like St.Helens is going to erupt? It may erupt every ten thousand years or so but ... "

Jenkins suddenly became very serious. "Earthquakes, eruptions, floods, and stuff like that are all things the Commies get riled up about to shake our confidence in the free enterprise system that has made this country so strong.

Say, this guy that works on the survey crew that you mentioned, he isn't out of the University of Washington by any chance is he?"

"He might be," I said with a little caution.

"See what I mean? That place is a hotbed of commies. They're going to have a hearing up there soon and clean that rat nest out. You can see how those bastards work. They plant seeds of doubt. When the General is elected they better pack up and leave. Hey, it's getting late and I have been rambling a bit. I'm going to have to lock up. That's enough for one time anyway. But tell me before you leave, where did you come up with that line about 'not working in a tunnel but building a dam?'"

"I'm not sure what made me say that."

"It was a good line and old man Henderson fell for it like a ton of shit. But Henderson has you marked, kid, and he'll take care of you."

"I have always taken care of myself but I do have one last question about the diversion tunnel."

"If you make it fast," Jenkins said.

"How do they know that the tunnel that we're drilling on from both sides of the mountain will meet in the center of the mountain? I can just see us drilling right past the crew coming from the other side. And if we do line up and meet, how do they know that both ends will be at the same level? One side could end up ten feet higher than the other."

"The tunnel damn well better meet in the middle. That's a first year engineering problem. Any freshmen could figure that out. Why don't you ask your pinko friend on the survey crew?" Jenkins said.

"I did. But all he said was that it was a simple problem to solve."

"Your friend is right about that. It is a simple problem. Why don't you ask him again."

"Good-bye Jenkins and thanks for your time. Tell my friend George that I enjoyed it," I said.

"Good-bye chucktender Mac. Get that damn tunnel done so the real work can begin."

Chapter 28

The Bore-Through

Bore-through was in the air. The 'bore-through' is to tunnel men what 'topping-off' is to steel workers who build skyscrapers. Our skyscraper was horizontal rather than perpendicular, but the thrill of completion must be the same.

When the miners from the east portal could shake hands with the miners working from the west portal we would have a bore-through.

For the last week the length of our rounds were reduced to only four feet. When we blasted, the men working from the other side had to clear out of the tunnel, and we did likewise when they shot. You could definitely feel the concussion of each blast on the opposite side through the thinning wall of rock that separated us. Rock was loosened from the crown every time they blasted on the other side. It would not be too smart to be drilling when this happened.

We reduced the length of the rounds to two feet and the excitement increased. Only the engineers had an accurate 'guess' as to how much rock separated the two crews, but we knew we were very close.

A bore-through 'pool' was organized. It was a five dollar pool. The pool was designed this way: for five dollars you could draw a slip of paper out of a box. Each slip of paper had a different time written on it. The times were in one minute intervals. There are 1440 minutes in a day, so if each slip was drawn the pot would be worth $7200. Not exactly small pickings. You could draw as many slips as you wanted to buy. To keep the AM and PM hours straight, a code was set up. Very simply, blue numbers were used from midnight to 11:59 and red numbers from 12:00 noon until 11:59 at night. [This would have been the perfect instance to use military time. So there would be absolutely no confusion. And if I'd still had by brother's watch with 24-hour face, I might have attempted to introduce the concept.] The point of the pool of course was to be lucky enough to be holding the slip with the exact time, or the nearest time to it, of the 'official' bore-through.

I bought my five-dollar chance and was thinking of going for more chances. Tennessee read my mind.

"Just buy one chance, Mac. That way you can be part of the fun but you'll never win the pool," he said.

"Why do you say that?"

"This is the seventh bore-through pool I've been in and every time it was won by either the Walking Boss or the Project Superintendent."

"You mean it is fixed?" I asked.

"I'm telling you that if it can be fixed it will be. You can be sure of that. Whiskey has a little plan of his own this time however," Tennessee said with a wink.

I wished Slim could be here. He would enjoy every minute of this.

I made it a point to watch as Whiskey's 'plan' unfolded.

The plan was simple enough and anyone could figure it out. Tennessee was the front man so to speak. Whiskey gave Tennessee a fist full of fives. Tennessee got in the pool line and kept drawing and paying for one slip at a time.

Suddenly he stopped drawing and stepped out, of the line of hopeful winners. They had the number they wanted. Tennessee and Whiskey poured over their slips in deep discussion. I wondered what the importance was of the one special slip. I found out soon enough. They had kept drawing until they got one that would occur in the second half of our graveyard shift. Say about four to six in the morning. This would be a period of time over which Whiskey Riley had some control. He could control the time by speeding up the blast or by delaying it some. The second half of the shift would be the best, because it would give him the most options. It cost them nine draws to reach the window of time they wanted. There were still some unknowns before the 'fix' could be assured. If Tennessee was right, the big brass had their own version of a 'fix' in place, and if the truth be known I would guess that the Shift Bosses on both days and swing shifts had schemes of their own going as well. This could prove very interesting.

Somebody knew an engineer who said that if both sides kept shooting two-foot rounds we would have a bore through on Wednesday or Thursday. Some quick calculations would tell us that we were within fifty feet or less of a bore-through.

It didn't happen on Wednesday. It didn't happen on day or swing shift on Thursday.

Now it was our turn. We had a shot at the pool. Excitement was running high. The miners, who as a class, prided themselves in being unexcitable, were like a bunch of kids waiting to open their Christmas presents.

We drilled our two-foot round in the first two hours of our shift. Normally we would start to load immediately. But not tonight. Whiskey called a big conference at the face of the tunnel. He seemed to be waiting for something to happen. From somewhere two eight-foot steels appeared. We had not used eight-footers in two weeks. In fact the eight-foot steel was supposed to all be in storage by now. I don't think Whiskey was too surprised. He pointed at once to the four center holes.

"Boys, I think those four holes should be a mite deeper."

The four holes formed a wedge right in the middle of the tunnel. Whiskey Riley took over one drill with Turk as his chucktender and Tennessee took the other drill with Easy Money as his chucktender. It was funny to watch Easy Money and Tennessee change roles.

The fix was on. Every man knew that he had contributed five dollars or more to a cause he couldn't win, but we all cheered as Whiskey Riley and Tennessee began to race on the drill-out It was really a sight because those guys could drill. Now remember, they went from the authorized two-foot round to an eight-foot round. Four eight-foot holes loaded to the collars would surely punch a hole through, if the engineers' report was anywhere near on target.

When they finished the eight-foot drill-out they had another big conference. There were still four hours to go to get to Whiskey's time. They estimated an hour to load, and they would have lots of time to shoot at just the right moment.

The high level-calculations were interrupted by a pickup racing into the tunnel with lights blinking and its horn blaring. Fortunately everyone heard this maniac bearing down on us and we had time to run to the ribs of the tunnel. It was the Nipper.

"Hey, Whiskey look what I found," The Nipper yelled.

Protruding from the bed of the pickup were two of the longest steels I had ever seen. The Nipper had gone someplace and 'high graded' two eighteen-foot steels, which are used by wagon drills for road construction and quarry work. After working all summer and only seeing four and eight-foot steels these eighteen-footers looked unbelievably long. The two steels came off the pickup in a flash and the pickup raced out in the dark as if it had never been there,which of course it shouldn't have. You don't drive a gas rig into a tunnel but the Nipper had done it.

The drill-out began again. Whiskey signaled to Truckee to get to the portal and make sure that no one came in who wasn't on our crew. He didn't want someone else to barrel in, the way the Nipper had done. The next pickup might not be as helpful. Truckee pointed to three other guys and they all went on the run to the portal. No stranger would make it past that front line.

Time was becoming an issue now. The chucktenders started carrying the powder in even before the drill-out was finished. Whiskey Riley waved them back for more powder. Whiskey and Tennessee finished the eighteen footers within three minutes of each other, with Whiskey winning the race. By some signal the Nipper came roaring back into the tunnel blinking his lights, but he laid off the horn this time. As the Nipper was turning the truck around with a tight U-turn the wagon drill steel was slid onto the bed of the pickup and cinched down with rope, and the pickup roared off disappearing out the end of the tunnel and into the night leaving only a blue cloud of smoke.

The slant of the holes originally planned for two-foot and now nine times that deep were sure to be crossing over each other.

"Boys, load them to the collars," Whiskey ordered. "We will either punch a bore-through or we will bring this whole damn mountain down. This is going to be one hell of a pop."

Whiskey Riley personally checked the buzz wire connections, and then checked them again.

"Get that jumbo clear out of the tunnel. We don't need to have it in harm's way," Whiskey yelled.

We all jogged to the portal, the men with the spool of buzz wire running as fast as they could. The moment was near at hand. Whiskey had the Nipper call the other side to clear everyone out of the tunnel. I will never know just how the word got around the job so fast, but within the next half-hour every man from the other side of the mountain had arrived. Many of the swing and day shifters were there and a host of people I had never seen. Over 300 miners and assorted others were standing by to watch the bore-through.

Whiskey stood up on a wobbly keg of nails. "Boys, I want to say something."

"No speeches Goddamn it, Whiskey. You will talk yourself right out of the money," Tennessee shouted.

Whiskey looked pained. "All I wanted to say was there is $200 for each Jack man of you. This is one 'fix' where the men who did the work will get the dough. That's all I wanted to say," Whiskey said.

"Damn it Whiskey, we all knew that. Now get your hand on that detonator," sqealed Tennessee in a voice two pitches higher than his usual screech. Nipper had called for the absolute time, so there could be no mix-up that way.

Whiskey yelled, "Fire in the hole. Fire in the hole."

Tennessee counted down." 7-6-5-4-3-2-1. Push that Goddamn handle."

It blew. I mean to tell you it blew. The rock bounced off the jumbo like shrapnel even at the distance it had been removed. We could hear the thunder from the blast roll and roll. Everyone cheered. We had done it.

Within no time Whiskey Riley's 300 pound frame was going up into the air, raised by his crew. It was just like winning the homecoming game in high school. Unfortunately, the men on one side of Whiskey had their half of Whiskey in the air but the other guys couldn't get Whiskey's leg high enough in the air to get it on their shoulders.The result was ten miners and Whiskey Riley all tumbled into a heap. The whole scene took on a carnival atmosphere.

Normally, after a blast the fans are turned on to blow the fumes and smoke out of the tunnel. This cleaning of the air takes at least half an hour under regular conditions. This blast could never be described-as 'regular.' It takes thirty minutes before you can breathe let alone see anything. To breathe powder fumes is certain to produce a granddaddy of a headache. There is no headache like a powder headache. It has been compared to the headache you get after drinking a milkshake too fast. Everybody has done that. Only a powder headache doesn't go away for hours.

Headaches or no, visibility or no, we were going into that tunnel. Whiskey grabbed a flashlight and went on the deadrun for the rubble pile that would surely be inmense. The story was later told that Whiskey went in dodging the still falling rock. That wasn't quite the truth but we did go in away too early. But we were going to see a little piece of history in the making, and we all couldn't wait to be there. We skirted big boulders as we ran like we were crossing a minefield. Up and over the rubble pile on our hands and knees we stumbled, feeling our way to the face. It was impossible to see much. Whiskey Riley was the first to reach the face and to see the expected hole to the other side. Flashlights played back and forth over the face of the tunnel. There was a big wedge blown right out of the center of the face. Why the blast didn't fracture the crown I'll never know. Not a sound could be heard other than grunting as men climbed over rock to get a better stab with their flashlights. It slowly began to sink in for one man after another. There was no hole. There simply was no hole through the tunnel. We had missed. Whiskey was beside himself, and called for picks and bars. Whiskey started swinging a pick with all his might. Tennessee picked up a bar and went to the aid of his Chief. The rest of us stood there stunned. How could it not have gone through? One by one we all started toward the fresh air. No one was talking.

The last thing I remembered as I gasped for air was the ringing of Whiskey Riley's pick against the solid rock.

The actual bore-through came at 9:08 on the day shift. The Portland *Oregonian* was there to record the event as men from both sides of the mountain met in the middle and shook hands through a hole about the size of a washtub.

From the picture I saw in the paper it looked like everyone was there. Not that we were missed, but few if any from the graveyard shift were there. We slept right through the whole affair. We had lost interest by then.

Someone came into the bunk house and announced that the bore-through pool had been won by the Walking Boss.

"Now that's some coincidence for you," Tennessee said.

Later we learned two things: that we had punched to within eighteen inches of getting our bore-through, and that when they counted the money in the pool about half of it was missing.

So many times I had asked different people, who I thought should know, to explain to me how they could be sure that the tunnel would actually line up when it finally met in the middle. How would they be sure that the ends being drilled from opposite sides of the mountain wouldn't miss each other? The answer I always received was, 'It's a simple problem,' anyone can figure that out,' no worry about that happening, and so forth. Well by God, it was such a simple problem that it didn't get solved. That's right. The ends did not align. The tunnel from the west was ten feet to the south of the tunnel coming from the east. That is ten feet off, with a tunnel forty-two feet wide. They missed by one-fourth the width of the tunnel. Within twenty-four hours chipping guns and jackhammers had removed all hints of the error. Unless you wondered why there was such a strange widening of the tunnel in one place, you would never know any thing had been done incorrectly.

But I knew, I saw it. I was there.

Chapter 29

DeDe

The summer was fast coming to an end. The evenings were crisp. We built a fire in a fifty gallon drum nearly every night to keep warm at lunch time. In many ways this summer seemed like a lifetime, and yet at the same time it had gone by very fast.

But summer was definitely giving away to fall.

DeDe had called and left a message for me to give her a call but somehow I never quite got around to calling her.

Labor Day would be September third this year. I wanted to work the holiday to get the double time. I found that out on the Fourth of July, which had also been a weekday. Those double time days counted up fast. My plan was to work through the tenth of September. I knew that registration at school was the 13th and 14th. This way I would get one more Sunday in on the ninth of September. I asked Tennessee how much notice was proper.

"What's a notice?"

I explained it to him and he just laughed. "Notice is when you tell the paymaster you want your time," he said. "If you want to take your check with you, tell the paymaster one shift before you leave. If you don't mind having your check mailed to you then tell him about fifteen minutes before the end of your last shift. That's notice."

I knew when they started the penstock tunnels there would be work for every miner. The problem was, there

was going to be about a two month 'down' time between
tunnel jobs. Some of the crew were concerned because they
had moved their families up, expecting the job on the diversion tunnel to last longer. Layoff was in the air.

Since I knew I would be leaving in two weeks I thought
it would be more fair to lay me off rather than a man with
a family. So even though Tennessee said that a 'notice' was
not expected in construction, I wanted to tell Whiskey of
my plans to leave and why. I didn't want him to think I
was just quitting because I was tired.

Whiskey seemed impressed with my plans to go to college. I had not shared my college plan, with anyone on the
job. He was also pleased that I would volunteer to be laid
off early if it meant saving a family man for a few more
shifts.

"I appreciate your thoughts, Mac, but I will see that you
have work somewhere until the hour you say you're leaving."

"Jees, you mean you're going to go to one of those regular colleges?" He shook his head in amazement. "Some day,
I'spect that I will be telling people that I worked in this
hole in the ground with Mac McGowan,who got an
eddycation." And I'll say, "when I knew him he was just a
local yokel."

He turned silent and seemed to be in deep thought. "I
hope you make it to school Mac, but I would like to have a
penny for every stiff I've known who was going to quit the
game after they had earned a grubstake for something or
other. Something always seemed to happen and they need
to work just a little longer. Just one more tunnel. That's all,
just one more. Hell, Tennessee has quit three times to buy a
little piece of ground to farm. He wants to be a farmer, can
you beat that? But he always comes back to drilling before
long. Something always happens."

"I want to go to college very much Whiskey. And I can't think of anything that can stop me now."

"I hope you do go, son, but if things don't work out for you, where ever I'm at, you got a job if I'm in a position to say. If I'm not here I will be somewhere digging holes into rock. Just look me up. Now I mean that."

"Thanks, Whiskey. I will probably see you next summer. I can't think of a better man to work for than you. I mean it."

"I don't know too many eddycated people, but some that I have met are assholes. Don't become an asshole, son. Remember where you came from, and those that have sweated with you and pulled a shift with you on the way up. Most of us are just plain hillbillies but we all have something to offer. Don't forget us too soon."

"I'll never forget you Whiskey Riley, "I said. "I know you and Tennessee sort of watched after me. That's what my brother would've done if he hadn't got killed. He would have liked you Whiskey. I will never forget my brother, and no, I will never forget you either."

"Don't you have some work to do? How about you getting closer to it. I want to sit here a bit. Now you go on," Whiskey Riley ordered me.

As I left and glanced back I saw the biggest and strongest man I would ever know wiping his eyes and blowing his nose into his big red handkerchief.

Whiskey's words about future work were good news for me. I knew that some day another dam would be built upstream from Yale. I knew there would be several huge dams built on the Columbia, and then there was the talk of dams on the Snake River too. Also recently the big news had been about the Feather River Project in California. They have some water rights to get straightened out by the courts, and then that project will be ready to go. It might be possible to work each summer on a major dam in the Pacific Northwest.

My little red bank book was nearly worn out from my studying it so much. Counting the bonus, which amounted to two hundred and sixteen dollars, I had earned a total of $2169.20 this summer. I had $1674.20 in the bankbook plus a little coming in interest. I had spent $495 dollars this summer and most of that was for my room and food in camp. At this rate I could save $6600 in a full year's work. If I worked a full year I could go to any school I chose. But now I was thinking just like the thousands of other construction workers Whiskey Riley had been talking about. Men who planned to quit but never did.

I had ample money for my first year of college the way I planned to do it. There would be no stopping me. I will quit on schedule.

For some reason, or maybe for many reasons, I had put off getting in touch with DeDe. I still had the piece of paper on which she had scribbled her telephone number the night of the rescue from the cave-in. It is strange but even though I had known DeDe a long time, I had a hard time remembering exactly what she looked like. I wanted to see her, yet I dreaded it in someway.

I returned to camp as usual after the shift to find a note from DeDe pinned to the door of my room. The note was short:

> Dear Jerry,
> I have just received some bad news that I must share with you. It would be better if I could tell you in person. Please give me a call soon.
> DeDe Driscoll

Seeing my name written out seemed strange. I had not used the name Jerry for so long it didn't seem natural any more. Her note interested me enough to overcome other reservations so I went at once to the public company phone.

I reached someone at the number on the second ring and I asked if I could speak to DeDe.

"Whom should I say is calling?" the nice voice asked.

"Tell her Mac McGowan," I said. I had a very strong impulse to quickly hang up but before I had much time to think about it I heard DeDe say, "Hello, this is Dee."

"Hi DeDe. This is Jerry McGowan."

"Thank you for calling," she said. I thought I detected a slight catch in her voice.

"You said in your note that you had some news," I said.

"Yes I do. Say, could you ... would you be interested in seeing a Sunday matinee at the BeeGee theatre? We would be back in time for your shift. There's a good movie playing called 'Broken Arrow.' I think you would like it." She misunderstood my hesitation. "We would go Dutch of course,"she quickly added.

"That sounds swell to me DeDe. I can borrow a pickup from a friend I know here. What time should I pick you up?"

"The movie starts at two. Why don't you pick me up at noon," she sounded much relieved.

"O.K. I will see you at noon tomorrow. Oh, DeDe? Could I meet you on the road?" I asked.

"Sure. I will walk slowly toward Amboy if I get to the road before you arrive. Otherwise wait for me at the intersection.

I will be there at noon. And Jerry? Thanks for calling me back."

"I'm looking forward to seeing you DeDe. Good night."

My hands were sweaty as I hung up the phone. What the hell was the matter. I don't recall being this scared even during the cave-in.

Red said I could use his pickup. I said I would fill it with gas, but he said not to worry about it. He didn't ask where I was going, or why, or with whom, and I didn't volunteer any information. That was a trait that I had discovered to be unique to construction men. That is, no questions asked, no justifications and no explanations needed. If they trusted you that's all that really mattered. It was a trait I had come to appreciate.

I showered when I got off shift and again about ten o'clock. I don't know why. I borrowed some Acqua Velva from Tennessee and put on my only dress shirt. It was the same white shirt I had thought I would be wearing when I found out that chucktenders don't work in the mess hall. I thought my jeans looked better than the cheap slacks I brought in with me. My crew cut was way too long. Nothing I could do about that now.

At eleven I went out to start Red's pickup and to check the oil. I wanted to be sure it would start O.K. It did with no trouble. I went back to my room to wait.

"My don't you smell nice," Tennessee observed. "What time does church start?"

"I'm not going to church," I said.

"You could sure fool me. I never saw you so slicked up before. What shall I tell Whiskey if you don't show up for work tonight?" he said.

"Don't worry. I will be there on time."

I saw her as I turned on to the road to Amboy. I was actually a few minutes early but she had already walked about a quarter of a mile past the intersection toward Amboy. She was wearing tight blue jeans and a white blouse. By coincidence we were dressed almost alike. But my white shirt was not crisp like her blouse. When she saw that it was me in the pickup she turned and smiled and gave me a little wave. She was really a beauty. I had not thought too much about how beautiful she was before. She was just DeDe before. But now I saw her as the knock-out she was.

On an impulse I stopped the truck right in the middle of the gravel road. I set the brakes and ran around to where she was standing. I hugged her and swung her around and around with her feet off the ground.

"God, it's good to see you DeDe."

"It's good to see you too but give me a little more warning before you do that next time," DeDe laughed.

I held the door for her and she popped into the pickup like a butterfly. Unfortunately, I had forgotten I had set the brakes and promptly killed the engine. I slowed down as we crossed the high suspension Yale Bridge and pulled over onto the gravel apron on the other side.

"DeDe do you really want to see a movie?"

"Not if you don't."

"We can't talk over the noise of the truck. It will take us over an hour each way and then we can't talk during the movie. And we have a lot of talking to do," I said.

"What do you suggest?"

"I don't have any plan exactly, but have you ever been to Merrill Lake?"

"No."

"Neither have I but it is only about ten miles I think. We could be there in 45 minutes and it would give us lots more time to talk."

"Let's go to Merrill Lake," she said, and jabbed her thumb in the direction we had just come.

I spun the truck around and headed back. I was going at a pretty fast clip as we shot through the intersection at Nelson's Cat House. I glanced sideways at her. She did not turn her head to look. I could not help but think of the last time I drove through that intersection. I was driving a Caddie, not an old Ford pickup. We soon came to the Woodland-Cougar road and turned right. A few miles later we were in the town of Cougar, Washington. It actually had quite a growing spurt since I had been here earlier in the summer with Tom Kyle. There were two large trailor parks right outside of Cougar that had not even been there before. I told DeDe about my trip with Tom to meet Ole Peterson. She was very interested in the adventure. I drove past the Cougar store and showed her the sign placed by Ole.

"Give My Regards To Civilization—Ole Peterson," she read. "He must be quite a character."

We stopped at Reese's Store and bought some potato chips, a dozen oatmeal cookies and two bottles of Nesbett's Orange pop. The owner was pleasant and seemed pleased to give us directions to the turn-off to Merrill Lake. Only we found out that the locals call it Lake Merrill.

The road into the lake started as gravel but soon turned into a dirt road. It was rough and bumpy with a steady uphill grade for most of the five miles to the lake. The lake was well worth the effort. As we topped the final rise we could see the peaceful narrow lake nestled below us in the timber. The lake looked like a long torquoise pendant on a piece of green velvet. The trees came to the water line. We hoped to get a good view of Mt. St.Helens driving into the lake but it may have been a case of being too close to an object to see it. We did have a good view from the Woodland-Cougar road. At the lake we were less than ten miles from the mountain but we could not see it.

For ten months of the year Mt. St.Helens looks like a giant icecream cone to me. Mt. St.Helens is often compared to Fuji in Japan for its beauty. We had a special attachment to this mountain because from the Valley where we were raised we could see Mt. St.Helens so clearly and that is forty-five miles away. But here we were right at the base, and we could not get a good view. From our Valley we could also see Mt. Hood in Oregon, Silver Star,Davis Peak, and on rare days even Mt. Adams. But I think St.Helens was the favorite.

We stopped the truck on a promontory overlooking the lake. There was very little beach area, as the timber came almost to the water's edge. There was a plateau extending about ten feet above the water which we chose for our picnic site. We sat down with our backs against a huge hemlock wind-throw. The tree had been down for many years and the mossy trunk of the tree formed the perfect incubator for thousands of frilly little hemlocks all vying for the right to replace the fallen giant. We sat in the sun warming our faces as the water reflected the fall sun off the lake. We shut our eyes and played the game we had enjoyed in grade school called 'listen and name the birds.'

Our beloved teacher could always quiet her flock of unruly country kids with this game. She had small prizes for the student who could correctly call out the names of the birds by the sound of their calls. DeDe suggested the game as we heard the familiar ruckus of the belted kingfisher even though we did not see it. We heard many bird calls but we had some difficulty in identifying them. The bird life at this altitude must be different than what we had learned to know in the Valley. We knew we would not hear the blue jay because they had already sent out their warnings as we first arrived. We would hear the blue jay only if we got up and moved about. Then they would feel obligated to warn all their woodland friends all over again.

We saw a mallard family and what we thought may have been a wood duck. Osprey were fishing very successfully and we saw a red tailed hawk circle the entire area in slow sweeping circles without ever moving a wing, just gliding. We heard a loon and several songs of the sparrow family, but we could not really identify them. We were both sure that we heard the distinctive five-note song of the western meadow lark. Once you have heard the meadow lark there is no mistaking the song, although we were surprised that they were this high in the Cascades.

This was the life. A warm peaceful fall afternoon, a beautiful girl, and not a worry in the world. Not a worry except for some conversation that I knew was yet to come. Conversation that we were both avoiding. We scooted along the hemlock as the sun moved because the no-see-ums, a tiny, tiny mosquito, were getting downright aggressive in the shade. On one of these scoots to the sun I held my brown arm out along side of her stark white arm.

"I thought you always prided yourself on your famous golden tan. You know, when all the freckles finally run together."

"You know how it is with us redheads. We burn, we don't tan."

"But you're not tanned, burned, or anything, you are white-white."

She appeared a little irritated. "What did I say?" I asked.

"Oh nothing."

"No, I said something I shouldn't have, " I said.

"In my line of work they prefer that your skin be lily white," DeDe said.

"I didn't know that." I thought a bit. "Why is that?"

She didn't answer but then right out of the blue she said, "Why didn't we go into Battle Ground to the movie like we had planned?"

Her voice had a sharpness to it that I had not heard until now.

"We could have. I just thought this would give us more time to talk. Aren't you having a good time?" I could hear panic in the corners of my words. I had wanted very much to show her a good time.

"I was having one of the nicest times since I can remember. But then you started lying to me, and to yourself. So suddenly I am not having as nice a time," DeDe said.

"Lying? What did I lie about?" She was getting under my skin. Something was going sour fast and I didn't know what to do about it.

She must have sensed my distress. "I'm sorry for calling you a liar, Jerry. If I were a man and called you a liar, I expect I would be picking myself up off the seat of my pants," she said.

"The thought did cross my mind, "I laughed.

She whipped her arm around my neck in a head lock and wrestled me down in a feigned death struggle. "I whipped you the first time when we were five years old, the second time was in the second grade, and I could do it again right now," she said.

"First of all, you would never have beaten me in the second grade if your big brother would have kept out of it. I can't remember the first time you mention but you probably cheated."

"Well I can tell you my dear old friend, my brother would not challenge you now or ever again. He would have to stand on his toes to come up to your shoulders. And speaking of shoulders, what have you been doing? Eating Wheaties twice a day?" She put both of her hands on my shoulder and squeezed. The hair stood up on the back of my neck and I could feel my face getting red. The sensation was short lived because she had not lost her train of thought by this wonderful interlude.

"I don't think you were being strictly honest with yourself. Maybe without even realizing it," DeDe said, in almost a whisper, "and this may be as good a time as any to talk about it," she added.

This was going to be the conversation I had dreaded. But maybe, she was right. Perhaps we do need to talk about it and not around it.

"I cannot lie to you or myself and say I wasn't curious or that there aren't some questions I need answering," I admitted

"I think we didn't go to the BeeGee theater because you were afraid we would run into someone you know. Or worse yet, someone who knows me," DeDe said. "You are ashamed of me and what I do. Well Mac, you will have to come to grips with that because that is your problem, not mine."

" How can you work in a place like Nelson's?" I just blurted it out. "You're a girl from the Valley. Do you have no consideration for your folks or the rest of us."

"Hold on just a minute cowboy," she flared. "I know for a fact that there isn't anything you wouldn't do to get a chance to get out of your beloved Valley. That includes lying about your age. You took a chance. You had the courage most of the others lacked. Can't you bring yourself to see the same in me?"

"I didn't go to work in a whorehouse," I said. I wished I would have phrased that differently, but the words were out. The silence that followed was agonizing.

"I didn't intend to either," DeDe broke the silence. "But believe it or not I have no regrets. I mean, none."

"But how did you ... I mean how did you even know there was a Nelson's Cat House? I don't understand how that all happened."

"Do you really want to know?" she asked.

"Yes, I really do. I want very much to understand. It is important to me, " I said.

She turned to face me squarely, and gently took both of my hands into hers.

"I came over the back trail to your place about ten in the morning on the day Slim and you left. Your mom said you were going to try to get on at Yale Dam. She said that you had turned down a 'good' job with the Kilmers. She had guessed that you were up to something when she heard you packing your work clothes."

"I never could fool Mom for long."

"She was very glad that Slim, I mean Jerry Curtin, was going with you but she was still worried. I could tell that. I don't know what else your dear mother said to me because I was totally preoccupied. My heart was broken. I thought I would never see you again. I ... I loved you so much I could hardly stand it. I just thought you would always be my boyfriend and best pal. I thought it was just the way it was meant to be."

"I never had any idea you felt that way, exactly," I mumbled. "It's funny because Mom scolded me for not saying goodbye to you and for not letting you know I was leaving. In fact, as I think back on it, her first thought was that we were leaving the Valley together. She even asked me if you were going with me."

"I think your mother always liked me. I know I think the world of her."

"She does like you. You are right there, but go on with the story."

"I can tell you I didn't sleep much that night. I caught the Yacolt Stage into Vancouver the next morning."

"You tried to find me?"

"Don't flatter yourself," There was no humor in the remark.

"I knew if I was going to get out of the Valley I had to do it on my own. You weren't the only one to have dreams. I had the dream of going to college too. I had a newspaper ad for a secretarial position with an insurance company. I wore my 'eighty-word' pin and my second year of short-hand scroll, so I thought I was prepared. They interviewed me and gave me a typing test, which I sailed right through. But as it turned out the opening would not occur for two more weeks. The pay was outstanding I thought, sixty dollars a week. I tried seven other places like the banks and other insurance companies but with no luck. By the time I had decided to head back to the bus station it was after five and the bus had left. It was probably the first time and only time that the bus left on time. I was in a real fix now. I didn't have any money for a room and I was starved to death. I was in the process of figuring how long it would take me to walk the nine miles home and whether my shoes would hold up in the rain, when this nice-looking older man asked me if I had missed the bus. I told him I had. He asked me if I was in town looking for work. Normally I don't strike up a, conversation with a complete stranger, but this man had a kind face and he showed genuine concern. He asked me what kind of work I did. I said that although I lacked work experience, I thought I could type as well as anyone. He then asked me if I would be interested in reception and hostess work. I thought he must be heaven sent. The man, as you must have quessed by now was Mr. Nelson."

"So Nelson saw a perfect chance to exploit a girl in a jam," I said.

"Not at all. Not then, or at any time since," she corrected me." He sent me to the Evergreen Hotel and told me to tell the person at the desk that I was to have a room on Nelson's account. He told me to go to the restaurant and order dinner for myself and have it put on the room bill."

"Now don't tell me you weren't just a little suspicious," I said.

She ignored my question and went on with her story.

"Mr. Nelson said I would be sharing the room with another girl and he hoped I wouldn't mind. He said he had another business appointment right then but to come down to the coffee shop with the other girl at eight in the evening and he would tell us more about the job. If we were interested after we heard more and if we wanted the jobs we could start the next day. The pay he said, now get this, the pay he said was 'only' three hundred a week to start but he said a person could advance rapidly."

"My God, did I hear you right? Did you say three hundred a week? You mean a month," I said.

"That's exactly what I thought. I was afraid to ask him to repeat the amount. I thought he was mistaken.

Anyway, I found the hotel room at the Evergreen Hotel. That was the first time I had ever been in a hotel room. Have you ever been in a hotel?"

"No I haven't. I stayed in a motel in Woodland once, but I have never been inside a hotel," I said.

"You can't imagine how thick the carpets are. Each room has its own radio. There is even one of those TV's in the lobby which anyone who stays at the hotel is welcome to watch. I met the other girl, who appeared to be older than me. She seemed very nice. She was from Stevenson, up the Columbia River. She had been to Portland for two days looking for work. But she couldn't type or take shorthand. She had no skills but she was very attractive and had a nice personality."

"Yeah, I don't suppose that 'nice' Mr. Nelson was picking up any fat ugly girls," I said, "but go on."

"We were still eating when Mr. Nelson came back. He explained that we would be taking appointments, arranging schedules, and collecting fees. He said the customers were hard working construction men at a very large project. He said that for the most part the men were gentlemen but if any were not gentlemen we would never see them a second time. He asked us to think about it overnight. He would see us for breakfast, and if we were still interested at that time he would give us an advance for the first week and an expense allowance. If on the other hand we weren't interested, then we could have breakfast on him and we would part friends."

"He sure was smooth. Talk about setting the hook, he is a master," I said.

"I knew it was too good to be true but on the other hand I don't think he would have minded if we would have said 'No thank you.' My new roommate and I talked about it in the room. We were both suspicious so we drew up a list of questions to ask him in the morning. But we didn't determine who would ask which questions or who would ask the first one. The next morning Mr. Nelson breezed in right on time and whipped out his wallet before we had time to ask question number one. He gave us each the three hundred dollars just as he said he would. Then he said he had almost forgotten that he had mentioned expenses and gave us each another hundred dollars, in tens. Jerry, there I was with more money than I had ever seen in my life, and it was right there in my hand. I didn't ask any of the questions, and neither did the girl from Stevenson. He said he would pick us up at eleven and suggested we might want to do some shopping or get our things together, And he specifically said, if we wanted to, this would be a good time to make any phone calls.

My new friend had an overnight case but I had only the clothes on my back such as they were. So we spent the next two hours shopping at J.C. Penny's. Well you can pretty much guess the rest."

"I can see how three hundred dollars a week would be tempting, but did you think about what you would be losing?" I asked.

"Three hundred a week? Are you kidding? We make that much just on a Saturday night with the tips. And no, I didn't spend too much time thinking about what I might lose, as you say. I had lost all I had to lose, at the hands of my stepfather right in my own home. At least construction men are kind, and Mr. Nelson is right; for the most part they are gentlemen."

"Three hundred a night? That's incredible. That's a lot more than I can make in the tunnel."

" Guess what: I'll be going to the University of Washington in a pre-med program. I have already been accepted. Mr. Nelson gave me time off to go to Seattle to make all the arrangements, like dorm reservations, and registration, and all those things. Did you hear me? I said I will be going to college."

"I heard you. In other words the ends justifies the means. Why didn't you go out and rob a bank or something?"

"Why didn't you?" she replied. "Why did you and Slim risk your life going underground when you didn't know sick-um about tunnel work? Why didn't you go rob somebody? Why didn't you pitch hay all summer? It certainly would have been safer, and some would say more noble;

but I can tell you one thing for sure, you wouldn't be going to college. So you took a shortcut, didn't you. Are you going to work underground all the rest of your life? No, you're not. Well I'm not going to whore all my life."

I wished she hadn't used that word. It just didn't sound right coming from a girl.

"Jerry, I am going to be a doctor. Mac, am I really so different in what I've been doing than all the girls we both know? The ones who marry in the Valley just so they can get some man they can hardly stand, to pay their keep and raise their kids?" she asked.

"The main difference as I hear you saying it is that those girls will have to sell themselves for years and, you won't have to because you will be a doctor. And if I know you, the best doctor in the whole damn state."

I suppose it was twenty minutes before either of us spoke another word. I broke the silence. "DeDe, I have met a great guy up here. They call him Whiskey Riley. He told me once that just because a girl works at Nelson's doesn't mean she is a 'bad' person. Whiskey Riley is a wise man, DeDe. I now know what he meant, and I believe it with all my heart."

DeDe slowly put her arms around me and squeezed me as the tears began to flow. She made no attempt to hide them.

"Jerry McGowan, you are a rare one if you really mean that," she whispered. "You have taken a 100-pound sack of potatoes off my shoulders."

I hugged her back and our tears joined as our cheeks pressed together. The spell was broken by my running nose. I had to honk on my handkerchief.

"Is there anything else you want to know, Jerry? Anything at all? Just ask me and I will try to answer the best that I can," DeDe said.

"No, I don't think so DeDe. As far as I am concerned you're still the nicest and the best-looking girl from the

Valley, and you're damn sure the smartest. I'm not saying that this conversation won't come up again, but if it does, it will be from you. And if you do bring it up we will sit down and talk about it then. Right now, as far as I am concerned we have better things to talk about."

Time had gotten away from us. Darkness comes quickly in the mountain forests and canyons. Light was still reflecting off the lake but it was too dark to walk at anything but a snail crawl. We stumbled several times climbing the bank off the lake to where the truck was parked. I must have had my mind on something else when we arrived because I had left the ignition switch on. It was one of those switches where if you turned the key one way the motor turns off, but the other things on the truck were still on, such as the radio. In any case, it continues to drag on the battery. So the battery was as dead as a doornail. Fortunately the truck was sitting on a slope that ran for about fifty feet before the road started back up hill. We would have to push the truck and hope that it caught on the first try. DeDe got behind the wheel and I pushed with all my might. A lot of girls wouldn't know what to do, but DeDe had done this a thousand times on her stepfather's farm. She popped the clutch at just the right time and the engine caught.

"Could I drive it out to the main road?" she asked.

"Sure, why not?"

She drove very slowly with the lights out for about twenty minutes. Then she flipped on the lights which jumped into the night and she jumped on the gas. We came hauling down out of the mountains like the Super Chief gone amok. How she loved to double clutch as she geared up and down. A family of deer crossed right into our lights. They were lucky DeDe was at the wheel. We picked up some hazel brush and bounced back on to the road. She squealed but didn't slow down one bit. She glanced sideways at me. "What are you doing?" she yelled.

"What am I doing?" I shouted back. "I'm up to the tenth bead and I'm not even Catholic." Her laughter was like a tonic.

"Will I see you tomorrow?" she asked, as we slid to a stop at the intersection of the service road and Nelson's.

"That would be great. Only I don't know if I can get any wheels."

"Would it be too far for you to walk down to the inter-section?" she asked. "I could meet you there and maybe we could hike down to the Yale Bridge. That is such a beau-tiful place and I could pack us a 'real' picnic. What do you say, Mac?"

"I think maybe I could walk that far," I said. I didn't mention that I had already walked it in the rain and had gotten nothing but ants in my pants for my trouble.

"I still need to tell you about something," she said.

"You mean all that jawing at the lake was not what you had on your mind?"

"Only partly," she said. "But we have been serious enough for one day. I'll tell you tomorrow. Bad news can always keep."

I stuck out my hand and she gave me a good hard grip. "So until tomorrow, goodnight my friend."

"And goodnight to you, rare one."

There was no goodnight kiss, just a warm handshake. I left in a cloud of dust blinking my lights to her several times. I managed very little sleep before I had to roll out to catch the jitney to the tunnel. I kept turning one of her com-ments over and over in my mind regarding her stepfather and what must have happened in her own house. I had never heard of a thing like that if I had caught her meaning and I think I did. A deep feeling of compassion for her came over me.

Chapter 30

Sad News

I was still self-conscious about being seen with a girl from Nelson's, so I slipped through the woods again.

Unlike the other time, when I sneaked through the woods to the intersection, this time I jogged. I found myself springing over, the downed logs like a deer.

I figured that I would be getting to the intersection too early, but DeDe was already there and waiting. She had a wicker basket filled with sandwiches and all sorts of good things. I took the basket from her and she took my other hand in her's, and we strolled down the gravel road toward the bridge over the Lewis River. From the deck of the high suspension bridge and looking west you could see the upper reaches of the Merwin Reservoir. The view to the east was of the strip of untamed river pouring into the reservoir.

We sat down on a flat rock projecting high above the river. Even from this distance the melody of the rushing white water could easily be heard. You would think that the water running over the very same rocks and riffles would make the same sounds all the time. But if you listened carefully, the sounds, the tones, and pitches are ever changing.

"I would really like to fish the water off that point down there," DeDe said.

"We could do it tomorrow if you have the time. I can get us a couple of rods and gear in camp. I learned to fly fish this summer. Are you interested in learning? There are some little tricks but they're none too hard to pick up."

"I would love to. You're on. I would need to get back at least an hour before day shift gets off work if you think that would be possible," DeDe said.

"It's settled then." I still wasn't quite used to the idea that her 'work' had time commitments and standards to meet too.

"But come on now, what's the news that you've been putting off telling me? That was mean to leave me dangling last night."

She hesitated. "I don't know any easy way to tell you, except just straight out."

"That's usually the best way," I said.

" Slim, Jerry Curtin, was killed in an accident."

When I had thought of the various possibilities she might have in the way of 'news' this had not even been considered. I had thought of several types of 'bad' news but all of them had been about DeDe in some fashion. I am ashamed to admit that my first reaction was actually one of relief. But then her words began to sink in. I found my voice and whispered, "How? How did it happen?"

I sunk down to one knee and she knelt beside me.

"He was trying to work that steep side hill behind their place with the John Deere. Everybody knows the reputation for stability the John Deere has. Anyway, it tipped over on him. They found him when he didn't come in at dark. I will spare you the details," she said.

"Please don't. I want to hear all you know."

"He bled to death," she added.

"Oh, Sweet Jesus. I don't understand why he was trying to work that ground in the first place," I said. "It was too steep. That's exactly why it had not been worked before. He knew that. But what do you mean he bled to death?"

"He was impaled by the gear shift when the tractor turned over. Some think that if he would have stayed still until help arrived that night, he might have survived but he fought to get loose. The gear shift was like a spear holding him down. The more he fought to get free the more damage he did to himself and the more he bled."

"But does anyone know what he was doing on that damn side hill in the first place?" I said again.

"Grapes."

"What the hell does that mean? Grapes? What about grapes?"

"The land was too steep to grow anything but grapes. That is what he was planning to put in," DeDe said.

"Grapes? No one plants grapes in the Northwest."

"He had already planted seven acres and he was trying to get more land ready, higher on the slope. He had an idea about making wine to sell I guess. They say he had gathered weather reports from the last twenty years and tons of research like that. He said our weather, soil, and all critical factors were almost a carbon copy of the fine wine 'producing areas of Europe. He had some scheme that he had talked to my brother about, having to do with selling stock in a wine making company or something like that."

"That was his downfall. He was always looking for the get rich quick schemes. He took one chance too many. One too many gambles," I said.

We had been the best of friends all our lives. Until recently he was my best friend. We had gone through sports together. He had been my catcher in baseball, he played tackle and I was the guard on the right side of the line, and we even double dated for the prom. I remember he had arranged to have us march together at graduation even though our names did not follow each other alphabetically, which was the order in which we were supposed to march.

"We did everything together," I repeated aloud. "But you know when we came up here to the dam it wasn't good for him," I said.

"I know. I know."

"He changed didn't he? Several people told us, above all else, 'stay together'. But we didn't. I could have stepped in harder I guess, but it was like there was a side to him I didn't know."

"He did change, Mac," DeDe said. "He lied to you often, he stole from you ..." I interrupted her. " How do you know that?" I said.

"I just do," she insisted.

"I was really dumb. Imagine, I actually loaned him money so that he could spend it seeing you at Nelson's, and he never paid back the money. And worst of all he didn't have the guts to tell me that he was seeing you. I had to find it out the hard way."

"I heard about that. Red, Slim's friend, nearly got his head taken off, the way I heard it."

"Red pulled a knife on me and would have had the right to have defended himself with it if he had chosen to do so. I could have been cut or worse."

"I know, I know," she said. "If it is any consolation to you, all Slim ever got for his money was conversation. That was his choice. In fact, you were about all he would talk about. He admired your ability to set goals and not deviate from them. He could not seem to do that. He envied you for the admiration the other men have for you which they didn't have for him. You had character and he did not."

"Damn it all. He had character, or whatever you call it, before he started drinking too much and trying to find the easy way to get rich like gambling with a bunch of tin horns. I bet mom took his death hard. It would be like losing another son to her."

"Your mom sat with the family at the funeral."

That really got to me when she said that.

"I would have gone if I would have known ," I mumbled.

"Everyone knows that, Mac."

"Was it a big funeral? "

"Not very big. There was hay in the fields and a rain was coming. Most of the men were trying to get the hay in before it got wet. But most of the womenfolk were there."

"That's O.K. Slim would understand that."

We sat looking at the river.

"Do they really think he would have lived until help arrived if he hadn't tried to free himself?"

"That's the story in the Valley, but my brother says he died before noon and they didn't even start looking for him until after dark. My brother does not think he would have lived until help got there. I guess we'll never know. I don't know what my brother knows about it but he seems to think Slim lived for about two hours. That's all I know."

"Dee, I will say this only once, and please don't ever repeat it. I'm glad Slim fought the gear shift even if meant shortening his life. It tells me he wasn't going to just lie there and wait to die. The real Jerry came back. He wasn't one to wait around for someone else to do the job. He had to try while he could, and by God, he did try."

"I have thought along the very same lines, but then I'm disturbed because his 'fight' was meaningful and methodical, which means he was conscious until he bled to death. I can't think on that too long."

"DeDe, would you mind a lot if we went back now? I would like to go back to camp, " I said.

"No, I don't mind. I understand. To tell the truth I am out of the picnic mood too."

We picked up the unopened wicker basket and walked slowly back to the intersection, each in our own thoughts.

"Will I see you tomorrow?" DeDe asked.

"You bet. I will get us a fly rod a piece if I can. Tomorrow will be a better day."

"Mac, I know you must be down to your last few shifts. Be very careful. I have heard the stories the same as you have that the last shifts are always the most dangerous. Many workers get wiped out on their very last shift. So be careful."

I nodded. But I had never heard that old wives' tale until just then.

I waited until DeDe had rounded the curving driveway and was out of sight before I dashed into the brush at the side of the road for my sneak back into camp.

The old wives' tale, maybe had some validity. As always you must think about the job and only the job when you cross the portal to enter the tunnel. If your mind is on what you will be doing the first day after you quit, you may not get to quit. So I pushed thoughts of Slim out of my mind. Pushing DeDe out of my mind was harder however.

The drilling was over. There was a lot of clean-up work and things to do, but our concentration was not the same as when we were drilling. Many of the miners were getting restless because the work we were doing now was no longer 'miner's work'. Most of the miners were talking about moving on.

I had never thought much about death. Not even when my Dad died, because his death was not a surprise. I did think about it some during the cave-in. Now Slim is dead. I would never see him again. I will miss him in so many ways.

I wished to God that my last words to him as he was driving away in Longview would have been different. In effect I forced him to admit that he was a thief. That he had stolen my watch. That exchange was totally unnecessary. But at the time I thought I was being rather 'clever'.

I wondered what Slim had thought about as he lay there bleeding to death. I wondered what he thought about as he was getting weaker and realized that this was one jam he would not overcome. I wondered if he thought of me. If he did, I hope it was about the good times because we sure had many..

But it was now time to think about the job.

Chapter 31

Another Good-bye

The fishing was just so-so. We had not started early enough in the morning. DeDe wasn't catching on to fly fishing very well or perhaps I wasn't as good at instructing as Tom had been with me. But we each had several fish on, so overall it was just a good time.

It was a sparkling fall day. There had been several nights of light frost and the first heavy frost would not be far off here in the foothills of the Cascade Mountains. The vine maple was ablaze and many of the other leaves were beginning to turn.

I had lost a little interest in fishing and was just standing at the water's edge watching DeDe trying to work a none-too-cooperative line. It was too bad that the girls didn't have a sports program in school, because I was sure DeDe would have been a terrific athlete. My eyes must have burned a hole in her back because she suddenly turned around and caught me staring at her. She quickly scooped up a rock and skipped it about three feet in front of me.

"Hey! Watch it there. You'll scare all the fish," I shouted to her over the noise of the rushing water.

She put on a strange little smile and deliberately picked up her feet and splashed her way over to where I was standing in the water. She was reeling in as she came and she tossed her pole up on the bank. I could tell by the look on

her face that something was going to happen and I suspected that something meant I was going to get one heck
of a lot wetter. I quickly tossed my pole up on the bank
along side of hers and turned to prepare myself for whatever was about to come. I did not expect what happened
next. She stood high on her toes and kissed me on the lips.
I returned her overture but not with an innocent little peck
as she had given me.

Her response was to kick my legs out from under me
and then push my head under the water each time I tried
to come up for air. It was so much fun being with her. We
sat in the cold water on the seats of our pants laughing like
a couple of kids without a care in the world. It was clear
that fishing was over for the day. We climbed to our flat
rock overlook and dried ourselves off in the warm fall sun.
We had the whole world to ourselves. I dozed off awhile,
but woke up to find her looking at me. I winked at her. She
showed mock alarm.

"You sir, are an undaunted hustler, a real scalawag . That's
what you are," she teased.

"No, but that is what I wished I were sometimes."

She got very serious. "I pray you never change," she said.
"Your a country boy and I hope you stay that way forever.

Now, tell me about your school plans. What are you going to study? Not law I hope. "

"Well as a matter of fact law is my eventual goal but I
will take an end run to get there. I am first going to get
certified as a teacher. I will save my money teaching so I
can go to law school. My last shift here will be next Sunday. That way I can get in one more double time day. I will
register at Clark Jr. College the following Wednesday. My
plans are to go to Clark for two years."

"Clark Jr. College? Why?" she asked.

"I don't think I'm ready for a big mainline college, even
if I could handle the costs. I listened to Spade, who goes to

the University of Washington. DeDe, they have classes up
there that are larger than our entire high school."

"Is it the expenses, Mac?" she asked.

"Not totally. With what I have saved this summer and
by getting some part-time work I could probably swing
it." I said.

"We could pool our resources and ... "

"No we couldn't," I interrupted. "It is a generous thought
Dee, since I suspect you would be contributing a lot more
to the 'pool', but you know we couldn't do that."

"No, you are right. We couldn't do that because of your
pride. Couldn't just for once..."

"And our sense of what is right," I said.

"Maybe."

"And then there is Mom. I could get an old car to drive
to school and live at home. I am the only one she has now,
and she is getting along in years. It's the little things, like I
hate to think of Mom trying to keep the wood box full this
winter. The feed man will deliver her groceries from the
co-op, but this way I could take her shopping. I didn't feel
too bad about leaving her alone this summer but that's not
the same as going through a winter in that old house. Anyway, I miss her pancakes."

"You haven't tried my pancakes, But I do understand
what you are saying," DeDe said. "Will you tell your Mother
about me?"

"No DeDe, I won't. If she asks me if I saw you I will say
yes. If she asks me anything about what you did for work,
I will say you worked for the Director of Personnel, which
is the truth, I guess."

"Thank you. I hope your mother never knows the full
truth."

"Enough about me and my plans. Let's talk about you,"
I said. "Like when is your last shift, or duty, or whatever
you call it?" I asked.

She laughed, "We call it a shift the same as you do. And the answer is last night."

"What? Last Night?"

"Last night was my last shift," she said. "I am all packed. I leave as soon as I get back today. Another girl will drive me to Longview where I catch my bus to Seattle."

"You are leaving today?" My heart was in my throat. "But I thought we would have a few more days. I was having such a good time. I was looking forward to seeing you tomorrow and each day. Do you have to go so soon?"

She reached out and took both of my hands in her's. "I have enjoyed these days too. I will always cherish this time we have had together. But the time has come for me to go..."

"I will miss you very much," I managed to mumble.

"I have missed you for a long time Jerry McGowan, but we both must do what we must do, at least for now. Don't worry we will have many more great times."

"Do you really believe that we will?" I said.

There was a long, long pause and I thought I saw her eyes start to well up. "The truth?" she asked.

"Always the truth between us. "

"The truth is, I doubt it."

"Seattle isn't at the end of the world. It's not that far away," I said. There was another long pause.

"I think Seattle will be a very long ways. I better get back now. Would you mind if we said- goodbye here?" she said. "I think I would rather walk back alone."

I could feel my chin twisting up like it always did as a boy when I tried so hard to hold back tears. I always hated that. I pulled her to me and gave her a long hug. "You give them hell in Seattle," I said.

She turned and scrambled up the bank without ever looking back. I sat down on our rock, because I was not sure my legs would hold me. Should I run after her? Could I just let her go out of my life like this? But what could I really do? "Hell, Seattle is not all that far," I said out aloud

I had a premonition however, that I would never see her again. I think she felt this too.

Chapter 32

Going Home

"Professor McGowan, there is a graduate student to see you.

"I will see her Jonsey, if it doesn't take too long. I have a critical appointment with the Dean and I shouldn't be late.

Show her in."

"Dr. McGowan this is Elizabeth O'Connell," Mrs. Jones said.

"Thank you for seeing me with no appointment," Ms. O'Connell said. "I have been meaning to see you all quarter but frankly I didn't know what to say."

"My goodness, don't tell me I'm your advisor. I try to meet each of my advisees early in the first quarter but I don't believe I have had the pleasure of meeting you Ms. O'Connell."

"I wish you had been my faculty advisor, from what the other grad students have told me about you."

"That is very nice of you to say. Now how can I help you?"

Ms. O'Connell did not seem to be sure how to start.

"I promised my mother that if I ever had the opportunity while in grad school to say hello to you, I would do so.

"Well isn't that nice. I'm flattered."

"Actually, I have had many opportunities to have said 'hello' from her but I have felt a little awkward."

"Have I met you before? You look so familiar," I replied.

"In the Fall Lecture Series you presented a paper in the graduate research seminar and... "

"I remember you. You challenged my statistical procedures. Yes I remember you."

"I apologize for that. I should not have done that," she said.

"I do remember you Ms. O'Connell. By God you sure made the Dean nervous. You were right you know. Thank God the mistake was picked up before I published it. My conclusions were correct but the error would have certainly put a shadow over the entire work. I hope you don't think it was necessary to apologize. I tried to indicate at the time that I appreciated your comments, and I was sincere when I said that."

"You were most gracious at the time Dr.McGowan."

"I know your mother, you say? And what is your mother's name, may I ask."

"My name is Elizabeth Mary O'Connell. My maiden name was Driscoll."

I had been standing up to this point because I thought it would speed up the conference and I did have to see the Dean soon, but I slowly sat down. She sat down too. Mrs. Jones swept around the corner to dutifully remind me of the time, but she stopped in the doorway, surprised at the sudden cessation of conversation in the office. With Jonsey protectively looking on, I got up and walked around my desk with my arms open wide. Ms. O'Connell quickly rose and met me over half way with equal enthusiasm. We hugged until this old man needed a breath. Jonsey cleared her throat to get our attention.

"Dr. McGowan, the Dean ... "

"Jonsey, call the Dean. Tell him I am in the middle of a long term recall exercise."

"But Dr. McGowan, the Dean..."

"Jonsey, I am going to ask this beautiful young lady if she will have dinner with me. If she can, then I want you to tell the Dean that I won't be late, I won't be there at all."

"If that's an invitation to join you for dinner, what ever plans I may have had, have just been changed," Ms. O'connell said. "I would be honored to have dinner with you," she said.

"There you have it, Jonsey. Go tell the Dean."

Mrs. Jones reluctantly walked backwards out of the room.

"Now tell me Elizabeth, if I may call you that, how is your dear Mother? How is DeDe?"

"Mother passed away last December."

"I am so sorry to hear that. I am so sorry that I never got to see her since, well I guess it was the fall of 1951."

"It was 1951," she said.

I thought about your mother many times over these many years. I wrote her once.

"I know. I have read the letter many times." she said. "Mom had just completed her residency and that was the occasion of your letter I believe."

"You are the spitting image of your Mother," I said. "Only DeDe's hair was a darker red as I recall. Jonsey, you may go call the Dean."

"What did you say I should tell him?"

"Anything you like."

"Mom gave me something I was to give to you if I should ever meet you." She took a small square box out of her purse and handed it to me. In the box encased in chamois cloth was a watch. It was my 24-hour military watch. My hands shook noticeably as I put the watch between my palms and twisted the back off as I had done so many times before.

"Here Jonsey, it says right here, 22 jewels. Not 21. This was given to me by my brother who was killed in Korea." My eyes clouded from moisture. I couldn't help it. Mrs. Jones produced a Kleenex and I gave the watch to her to screw the back on for me. I did not trust my own hands to do the job. Jonsey gave Elizabeth a Kleenex and then took one herself.

"I think I can call the Dean now," Mrs. Jones said. She carefully handed the watch back to me. I sat down looking at the watch and turning it over and over. A flood of memories came back to me.

"I wonder how DeDe got the watch?" I mused.

"I thought you had given it to her," Elizabeth said.

"No, not exactly. Tell me everything about DeDe. I want to hear it all. I know she became a noted pediatrician in Seattle. I know she was credited with major research in leukemia."

"Yes, she performed one of the first bone marrow transfusions. Which makes it ironic that she should die of cancer. So you followed Mom's career over the years," Elizabeth said.

"No one could be prouder of her than I was. I wished I would have told her so. Imagine a girl from the Valley becoming a famous Doctor of medicine. Do you have any idea of what that means?"

"I think I do. And, Dr. McGowan, you have done fairly well for yourself, considering you were just a boy from the Valley. Mom kept a scrapbook on you."

"She did?"

"She was very proud of your work as the Undersecretary of UNESCO. And when you were with the U.S. Office, she referred to the Morse/Carey Amendment as the Morse/Carey/McGowan Amendment."

"My goodness, I don't think there is one person in a million that has even heard of the Morse/Carey Amendment."

"You are right I'm sure, but Mom followed it. First, I suspect because of you and your involvement, and secondly because of her work and interest in disabled children."

"I would like to see that scrap book some time."

"So would I "Mrs. Jones said.

"Do you have any pictures of her?" I asked.

"Yes, many of course. I even have two pictures of you." Elizabeth said.

" My goodness," Mrs. Jones said. Mrs. Jones had returned to the doorway, and was hanging on every word.

"I have your high school graduation picture, crew cut and all."

"I remember that picture. I borrowed Slim's suit jacket and tie for that picture." I said.

"Mom had his picture too. It looked like half the class wore the same tie and jacket," Elizabeth said.

"But the other picture is the one I always liked. It was taken at Yale Dam. You were on a stretcher and mom was leaning over you. The aspect that makes this picture a classic is the tear that you can see on Mom's cheek."

"That was a picture that the Portland *Oregonian* took, "I said. "I remember the situation very well, but I had forgotten about the picture. I would give anything for a copy of that picture, if you don't mind."

"I will see that you get a copy," Elizabeth promised.

"Tell me more about your Mother," I said.

"Yes, please tell us more, "Mrs. Jones said.

"Jonsey, isn't it a bit past your usual quitting time?" I said.

"Oh, that is no problem," she said.

"I see."

"What would you like to know?"

"Well, tell me about your father," I said. "Did she meet him at the university, or working in the hospital? Is he still alive?"

"Mom never married. She raised me as a single parent, which as you know in the 1950's was very unusual," Elizabeth said.

"Isn't that interesting, " Jonsey said. "How old did you say your Mother was when you were born?"

Elizabeth turned to face Jonsey. "I was born June 3rd., 1952, if that is your question. I don't know how she was able to manage it but she did. She was a great mother."

"She couldn't have been anything else," I said. "She had always been very goal oriented. Your Mother was smart. She was valedictorian of our class you know."

"Yes. I knew that."

"Not only was DeDe smart but she was 'wise' too, if you get the distinction. Wise beyond her years."

"It is still strange to hear her called DeDe," she said.

"That was her childhood name. That is what everyone in the Valley called her. She was admired by all as a girl growing up, "I said. "I can tell you my own dear mother thought the world of DeDe."

Elizabeth nodded . "I know that. Mom often quoted your mother and when things got tough, Mom would describe what it was like to raise a bunch of kids in the late 30's and 40's Dr. McGowan, I actually met your Mother on several occasions."

"Well I'll be darned. I didn't know that."

"DeDe Driscoll must have been an outstanding person," Jonsey said quietly.

"She really was. DeDe Driscoll was one of those rare gems that comes along only once in a lifetime."

"You should have married her," Mrs. Jones said.

"Well, we had separate goals to achieve, and we just took different trails."

"You should have married her, "Jonsey said.

"I heard you already," I responded. Jonsey had plunked her self in the remaining chair and showed no signs of leaving . "Don't you have a phone to answer or something?" I asked.

"No, I have it on the message phone."

"Mom was way ahead of her time in many areas. She must have been one of the first women to have a job in construction," Elizabeth said.

I smiled. "Your mother played a significant role in construction I am sure. At least in the construction of the diversion tunnel at Yale Dam. If you met my mother, that means DeDe must have returned to the Valley," I said.

"Mom went back a number of times. She anonymously sponsored the Girl Scout Troop at the new school. They didn't have scouting in the Valley when Mom was growing up and she had always wanted to be a Girl Scout."

"What did the Valley look like to you?" I asked.

"It just reminded me of a typical suburban community as far as I could see," she said. "You never went back?"

"Only when my mother passed away. The funeral was in Vancouver but I drove out and looked around. It wasn't the same."

"Well, Elizabeth Mary, we could talk all night, but if we are going to have dinner we had better get started. Elizabeth Mary will be easy for me to remember. You see, that is just the reverse of my Mother's name. Her name was Mary Elizabeth."

"I know," Elizabeth said.

"Jonsey, wouldn't you like to join us for dinner?" I said.

"I already made the reservations for two, but I suppose..." Elizabeth interrupted us, "I will meet you there in an hour. I need to run by my apartment first."

We watched her run through the light rain to her car. Jonsey broke the silence. "I wonder how DeDe got your brother's watch?"

I don't know exactly," I said.

"I suppose I could join you for dinner," Jonsey said.

"That's O.K. I will tell you everything tomorrow."

"You don't have to tell me much more. I think I have most of the story."

"What do you mean?" I asked.

"You don't get this yet do you," she replied.

Chapter 33

Ghost of Youth

"Hold on a minute Jonsey. What are you trying to say?"

"There isn't much I 'try' to say ,Dr. McGowan. I just say it."

"You are right on that count. What is on your mind? "

"Are you about to bore that lady with a bunch of old construction stories? That is not what she came here to hear."

"I think she'd will be interested in some of the events her Mother and I shared. I think my stories-are pretty damn good if I do say so."

"She is hardly a girl. She is over forty five years old. There will be years to share those. Now I am sure she is curious about 'events' that you shared with her mother. That is the key to this evening. Make it a memorable one for her. It is her mother she wants to hear about. Tell her how her mother got the watch. Do you know for sure?"

"Not for sure. All I know is that Jerry Curtin stole it from me to pay off a gambling debt, or to get into a game I don't know which. How DeDe got it? Maybe from a tin horn gambler. I can only guess."

"You mean she was one of the Nelson girls?"

"Well sort of, I guess."

"There is no 'sort of' now, is there. You see I have remembered your stories. Elizabeth 'has no idea about that part of her Mother's life or she would never have looked you up. Keep away from that. Don't even get close. Lie if you have to."

"I could tell a few good stories without mentioning anything about Nelson's," I said.

"Then tell her how your hero Whiskey Riley died in a
California prison."

"That was just a rumor. I could tell her that Nick's is still
serving beer after all these years, and, ironically, Nick's
also serves as a Clark County Branch Library."

"Tell her why you think Ole Peterson was a more significant figure than that Johnny-come-lately, Harry Truman. I
bet, between that and Nick's, she will really be fired up
with your stories."

"As I have told you before, no one would have heard of
Harry Truman if Mt. St.Helens had not erupted. Or even if
Truman would have come off the mountain and not been
buried alive, do you think his legend would have lived?
But Ole Peterson, now there's a real legend. I think Elizabeth would be interested to know what happened to the
sign Ole Peterson hung at Cougar. You know the one."

"Yes, 'Give my regards to civilization' should have been
enshrined perhaps, but it wasn't."

"And speaking of Cougar..."

"McGowan, I know exactly what you are going to say,"
she interrupted. "Before the dam was built only about fifty
people a year ever visited Cougar, and last year over half a
million tourists went through that little Berg."

"That is a remarkable thing, Jonsey. I usually like to tell
about D.B. Cooper too. Do you know that he was the only
skyjacker the F.B.I. never caught?"

"And he presumably bailed out over Cougar with all the
money."

"That's true, Jonsey."

"Maybe it is true, but do you think this lady who carries
your own mother's name wants to hear about the legend
of D.B. Cooper?"

"I should have fired you ten years ago when you first came here. I should have tied a can to your tail the very first time you scolded me that way."

"It was seventeen years ago, and who would you have gotten to put up with you?" she said.

"Jonsey, what should I talk about? I'm as nervous as a kid on his first date."

"To start with, let's get something straight. Did you love DeDe?"

"Well I thought the sun rose and set on her, but we were just kids and ... "

"No, no, I mean did you make love to her. Do I have to draw you a picture? Elizabeth thinks you are her father. Could that be possible?"

"Well I don't know I, or I mean we, or ...well, it's possible, but."

"That is all I need to know," Jonsey said.

"To tell you the truth the thought did pass through my mind an hour ago. But if DeDe thought so, why didn't she say something all these years?"

"If she knew you as well as I think she did, then she would have known exactly how you would have reacted. Remember, we are talking about the 1950's and people thought differently then. She knew what you would offer, and she did not want you on that basis."

"She once accused me of having too much pride. She had a bit too much of her own, didn't she?"

"Elizabeth is not after anything from you. If I read her right, and I think I have, she just wants a void filled. She has heard about her father all her life, but she doesn't know it. She missed all of that. You need to carefully fill that void in the years you both have remaining. Did she say whether or not she has any children?"

"I don't think she mentioned it one way or the other," I said.

"Ask her. You may be a grandparent. If she has children they have a right to know you."

"A right? This is all coming a bit too fast for me. I don't even know if this girl is my daughter."

"She is not a girl, she's a grown woman. And you say she is the spitting image of her mother. Well I say she is the spitting image of her Father. You have the opportunity of a life time you old fool, if you don't blow it."

"Can't I tell her about Slim's winemaking scheme being ahead of its time and now wine making is a significant industry in the Northwest?" I pleaded.

" Sure tell her, I don't care. She will be polite enough to listen I'm sure and if you pause long enough she will laugh at your jokes. But, hey, stay away from that Beatrice Rosen person and how you got her to white-wash the cave-in investigation. Please, leave that one alone."

"Jonsey I should have married you after your husband died," I said, and gently shook her by the shoulder.

"College professors never interested me. But where was Whiskey Riley when I needed him?"

We hugged and laughed and hugged again.

"Professor McGowan?"

"Yes Jonsey."

"Don't wear your green tie tonight. Not the green one."

THE END